I0652881

ALIEN MINDS

BOOK THREE OF THE DIMENSION DRIFT SERIES

CHRISTINA BAUER

CONTENTS

ALIEN MINDS

ALSO BY CHRISTINA BAUER

SAMPLE CHAPTERS: ECHO ACADEMY

NEW APPENDIX OF TOTALLY AWESOME GOODIES

STANDARD APPENDIX OF STUFF THAT'S STILL PRETTY COOL

COPYRIGHT

Monster House Books
Brighton, MA 02135
ISBN 9781946677273
First Edition

Copyright © 2019 by Monster House Books LLC
All rights reserved. This book or any portion thereof may not be reproduced or used in any manner whatsoever without the express written permission of the publisher except for the use of brief quotations in a book review.

DEDICATION

For All Those Who Kick Ass, Take Names
And Read Books

Dimension Drift

Dystopian adventures with science, snark, and hot aliens

1. Scythe
2. Umbra
3. Alien Minds
4. ECHO Academy
5. Justice
6. Slate

Angelbound Origins

About a quasi (part demon and part human) girl who loves kicking butt in Purgatory's Arena

1. Angelbound
2. Scala
3. Acca
4. Thrax
5. The Dark Lands
6. The Brutal Time
7. Armageddon
8. Quasi Redux
9. Clockwork Igni
10. Lady Reaper

Angelbound Offspring

The next generation takes on Heaven, Hell, and everything in between

1. Maxon
2. Portia
3. Zinnia
4. Rhodes
5. Kaps
6. Mack
7. Huntress

Angelbound Lincoln

The Angelbound experience as told by Prince Lincoln

1. Duty Bound
2. Lincoln
3. Trickster
4. Baculum
5. Angelfire

Fairy Tales of the Magicorum

Modern fairy tales with sass, action, and romance

1. Wolves and Roses
2. Moonlight and Midtown
3. Shifters and Glyphs
4. Slippers and Thieves
5. Bandits and Ball Gowns
6. Fairies and Frosting

Pixieland Diaries

Sassy pixie Calla loves elf prince Dare. Too bad he hasn't noticed her. Yet.

1. Pixieland Diaries
2. Calla
3. Dare
4. Winter Prince
5. Ley Queen

Beholder

Where a medieval farm girl discovers necromancy and true love

1. Cursed

This is a completed series.

ALIEN MINDS

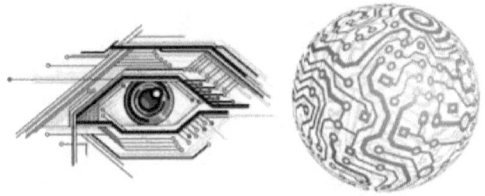

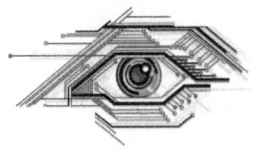

IN THIS MOMENT, I know four things.

One, I just woke up in a hospital bed.

Two, I don't remember anything about my life before today. *Hello, amnesia!*

Three, I want out of here now because …

Four, there's a creepy couple in my room—Luci and Josiah—who claim they're my sponsor parents. According to them, I'm a seventeen-year-old science prodigy called Wisteria Roberts.

Huh. That name rings zero bells.

Plus, these two make my skin crawl.

"We sponsor you *financially,*" explains Josiah. "Then in the fall, we'll fund your senior year of high school at ECHO Academy." Josiah's a lanky guy with slicked-back hair, a frayed suit, and an overly large Adam's apple.

"Afterward, you'll pay us back with interest," adds Luci. "Forty percent. Compounded annually."

Luci is tall and willowy with white-blonde tresses. By contrast, I'm a curvy girl with brown hair and ebony eyes. I'm also wrapped up mummy-style with bandages. According to Luci and Josiah, I took a spill on Newbury Street and lost my memory. So sketchy.

Some small voice in my head cries that I should be terrified right now. Instead, I just feel numb. Must be a happy side effect of having no memory. Like an amnesia bonus.

"You'll love living in our dorm," says Josiah. "In fact, think of me more as your sponsor *friend* than your sponsor *parent*."

At this point, that small part of me screams how Josiah is a disgusting pig. But more of me is still happily numb, so the warnings go nowhere.

Screech, screech, screech!

A chorus of alarm bells sound. Red lights flash in the outer hallway. An overly calm female voice drones through hidden speakers. "Cleansing search commencing ... cleansing search commencing. All hail the Authority ... All hail the Authority."

With that, the inner cogs of my brain connect and whir. Feelings return. My blood chills over with fear. I may not recall my personal history, but I do remember how our evil government—what we call the Authority—conducts cleansing searches. They find the sick or poor, label them as *undesirable,* and slate them for *cleansing.* It's a fancy word for murder.

The alarms wail louder. My heart rate skyrockets. If there's a cleansing search, I'm a slam dunk to be undesirable.

A cat-like animal slinks into the room. My eyes almost bulge out of my head. This is one of the Horde, which are genetically altered attack animals. In this case, the creature has a feline body paired with the hide of a serpent and bat wings. A golden collar encircles its throat. The creature sniffs at me once before letting out a high-pitched howl.

Yee-oooow!

I grip my sheets and shiver. At this point, I'm only inches away from death. The way cat-snake-bat yowls, the animal is calling for its master.

Sure enough, a warrior bursts through the door. He wears black body armor that's patterned with charred-out bones and paired with a skull-like helmet. I know that particular uniform. This guy is one of the Merciless, warriors who specialize in cleansings.

I'm so dead. Literally.

"I'm Captain Vargas." The Merciless gestures toward the cat-snake-bat. "This is Marro." He then points straight at my nose. "My animal called me here because it scents you as undesirable."

Bolts of worry move through my torso. This is not good news.

Vargas lifts a gash gun from the holster at his waistline. "Prepare to be cleansed."

I look over to Luci and Josiah. In response to the threat to their supposed *sponsor child*, they gasp, pale, and retreat to a far corner. *Thanks for nothing.*

Closing my eyes, I wait for the inevitable.

No blast sounds.

Instead, the alarms fall silent. Reopening my eyes, I see a wisp of a man stroll into the room. Tufts of gray hair encircle his balding head. Small round glasses sit atop his thin nose. The name tag on his loose lab coat reads *Dr. Godwin.*

My heart sinks.

Yup, it's *that* Dr. Godwin, the guy who runs the attack Horde, of which Marro is only one example.

Although Godwin stands far shorter than Vargas, the doctor swaggers toward the towering warrior.

"What are you doing here?" snaps Godwin.

"Routine visit," replies Vargas.

"Then why are you holding your gash gun?" asks Godwin.

Vargas quickly reholsters his weapon. "No reason."

I raise my hand. After all, Godwin seems to be on my side here. "He was totally about to cleanse me," I state.

Godwin frowns. "We've been through this a hundred times, Vargas. You are forbidden from killing my patients."

My eyes almost bug out of my head. *I'm Godwin's patient?* Luci and Josiah said I'd gotten in an accident, but not *who* was treating my memory loss. Godwin's on the government's Star Council, which means he's the nastiest of the nasties. Having him as my doctor will not end well.

"Did your animal bite her?" asks Godwin.

"Not yet," replies Vargas.

"Good. Be sure to keep your beast away from my patient." Godwin glares at Vargas. "And don't *you* go near her again, either."

For the record, I like the direction this conversation is taking. *Not being killed by Vargas* is a good plan, even if it does come from Godwin.

"Near or not, I'll keep tabs on her." Vargas pulls out a metal cuff from somewhere. A second later, he snaps the device on my wrist.

Cool steel presses against my skin. I have to hand it to Vargas—the guy moves pretty quickly for a massive dude in heavy black armor.

Still gripping my forearm, Vargas lifts my wrist up for a closer examination. For the first time, I notice a small screen embedded into the metal. The display reads: *Wisteria Roberts, private staff for Dr. Godwin, goal loading in process.*

I try yanking my arm free from Vargas's hold. The guy's grip is like iron.

"I didn't give permission for that," snarls Godwin.

Vargas folds his arms over his chest. "Everyone gets a wrist cuff, even if they're a legitimate citizen. If you don't like it, take it up with Humboldt." General Humboldt runs the Merciless; Dr. Godwin leads the Horde of genetically enhanced killer creatures. The two have a hate-hate relationship.

Turning away from Godwin, Vargas focuses on me once more. "Now I can track your every move," he explains.

"Oh." That numb feeling returns. It's like I'm a mindless pawn on a chessboard—no idea what the players are doing. I find myself staring at the cuff. "This says something about goals."

"Soon you'll receive updates on the Liberation Celebration." Vargas sighs, as if simply saying the words Liberation Celebration were some kind of prayer.

His attitude is not a shocker. Every August, the Liberation Celebration commemorates the day the Authority took power. It's a huge deal.

"This year, we're adding a contest to the event," adds Vargas. "It's between the Merciless and the Horde." Vargas nods in the doctor's direction. "Godwin's side is losing."

"Leave," orders Godwin.

"As you command," says Vargas.

With that, Vargas marches off down the outer hallway. Marro slinks along behind him, the little creature's bat wings fluttering with each step. Poor Marro. If that golden collar were off, then he'd probably scamper away to chase mice. Horde animals aren't naturally mean.

"Impossible man." Godwin steps back to my bedside. As the doctor moves closer, my skin prickles with fear. Although I can't remember where we met or anything, I know one fact.

Godwin is a dick and I hate him.

"It's true that I'm behind in terms of the competition," continues Godwin. "But in order to take the lead, I need top scientists. You're supposedly a prodigy, so I've spent weeks rescuing your mind. Now you owe me everything. Will you help me win?"

I pretend to consider this before replying. "It's tempting, but no thanks. Just send me back to where I came from, and I'll be fine."

Under the bedsheets, I cross my fingers. *Please send me back.*

Godwin points toward Luci and Josiah. "You met your sponsor parents. Don't you want to live in safety and comfort while attending ECHO Academy, the world's greatest school for science? In return, all you need do is provide a little assistance for the celebration. Swear to help me and it's all yours."

I wince a bit, like I'm seriously thinking this through once more. "Nope. Still not interested. I'm just—" I pat my head bandages "—recovering from brain surgery and everything."

Godwin rounds on Luci and Josiah. "You two. Out."

"What do you mean?" Josiah's mouth falls open. "Wisteria's not our sponsor child anymore?"

Godwin's thin nostrils flare with rage. "Wisteria will stay under my personal care. If I have need of you, I'll let you know."

Luci slumps. "But I thought—"

"Go!" orders Godwin.

In another display of fake-parent awesomeness, Luci and Josiah skitter from the room. A pang of disappointment fills my soul. It's as if I knew Luci and Josiah, but expected more from them.

A sneaky look lights up Godwin's bland face. "Since you aren't willing to help, I must resort to more brutal motivations. I've found a private guard for you." He snaps his fingers. "Enter."

A boy stalks into the room. Wearing fitted black body armor, the guard looks about eighteen years old with broad shoulders and a lean, muscular body. His hair is cut short—military style—and sets off the heavy angles of his face. But what stuns me are his eyes.

Large.

Blue.

Soulful.

My breath catches. *I definitely know this boy. He's important.* Every cell in my body wants to remember more. Stupid amnesia.

Godwin sets his hand on the guy's shoulder. "Introduce yourself."

If the boy recognizes me, he doesn't show it. His eyes stay cold as his gaze locks with mine. "I'm Thorne Oxblood."

My throat tightens with grief. I don't remember this guy, so why does this moment feel like such a betrayal? After all, I handled waking up with amnesia no problem. I sailed past the *Luci and Josiah Show* like some part of me was expecting it.

But Thorne? His empty stare hits me like a body blow. Despite my best efforts, a whimper escapes my lips. *This is horrible.*

I glance over to Godwin. The word *smug* pretty much sums up the doctor's face. "Now, that's more the reaction I was expecting." Godwin focuses on Thorne. "Tell her what I've hired you to do."

"I'm here to ensure your compliance," states Thorne. "Dr. Godwin requires your unique services to meet his goals for the Liberation Celebration. You will help him or die."

All my sass melts through the floor. Something about Thorne tears at my soul in a deeper way than anything from Godwin, Luci, or Josiah.

This can't be happening.

Once more, Godwin claps his hand on Thorne's shoulder. "Make sure the girl's ready for testing first thing tomorrow morning. I must confirm her skills before moving forward."

Thorne stiffens his stance. "Yes, sir."

"Did you say *testing*?" I sit up straighter. "Don't I need more time to recover?"

"Let me clarify a few things." Godwin's voice transforms into a sinister whisper. "I don't want your help. If I weren't so desperate for scientists, I wouldn't even consider you. And if you're any good, you'll become nothing but a whisper and a shadow. Every success you achieve will be attributed to me. I trust we understand each other."

Without waiting for a reply, Godwin presses a button on the wall. "Knock her out."

A young woman's voice sounds from hidden speakers. "Yes, Dr. Godwin."

Blue fluid fills my IV tube. I frown. That particular shade of drug is familiar.

Tranquilizer.

In this moment, one thing becomes clear. *I'll never help Godwin*

win at the Liberation Celebration. In fact, I'd love to explode the whole thing in his smarmy face.

Within seconds, my eyelids droop. A low whir sounds as the blinds auto-close on my bay windows. Godwin takes off. The door shuts behind him with a soft click, leaving me in shadows.

Thorne stands against the wall, silent and staring. He could be the cover boy for *Cruel Killer* magazine, the guy's so intimidating.

As my consciousness fades, I focus on my wrist cuff. Words flash in a dim green glow.

Update complete
Star Council Level Access: Godwin
Humboldt-Merciless Undesirables Tagged: 1,342,109
Godwin-Horde Undesirables Tagged: 443,808
Total To Be Announced At Liberation Celebration: 1,785,917

What in the ever-loving Darwin?

That's what this is all about?

According to this readout, Godwin and Humboldt are racing to tag the most undesirables for death ... with their grand totals to be broadcast at the Liberation Celebration. A sick taste crawls up my throat. President Hope has made a game from marking people for execution.

Maybe I don't know who I am, but I must have family somewhere. A word appears in my mind: *mother*. I don't know my mom's name or where she is, but I feel certain of one fact. My mother's an undesirable. To keep her safe, I must help the others as well. As my consciousness fades, my thoughts reel through options.

An idea appears.

Perhaps I can put Godwin in jail, escape this scary scene, ruin the Liberation Celebration, and save every undesirable—including my mother—all at once.

I just need a *team*.

As my eyes flutter closed, I notice how Thorne watches me with extra interest. Now that Godwin's gone, my badass guard looks all things wide-eyed and sweet.

That settles it.

He'll be my first team recruit.

"Intoxication with technology is the hallmark of an underdeveloped society." –
Beauregard the Great, *Instructions for Visiting Parallel Worlds*

AFTER SPENDING hours on guard duty, I can finally leave Mass General. Soon I'm tooling my hoverbike toward the outskirts of the Boston Dome. Overhead, a cloud-free sky is projected onto the plasma. Tall buildings loom around me in a maze of chrome, concrete, and blinking lights.

An image appears in my mind. Meimi—I never even *think* the false name Wisteria—lies curled on her hospital bed, drugged up and asleep. Every instinct in my soul says I should've stayed behind and guarded her while she rested. Not an option. An important appointment is coming up, and I can't miss it.

For Meimi.

Of course, Godwin doesn't know I'm leaving the city. Then again, the doctor doesn't know a lot of things about me.

Like the fact that I'm not from this planet.

Plus, I'm not just any alien. My father's the Emperor of the Omniverse, the universe of universes.

So what Godwin doesn't know about me is quite a lot, actually.

Glancing down, I check my smart watch. Based on the time, Godwin's still off chatting with President Hope. Those meetings last for hours. I'm good to leave the dome until dawn.

At the foot of Mass Avenue, I reach a line of arches set into the dome's glassy base. *Checkpoint Seven.* Electric cars, regular pedal bikes, and hoverbuses—all of them wait in long lines under the archways. One aisle always stays empty, though. It's reserved for Star Council members and their adjuncts, like me. I pull up there.

A Merciless warrior steps out. He's dressed head to toe in black armor with a helmet shaped to resemble a skull. A small attack animal creeps along at the fighter's side: a cat with reptile skin and bat wings. Only one guy keeps that particular attack animal handy. I stifle a groan.

Captain Vargas. He's found me. Again.

Vargas works for General Humboldt, a bigwig who loathes Godwin. Together, Humboldt and Godwin are both trying to undermine President Hope.

It's a really twisted situation.

Peeling off his helmet, Vargas marches over to my hoverbike. Like all Merciless, Vargas is in his late twenties, pale skinned, golden haired, and handsome. He's also been screened for certain psychological profile: no empathy, high intellect, and strong predatory instinct.

In other words, a successful sociopath.

Vargas flashes me a winning smile. "Lovely day. Eh, Thorne?"

No one's more charming than a sociopath. Best to keep every conversation to a minimum. "What do you want, Vargas?"

"Why so hostile?" He widens his eyes in the perfect replication of surprise. What the guy really feels is nothing. That is, unless he's attacking someone.

"Because you're tracking me when you should be tagging undesirables."

All traces of a smile vanish. Vargas doesn't bother to deny that Humboldt has him trailing me. "I could slap a wrist cuff on you."

"I'm an adjunct member of the Star Council. My boss has his own way of keeping tabs on me."

As a matter of fact, Godwin injected a DNA tracker directly into my bloodstream. I overrode it, though. Right now, those markers show I'm in Meimi's room. The only way Godwin would think otherwise is if he stopped by the hospital. And since the doctor's in with President Hope, he won't.

"Try again," I tell Vargas.

"According to data feeds, you should be at Mass General, looking over Godwin's *patient*." The way Vargas says *patient*, I know he suspects Meimi is something more. *Not good.*

"So?"

"Why are you leaving the city?" asks Vargas.

"Want my plans? You know the protocol. Ask Godwin."

Vargas chuckles. "I already know what you're up to. You've a suite reserved at the Berkshire Mini-Dome and Deluxe Resort. It's only a short ride from the city. Exclusive. Romantic. Perfect for a certain lady, eh?"

Whenever I leave the Boston Dome, I always set up a reservation at the Berkshire Resort, just in case I need an alibi. Vargas thinks he caught me sneaking off for a woman. Instead, he's only becoming part of my cover-up.

When I answer, I take care to keep my face blank. "Wave me on, Vargas."

"Not a chance. Godwin ordered you back to Mass Gen."

I check my smart watch. There are zero texts from Godwin. Vargas is bluffing. This guy has no idea where I'm supposed to be or why. This is how sociopaths pass the time—playing mind games with the rest of us.

Or in this case, *trying* to play mind games.

I lower my voice. "Let. Me. Through."

There's a long moment where Vargas stares at me. His hands ball into fists, a movement that makes his armor crackle. It's an invitation to fight.

Every cell in my body wants to battle this guy.

Or since I'm from Umbra, it's more accurate to say every *sentient* does.

My people are unique because our bodies store sentient, the most powerful beings in the omniverse. Sentient may look like particles, but they're actually tiny cybernetic organisms that work as a hive mind to give us extra powers, like battle energy. Right now, my battle sentient are screaming for me to smash Vargas in the face. They communicate by sending me images of my fist crushing the warrior's nose.

And because I'm adjunct to the Star Council, I could get away with it too.

On reflex, I start the process of activating my sentient. I picture tiny black particles seeping out from under my skin, covering my body in heavy armor. Next, I imagine more lacing through my muscles to provide extra strength. The sentient stir inside me, but they don't appear.

My back teeth lock in frustration. For some reason, the Boston Dome blocks sentient from departing my body. It's infuriating. It's also why I must leave for this chat with my brothers. Normally, I'd just summon my knowledge sentient to contact them. But because of the dome, I must exit the city and connect at a specific time. All of which adds up to one thing.

If I want to take Vargas down, I'll have to do it human style.

Which wouldn't be too hard, actually.

In fact, a fistfight might let off some steam.

I kill the engine on my hoverbike. "Give me an excuse."

Vargas pauses for another long second, and then waves me on. "Fine. Go."

A little disappointing, that.

When it comes to battle, humans are no match for an Umbran like me. Even so, since Vargas has all that armor, he might have been interesting. I could have even freed Marro when I was done.

Ah, well. Another time.

Revving up my hoverbike, I take off at top speed through the dome wall. The moment I'm through, the road changes from smooth concrete into cracked asphalt. Gray skies loom overhead, filled with green-tinted rainclouds. In every direction, the landscape is nothing but rubble. The scent of rotten eggs fills the air.

Leaving the dome by hoverbike isn't a common choice. Most people prefer a fully enclosed vehicle. That way, you avoid breathing unfiltered air. And sure enough, bits of soot, grime, and other gunk float before my eyes. I swear, there are coal mines with better atmospheres than Reformed New England.

But since I'm out of the dome, I can easily fix the air-quality problem.

Finally, I contact my sentient again.

Fast as a heartbeat, I send them a mental image of an air-screening mask, goggles, and an earpiece. This time, my sentient respond instantly. Silver particles rise from my skin, quickly forming the shapes needed.

After that, my sentient send me a mental image of a man punching his fist high. That's their way of saying it's good to be useful once more.

"Missed me?" I ask.

In reply, the mental image turns into a crowd cheering.

"Yeah, missed you too."

I don't store a lot of sentient, but the ones I have? After years of training, I've gained close control over every particle.

For the next hour, I speed over broken roads. Eventually I reach the ruins of an old apartment complex. The spot reminds me of a doll house: an entire wall has been sheared off, revealing sixteen floors of people's lives the moment before the Authority took them down. There's a living room with a faded-pink couch that hangs over the ledge, a library with books strewn across the floor, and a nursery with a toppled-over crib. *Sad, really.*

Parking my hoverbike, I march up to the building's front door and step inside the lobby. It's pretty standard stuff for old Earth. There's a reception desk, now smashed. A wall of mailboxes stand nearby; they're also demolished. Yellowing envelopes and faded catalogs still sit in exposed boxes. Some couches litter the floor, all of them covered in mold and collapsing in on themselves. Greenish dust covers everything. In the twenty years since the Authority attacked, few people have stepped in this place ... which makes it the perfect spot to meet my brothers, Justice and Slate.

Still, the building sets my nerves on edge. It's too much like a cemetery. Out of habit, I peel off my human covering, allowing my sentient to come out and take their place. Within seconds, I'm wearing black body armor that's indestructible and made from sentient. No self-respecting Umbran meets his people in human clothes.

My earpiece beeps as Justice calls.

"Accept comm," I say.

"Slate and I are coming through." Even though he's universes away, Justice's deep baritone sounds perfectly clear. That's all the work of his sentient. Like me, Justice and Slate also command these cybernetic organisms.

"Check that," I reply.

My heart lightens. It'll be good to see my brothers again.

A hoop of silver particles appears in the air before me. It's the beginnings of a drift void, which is how we travel between universes. Since this circle is silver, the void's created by knowledge sentient. There are four kinds of sentient in all: black for battle, silver for knowledge, blue for second sight (meaning visions of the present or future), and red for danger.

The particles spin in heavier loops until the center transforms into a solid circle of gray. The sight reminds me of a silver plate hanging in midair.

Then Justice punches through.

From the other side of the drift void, my brother strikes. Justice's fist smashes through the center of the void, opening a portal between this version of Earth and my home world of Umbra. Justice steps through the round opening between our realities.

My older brother cuts a bulky figure in his long duster, heavy boots, and scarred face. Basically, he's a younger version of our father, Cole. Both are the perfect combination of intellect and a hefty right hook. Justice is a master of battle sentient, second only to the Emperor himself.

A moment later, Slate slips past the round portal. My younger brother is a tall and sinewy with a long face and shoulder-length white hair. As a master of second sight sentient, Slate wears a deep indigo jacket with a high collar and straight cut. Not for the first time, my brothers remind me of a cowboy and preacher from Umbra's Wild West days.

Or maybe it's Earth's Wild West days. So hard to tell. My family *guards and gardens the omniverse,* meaning that we encourage certain lines of parallel universes to expand while others die out. Over the millennia, it gets easy to mix up *what* comes from *where,* if that makes sense.

With Slate through the drift void, the portal spirals into smaller circles. Within seconds, the connection has completely disappeared.

Justice grins. His symmetrical smile highlights his rugged, twice-broken nose. "Thorne. Good to see you." He sets his hand on my neck. "I still can't believe it. A transcendent."

I grin. He means Meimi, of course.

A transcendent is someone you love deeply across so many parallel universes, that connection bleeds over into your current reality. We were raised that the very idea of a transcendent is a fairy tale.

Even so, it's true.

Meimi is my transcendent.

It still doesn't seem possible.

Since I command few sentient, I'm the weak brother. The extra prince. An unworthy guy who got a free pass to the royal table. If anyone found a transcendent, it should have been Justice. He's the one who'll someday become Emperor. How I ended up deserving an honor such as Meimi, I'll never understand.

I only know that I'll protect her with everything I am.

Justice leans over until our foreheads gently touch. There's no mistaking the deep smile in his voice as he speaks. "Transcendents exist. What a boon."

"Don't forget," I counter. "Meimi and I are *soul* transcendents. She's not Umbran. We only share thoughts and feelings, not sentient power."

Justice shrugs and steps back. "I'd take that. You're a lucky man."

My smile widens. *I am indeed.*

Standing ramrod straight, Slate grips his fists behind his back. "Explain," he declares. My younger brother's voice is resonant and, as always, only heard for a word or two. By saying *explain*, that's Slate's way of asking for full details on me and Meimi.

My little brother doesn't chatter much. I figure it's because he lives in multiple futures with his second sight sentient. Or it could be that he's the baby of the family, so he got used to me and Justice doing all the talking.

"Let me think." I pause, trying to recall the last time I spoke with my brothers. "I saw you right after Meimi was taken by Godwin." It's only been a matter of weeks, but it feels like years have passed since then. "Since that day, there hasn't been much to tell. Godwin erased Meimi's memory, just like I expected." The very thought heats my blood with fury.

No one should have touched a hair on Meimi's head, let alone erased her memory.

Still, I can be thankful I saw it coming and could do something about it. Blinking hard, I refocus on my brothers.

"Meimi's been unconscious in hospitals most of the time," I continue. "I wheedled my way into Godwin's confidence so I could watch over her. Now I'm her guard."

"What about her—?" Justice taps his temple.

"Before Godwin took Meimi, I was able to link with her mind and leverage my own second sight sentient. They're keeping her memories safe." I don't add in the part about having to kiss her to get the job done. My brothers know how blue sentient work. And my kisses are nobody else's business.

Slate frowns. Since his face is all high cheek bones and smooth lines, that grimace is like breaking up a sculpture. "Meet," he says again. That means he wants details from before Godwin entered the picture.

My brows lift. This is a lot of talking from Slate. And frowning? It's an avalanche of emotion.

"All right." I hold my hands up, palms forward. "When I first saw Meimi, our minds instantly connected. There was no push from my sentient. It just ... happened. I could feel her emotions; she sensed mine as well. And we both received visions of the future—of us dancing, riding hoverbikes, that kind of stuff." My heart warms just remembering the experience.

"Were you shocked?" asks Justice. Normally, I'd give him guff about all these questions about feelings. After all, Justice is a big bad warrior. But my older brother seems so genuinely concerned, I can't make any jokes.

His interest is cool.

More than that, actually.

It's sweet.

And for a rough warrior like Justice, that's a big deal.

"Oh, I was floored when the visions first came in," I reply. "But the whole thing became more overwhelming for Meimi, so I shut down our link. I only opened it up once more to save her memories. And since then, nothing like that connection has happened again." I scratch my cheek and wince. "I'm pretty sure she hates me now that she's awake. Not that I blame her. Godwin presented me as her badass guard."

"You can't give her back her memories?" asks Justice.

"Kiss," says Slate.

And there it is. They both know how it works.

"Not yet." Frustration tightens across my neck and shoulders. "My powers are blocked while I'm under the Boston Dome. No kissing—no activating her memories—until I get her out of Boston. Not that there's been a chance to help her leave. Until today, Meimi's been unconscious and in the middle of different *procedures from Godwin.*" There's no hiding the acid in my tone as I say that last bit. "But she's recovered and mobile now. I'll get her out soon."

"Override," declares Slate.

I look to Justice. "What does he mean?"

"Slate's seen some futures where you override that block. We're working on options."

"Thanks." This is good news. Umbran tech is far more advanced than Earthen. In fact, I'm amazed that humans came up with anything that could block our sentient in the first place.

Now that we've covered the happy subject—namely Meimi—it's time to cover darker topics.

"How's Cole?" I ask.

That's our father, Emperor of the Omniverse. To become ruler, Cole had to take in a ton of Crown Sentient, a super-powerful breed of these cybernetic nanocreatures. Crown Sentient allow my father to see multiple universes and dimensions, but they're also eating away at his mind.

"Cole's still Cole," says Justice. "The emperor's obsessed that I have a transcendent. Thinks it's the end of his rule."

My chest tightens with worry. When our father is sane, we call him Dad. When he's not, then his name's Cole. Sadly, he's been Cole more and more lately.

"Sorry you had to deal with that alone." I tap my earpiece. "Wish I could contact you when I'm in the dome."

"Not to worry." Justice adjusts his white Stetson. "Take care of your transcendent. Let Slate and I handle Cole."

Slate's gray eyes widen. "Coming."

"You mean Cole?" I ask.

Slate nods. My heart sinks. My father is following us here.

No, not my father. *Cole.*

And he's been obsessing over transcendents.

There's not much I can do to protect Meimi from him, considering how weak I am with sentient. Even so, what I lack in sentient power, I make up for in training, learning, and determination.

I can only hope this time, that's enough to save Meimi.

"Eventually, Crown Sentient destroy the mind of every emperor or empress who possess them. It is only a matter of time." – Hammurabi the Seventh, *Law of Sentient*

ANOTHER DRIFT VOID opens in the ruined lobby. When Justice visited, he used silver sentient, meaning the purpose of his trip was knowledge. This time, Cole's connection to this world is made from dark particles.

Battle sentient.

Seconds later, the whirl of dark molecules changes. Where there was once a loop, now a plate of sentient hangs in the air. A moment of hesitation follows. Justice, Slate, and I barely breathe, let alone move.

Crash!

Cole leaps through the drift void. The flat disc of sentient falls to the floor. The plate smashes into pieces before vanishing altogether.

He's here.

My father stands before us, his barrel chest heaving in deep breaths. As always, he wears nothing but black: short leather coat, wool pants, Stetson hat and tall boots. A dark patch covers his left eye. His face is crisscrossed with scars.

And he's definitely in Cole mode. Not my father at all. It's in the eyes. My father has large brown eyes that overflow with emotion. Cole's are harsh and calculating. Overall, the effect is like watching a reanimated corpse—there's something of the person you loved, but not, all at once.

A weight of sorrow settles in my heart.

Cole rounds on Justice. "What is this? Why are you here?"

"Tell us first," counters Justice, "why did *you* come here?"

Justice takes off his pale Stetson. Within seconds, the hat bursts into a small cloud of particles. The tiny bits then reenter my brother's skin. Like everything my family wears, our clothes are made of sentient. For Justice, removing his hat this way is another way of saying, *you want a fight? I'm ready*.

"I'm here because I sensed a transcendent." Cole pulls out a small square device with a tiny gray screen. This thing may look simple, but anything my father builds is both complex and powerful. "What do you make of this?" he asks.

Justice glances at the small square in Cole's hand. I can see the screen easily enough; it displays the date and time when I kissed Meimi. The device also gives the coordinates for this version of Earth. It seems that my first meeting with Meimi wasn't enough to set off any alarms with Cole. But protecting her consciousness with my kiss? That definitely got his attention. *Good to know.*

"That's a date and time," says Justice.

"No, it's a transcendent," retorts Cole. "I got a single read on this person. Since then, nothing. And now I find you three sneaking off to this planet." He points at Justice. "What are you scheming at?"

Cole only accuses Justice of having secret plans. My father doesn't see me or Slate as much of a threat. Well, perhaps Slate a little. I barely rank as non-furniture.

"Does it make any difference what I tell you?" asks Justice.

With a slow motion, Cole eyes my oldest brother from head to toe. "Nah," he exclaims at length. "I already know the truth, son. You want to be more powerful than I am. So you send the weakest in the family to watch over your girl." Cole hitches his thumb in my direction. "You sent your frail little brother to protect your transcendent. Admit it."

This is too much.

I step forward. "You taught us that transcendents are fairy tales," I say calmly. "They don't exist."

Cole sniffs. "Not for you, they don't."

His words drip with disdain. *Here we go again.* I'm the extra prince. The weak child. And honestly, I don't know what to make about having a transcendent. Beyond an overwhelming need to keep Meimi safe, I've no idea what consequences might be out there. Meimi and I can connect our thoughts and feelings, but that wouldn't make me more powerful with sentient. And controlling sentient is all that my father—or rather Cole—cares about.

"Respect," says Slate. It's his way of standing up for me. My chest warms with his effort. My little brother knows I focus on reading, research and practice to compensate for having so few sentient. He thinks it's a worthy pursuit.

Not so with Cole.

The emperor glares at Slate. "Get strong with battle sentient and you can say a word that I'll actually listen to." He returns his focus on Justice. "Don't pretend anymore. I've seen universes with transcendents. Plenty of them. But I had to erase them all. No transcendents. Nothing that will threaten my rule."

Justice's mouth falls slack. "You did *what?*"

"You heard me!" howls Cole. "I protect my crown." Cole thumps his fist against his chest. "I don't have a transcendent. And if I'm alone, then it's not safe for others to be paired up. Who knows when some couple would rise and attack me?"

Justice, Slate, and I exchange looks. We were all raised that transcendents were a myth. Yet can this be the truth? Father never found his transcendent ... so he wiped out everyone else's?

"I know how it works." Cole taps his temple. "Finding a transcendent gives you extra energy. More power." He steps closer to Justice. "You want to rule. You'll take my Crown Sentient, bond them to you, and usurp my throne."

Now, becoming emperor isn't a life goal for me or my brothers. We consider it more of a family curse than anything else.

Even so, there's no explaining that to Cole.

"I'll ask y'all again." Cole cracks his knuckles. "What are you three doing here?"

I step forward once more, this time moving so I stand right between Cole and Justice. I'm as tall as both of them. Since I now face Cole, there's no way he can avoid addressing me.

"I chose to come here to make good on *your* promise," I declare in a low voice. "Do you remember those two scientists, Rose and Truman Archer? The ones who hid your Crown Sentient so you could rule? They live on this world. You said you'd grant them one favor for risking their lives to help you. Rose called in that favor. She wants her daughter kept safe. So that's why I'm here."

Originally, Rose asked for help with her daughter Luci, not Meimi, but that's beside the point. And I won't get into that level of detail with Cole. I'll be lucky if he remembers the conversation about Rose and Truman in the first place.

Cole frowns. "Janais might've said something about that."

A little tension eases from my shoulders. Mentioning our mother, Janais, is a good sign. It shows that the emperor is moving away from being Cole ... and coming closer to becoming our father again.

"We discussed Rose and Truman weeks ago," says Justice. "It was you, me, and Janais. Don't you remember?"

"Maybe." Cole takes a half step backward. Like always, he looks right through me to Justice. "But you can't leave tech here. There are rules for going on missions to other worlds."

"I'm haven't left a thing in this version of Earth," I explain. "It's the same for Justice and Slate. We know the rules."

Cole isn't shouting more death threats, which means I'm making headway. At this point, he's just grasping at straws to find some excuse for his temper tantrum. Leaving tech behind is a big deal. That doesn't mean it happened.

"Go ahead," I say. "Scan the planet. We've left nothing here." I step closer, forcing Cole to meet my gaze again. "Rose and Truman Archer. They risked everything for you. I'm keeping your promise and protecting their daughter."

And all of that is true, by the way. Both Meimi and Luci are safe, thanks to my work.

For a fraction of a second, Cole meets my gaze. "Fine. We should keep our promises. That's what I always tell you boys." His grizzled mouth rounds into a soft smile.

There. That's the father I remember. The one who taught me to ride a quarter horse. Who loves his wife with the fire to light a thousand suns. And who always told me that it didn't matter if I had barely any sentient. His words echo through my mind.

Life is soul and smarts, my son.
You've got plenty of both.

Father raises his hand. Thousands of silver particles lift off his skin, floating up into the shape of a vertical loop.

He's opening a drift void.

Leaving.

Peacefully.

The silver particles solidify into a single round plate. Dad steps toward the drift void, then pauses. A visible shiver racks his body.

When my he turns around again, my father is gone.

Cole is back.

"No transcendents!" Cole whips out his Bowie knife. The drift void disappears. "I've seen my own death due to their power." Cole turns to Justice. "I'm killing your transcendent, here and now. I can track her down. Just try to stop me."

Fresh battle sentient seep out from Cole's skin. A heartbeat later, those particles form a dark lasso in Cole's free hand. Most sentient can't create tiny moving parts, so my brothers and I mostly create sentient swords and ropes. That said, you never know with Crown Sentient. Those can do all sorts of unexpected things. Only Cole knows their true capabilities.

"You're not killing anyone today," declares Justice.

In reply, Cole lunges straight at Justice's throat. My breath catches.

Without hesitation, I jump between my father and brother, raise my upper arm, and block Cole's strike. My father's blade pounds against the body armor on my forearm. Pain radiates through my limb. Cole's attack will leave a bruise, but at least my armor didn't break.

Yet.

Leaning over, Cole pounds my kidneys with a series of fast hits, followed by a heavy slam against my jawline. My body burns with agony. Cole's every strike is backed by millions of battle sentient, but the jaw hit is the worst. I go flying across the room, my back slamming against a far wall. Blood drips down my chin. Hurt radiates through my torso.

Here we are again.

Another fight with Cole.

Three against one.

But with Crown Sentient on the emperor's side, it's never a fair fight.

"There are five fighting modes for facing an opponent who wields battle sentient: water mother, wolf cub, weaving maiden, crow's bridge, and wailing ghost. For Crown Sentient, there is only one option: run." – Wu Zhao Zetain, *The Art of Sentient War*

PAIN RICOCHETS through my nervous system as I force myself back onto my feet. Meanwhile, every inch of Cole's body ripples with black battle sentient. Soon, my father looks more like a carved statue than a living being. His outline expands by at least a foot in height alone.

Assuming I'm out of the fight, Cole cracks his lasso in Slate's direction. The cord snaps across the room, pausing at my younger brother's feet. From there, the rope rolls up into the form of another warrior. Soon a seven-foot-tall, coiled-up cowboy looms before Slate, able to fight without Cole giving it a single command.

That's Crown Sentient.

Agony pulses through my limbs. Still, I force myself to hobble a few steps closer to Cole. Across the lobby floor, bits of sentient rope break free from the coiled-up cowboy and tangle themselves around Slate's throat. Other cords bind his feet. To counterattack, Slate summons a pair of Bowie knives to appear in his fists. My little brother cuts through Cole's ropes with superhuman speed. Those efforts won't last, though. Slate will wear down. Crown Sentient won't.

Meanwhile, Cole and Justice launch into a fistfight that tears apart what's left of the apartment building's lobby. The cracked reception desk gets smashed to bits. Both couches become used as battering rams. Before long, Cole pins Justice against the wall.

"I'll kill her," cries Cole. "You can't stop me!"

With rapid-fire punches, Cole smashes his fists into my brother's face. It's too much. Meimi is my responsibility. Justice shouldn't die for her.

I step up beside them. "Hey!"

Cole keeps hammering away, oblivious. Justice's head lolls to one side. His eyes are swollen and closed. My older brother is unconscious now. So is Slate. I'm the only one left.

A weak prince.

False royal.

And the last chance for Meimi.

I force in a deep breath past my shattered ribs. "HEY."

Cole rounds on me.

I hold his gaze.

There's only one choice when Cole gets this out of control. Fighting him with fists won't work. So I don't even raise my arms.

But I also won't back down. Cole wants to kill the transcendent. I have to stop his murderous rampage and send him back to Umbra. For Meimi.

Cole slams another punch to my chest. More of my ribs crack. Pain spikes down my spine. I hunch over, but don't fall.

I also don't strike back.

Somehow, I'm able to keep eye contact with Cole.

Cole hits my jaw again. Blood spatters across my chest.

Yet I stand still and don't strike.

More hits. Kidneys, skull, ribs. Agony erupts through me, delivering pain beyond anything I've ever known. Even so, I refuse to topple over.

I won't give up.

Meimi.

Cole's panting now. "Why don't you fall down and play possum? You've got no sentient."

I force out words past a fractured jaw. "Life is soul and smarts. Someone told me I've plenty of both." I'm almost totally hunched over now, yet I keep eye contact between us. "I'm fighting, just in my own way."

Inside my heart, I plead with whatever runs the universe. *Come on, let this work. Let my words touch whatever part of Cole is still my father.*

Cole slowly steps backward, his body reassuming its normal proportions. His skin stops resembling dark stone. His face falls slack with horror. "Oh, my sons."

And with that, Cole is gone. Dad is back.

I exhale. *Meimi is safe. For now.*

Father glances over to Justice. My oldest brother shakes his head as he comes back to consciousness. Sentient help us heal quickly. Father raises his hand. His black lasso whips away from Slate, who pulls in a deep breath while rubbing his throat. *Yes.*

I slump forward, bracing my hands on my knees. My own sentient start to rebuild my injuries, but it isn't pleasant. "It's good to have you back, Dad."

"How long was I gone this time?" asks Father.

Justice forces himself to stand. "A few weeks. Maybe more."

Panic shines in Father's dark eyes. "Janais?"

"Mom's fine," explains Justice.

"Okay, good. I need to get back. See what I ruined and what I can fix. I'm sorry, boys."

Father opens another portal, this time with silver sentient. He doesn't punch his way through, so it takes longer to pass beyond the circle, but soon enough he's gone.

That was close.

Justice, Slate, and I share a long moment of quiet. What's there to say? We're losing our father.

"We should leave." Justice rakes his hand through his brown hair. "We'll look into that situation with unblocking the dome."

"Much appreciated." I swallow past the knot of grief in my throat. "You didn't have to fight him, you know. Meimi's my responsibility."

"Brothers," says Slate. And I know what he means. If we're going to survive this, we must protect each other, no matter what.

Justice opens another drift void, steps through, and is gone. Slate starts to open one of his own, pauses, and then turns to me. He makes a bird-like tilt of his head.

"Transcendent." Slate packs all the meaning in the world into that single word. I realize what he's getting at.

"I'll keep Meimi safe," I say. "She's all that matters."

Slate nods and then finishes opening his drift void. After he slowly steps through, my little brother takes off as well. The void itself swirls into ever smaller loops.

Then it vanishes.

Once they've both left, I drag my hands over my face.

Cole's had some kind of vision. He's convinced there's a transcendent for Justice somewhere on this version of Earth. And he's created some device that might be able to track her down.

Keeping Meimi safe just got a lot tougher.

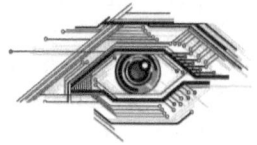

ONE BENEFIT of being pumped full of tranquilizers—you sure fall asleep fast.

In my dreams, I soar over a complex of brick buildings surrounded by gravel and blackened grass. Positive point: I'm wearing my hospital gown, so at least this isn't one of those *show up somewhere naked* dreams. A broken sign on the pavement reads *Ozymandias Chemical Factory*.

Although I have no wings, I fly toward the largest structure in the complex of buildings. It's a long brick affair that's two stories high and topped by an arched roof. One chunk of wall has been completely smashed in.

Swooping downward, I move through the factory's busted wall, stopping inside a small storage room. At one time, this place also served as a kitchen. Now the counters droop at odd angles. Smashed bits of porcelain line the floor. What was once a stove and fridge are now melted-down heaps.

This room should be deserted.

Yet someone is here.

A figure sits by the window, watching the sheets of green rain.

I move closer, my feet hovering inches above the ground. My dream-self knows exactly who to expect. "Mom?"

Memories appear. My mother always sits by this window. For years, she and I have hidden out in this very deserted factory. With each passing day, Mom becomes less coherent and more catatonic.

The Authority considers her *undesirable*. Unless we stay out of sight, it's only a matter of time before they find and kill her.

I step closer to the figure. "Mom? Is that you?"

The stranger turns away from the window.

This is not my mother.

She's me.

Shock skitters down my spine. I'm facing a perfect replica of myself, only this version is blue from head to toe. Plus, she's wearing indigo body armor. I blink, wondering if the vision will change.

It doesn't.

"Hello," says Blue Me. "I'm Meimi."

"I'm, uh, Wisteria."

For a dream, this experience now takes on a lifelike edge, outside of the blueness factor. Something tells me this has become something else.

Reality, maybe? Hard to say.

"What did you just call yourself?" asks Blue Me.

"Wisteria," I say.

"No, that's not our name." She gestures between us. "We're both called Meimi, only we got a split up. I remember some stuff about our past. You pretty much know zip."

"I know Mom and I lived here," I offer. "Maybe my memories are coming back."

Blue Me shakes her head, tossing her wavy blue hair with the motion. "I brought you here for a reason. Guess who knew the kitchen would bring back a few things? Me."

I take a half step backward. "So if you brought me here, what do you want?"

"We're the same person," replies Blue Me. "So I figure we should team up. Since one of us—*that would be me*—houses most of our memories, and another one of us—*that would be you*—has the ability to actually do stuff outside of random dreams, I thought you might have a few ideas."

My thoughts turn back to my last encounter with Godwin. "I do have one plan. The Authority wants to kill a ton of innocent people." An image appears in my mind. A woman seated by a window. Mom. She could be on that list of innocents. "I need to stop this by putting together a team."

Blue Me purses her lips. "We were never really into teaming."

"But I must protect people from the Authority." *Like Mom.*

"While we do this, could we get ourselves set up in ECHO Academy?" asks Blue Me.

"Well, I have no idea yet how I'm doing any of this, but sure. Why not add ECHO Academy to the list?"

Blue Me smiles. "In that case, I'm in. What do you need?"

"Scientists. People I know and can work with."

"Well, we certainly knew some smart folks in our past life. The ones most likely to help are Chloe, Zoe, and Fritz."

Closing my eyes, I repeat the list. *Chloe, Zoe, and Fritz.* "I need to recall those names when I'm awake. How do I get your—I mean *our* —memories back?"

"I'm working on it." Blue Me snaps her fingers. "Oh, there's someone else who might be useful. The Hollow."

"Seriously?" That's a shocker. The Hollow is in a maximum security prison and slated for death.

"Think about it," says Blue Me. "For decades, we were getting a new president every year or so. Then President Hope gets appointed by the Star Council. She's lasted a whopping three years. The secret to her success was..."

"The Hollow." I rub my neck, thinking. As a professor at ECHO Academy, the Hollow developed her own cyber implants for grabbing and sharing information. She could be super helpful. "But the Hollow has been declared an undesirable and slated for cleansing. Even President Hope couldn't save her. I don't think we can free her for our team."

Blue Me's body fades until the back of the kitchen becomes visible through her torso. I gesture toward her. "Something's wrong with your, uh, *you*," I point out.

Holding up her hand, Blue Me scans her skin. "Crud. I'm running out of time." She returns her focus to me. "I'll find a way to contact you while you're awake. Soon."

With that, Blue Me vanishes entirely.

Sadness envelops me, heavy as a cloak. For the rest of my dream, I float-walk through the chemical factory, scanning through bits of rubble, trying to find any part of my lost memories.

I never do find anything.

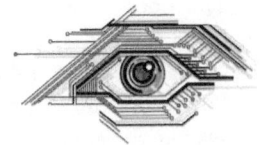

THE NEXT MORNING, I wake up in a crappy little cot. No more fancy-pants hospital. Now I'm locked up in a concrete block of a room. Turning on my side, I find that messages have been scratched into the wall nearest me.

ECHO Academy Underground
Tawana Rines, Chemist, 2219
Ian Rhodes, Drift Scientist, 2226
Jane Fisher, Engineer, 2232

I run my fingers across the letters cut into the concrete. Does this mean what I think it means?

This is *the* ECHO Academy Underground?

My skin prickles with excitement. The Underground is the most prized assignment for any researcher. The name pretty much gives away the location: a complex of rooms about ninety stories underneath the ECHO campus. But the stuff it contains is amazing. Supposedly, the greatest laboratory in existence can be found down here. Plus, the Simulacrum is here as well—that's a souped-up hologram generator that can run almost any scientific scenario.

So the tech toys here are cool. The accommodations? Not so much.

I scan the names again. The dates must mark when these scientists left here. But why carve their names in cement?

The answer instantly appears. This is the Authority, after all. I can't imagine you get a nice pat on the back and a chocolate cake when you're done being useful. This may very well have been their way of saying goodbye.

I shiver. Hopefully, I won't be another name on that list.

The door opens with a long squeak. Thorne steps through. It might be the bad lighting in here, but the guy's skin looks more pale than usual. He's also trying to hide a limp.

"Good morning," I say. In reality, I'm not sure if it's morning, but it feels like the a.m., so I'm going with it.

"Hey."

Not much of a reply there.

Thorne leans against the wall, staring into nothingness. The warmth in his eyes has disappeared.

Sitting up, I notice I'm no longer wearing my hospital gown. Now I'm in a button-front onesie that says Authority in big red letters. Gray Mary Janes sit on the floor by my bed.

"What's with my new outfit?" I ask.

"Better than the hospital stuff."

I tug at the collar of my onesie. "Who changed my clothes?"

No reply.

This guy is tough. Unfortunately, he's also my only chance for an ally. Maybe I should say something cute or flirty. That could build more bridges.

"If you were the one who touched me, I'll break all your fingers."

Oops. That sounded better in my head.

Thorne slices a look in my direction. "Not me. Nurses."

"Three words." Smiling, I pat at non-existent tears beneath my eyes. "Wow. I really feel we had a bonding moment there."

Thorne gives me what might be a wink, but it's too quick to be sure. He then goes back to staring at the opposite wall.

Boys are so confusing. They should come with a manual.

The door swings open again. This time, it's Godwin. He must have a closet that's filled with nothing but lab coats. It's all the man wears.

Godwin stalks right past me to approach Thorne. "How was the girl overnight?"

My guard's face stays stony. "Fine."

I raise my hand. "I slept like I was drugged up, then I awoke in different clothes and in a decidedly prison-cell-like setting. But I'm handling it all pretty well, thanks for asking."

The doctor keeps talking to Thorne. "Did you deactivate her wrist cuff?"

Thorne nods. "Can't take it off permanently, though. That would send an alert to Humboldt directly."

"That's fine," states Godwin. "As long as we're the only ones who can track her."

I raise my hand again. "I found that last statement to be both creepy and threatening."

Godwin's upper lip twitches with anger. Glad to see I'm getting through to the guy. After marching to my bedside, the doctor shoves a data pad at my face. "Review this code. Do you see anything wrong?"

"I take it I'm starting the testing now." I blink innocently. "Is that right?"

"Of course." A vein throbs along Godwin's temple. I take that as a personal victory.

"So," I continue. "If I take these tests..."

"*When* you take them," corrects Godwin.

"We'll see," I say. "After the testing stuff, will you then show me your master plan for the Liberation Celebration? Also, when you're sharing your evil schemes, I'd love it if you threw a good *mwah-hah-hah* in there. And also-also, please say, *we're not so very different, you and I*. After all, if you're going to play up the evil doctor, don't go halfway."

"If you fail any of these tests," snarls Godwin, "I'll slice your throat myself."

"And if I pass them?" I ask.

"I will indeed take you to the Simulacrum and reveal my scheme."

"Okay, I'm in." I scoop the data pad from his hands.

"As I was saying before," explains Godwin. "You must review this code. See if you can find any gaps." A smarmy light shines in the doctor's button eyes.

No question what that smarm factor is all about. Godwin totally thinks there is absolutely zero wrong with his code.

I scan the rows of tiny symbols. Blaring errors stand out. The mistakes are simply too irritating not to fix, so I open up an editing program and start rewriting.

Godwin leans in. "What are you doing?"

"This code is for powering up a magnetic enhancer," I explain. "It's way inefficient. See this start-up sequence? It's all over the place. You're sucking up extra rounds of processing time for no reason." I pause, an idea forming. "Did you try to reverse engineer someone else's work?"

Godwin's face turns pink. "I don't know what you're talking about."

In other words, he totally reverse-engineered someone else's stuff.

I tap the screen. "You can't calibrate the refraction index until you've connected and optimized all the magnetic energy source inputs." I don't even end the sentence by saying *duh*, which I consider another personal accomplishment.

Godwin grabs the data pad from my hand. "That's can't be right." He flips through screen after screen. "I'll have my men look over this later."

Which means I'm right.

I try not to smirk. But honestly? I don't work too hard.

"Anything else for me?" I ask.

Godwin rounds on Thorne. "Hand her the test," he says. "Just the way we discussed it."

Thorne marches to the door. A few seconds later, he tromps back with a hefty box balanced in his arms, which he then dumps out onto my bed.

Subtle.

"Assemble this," orders Godwin.

I debate telling him to ask nicely, but even Godwin has his limits for how much mouth he can handle. Plus, if the guy bursts a blood vessel, I'll never discover his evil plans.

Focusing on my bed, I pick through the pile of junk. In my mind, the pieces realign and connect. Within minutes, I've set the bits together into what looks like a wire octopus.

"This is a magnetic enhancer," I declare. "It goes with the code you showed before. But you need a bunch of parts to finish it."

"That's correct." Now a second vein pulses angrily atop Godwin's shiny head.

Someone's not a happy doctor.

"I've many more assessments planned for you," announces Godwin.

Thus begins a lot of tests that follow a repeated process that goes something like ...

Godwin question: What's this?

My answer: A blueprint for a blabbity blah.

Question: How would you make it better?

Answer: How long do you have?

We repeat this discussion for the following topics: drift void monoliths, quark tracker code, dimensional lenses, and dark matter brackets. Godwin also throws a toaster in there just to be a dick. I fix that, too, just because I can.

Next follows another set of software coding tests, after which we return to the *let's dump crap on Wisteria's bed* routine.

Hours pass. I'm pretty sure a full day goes by, although it's hard to tell down here. I haven't eaten a thing. Even so, I refuse to let Godwin see I'm hungry or tired as I assemble yet another pile of junk.

"This is a quantum detector," I announce. "Again, there are about twenty ways this could be better. Or even deliver basic functionality."

Godwin's constellation of head veins still thump away, but he doesn't say a thing. Over the course of the day, I've decided to call them the Poundy Bunch. Not a lot of chances for entertainment down here, so I'm taking my laughs where I can get them.

I clear my throat. "What's next?"

Thorne glances to Godwin, but my guard doesn't say a word either. That's pretty typical for Thorne. It's like I don't exist.

Did I dream that wink of his from before?

A theory appears in my mind. *Maybe this is early Stockholm syndrome.* Thorne is just a muscle-bound douchebag, and I'm tricking myself that he's more.

I switch my focus to Godwin. *Perhaps he's the one I need to recruit as a helper.* The Poundy Bunch start doing extra gross things on his shiny skull.

Thorne it is, then.

"Look," I say. "We can go around and around on these tests. There are two things you need to know, though. One, I'm hungry."

Yes, I was going to be badass and pretend I didn't need a meal. But then I pictured a sandwich.

"Two," I continue, "until I see your master plan, I won't really know if I can help you. So, let's get this over with. Show me your stuff. I'll tell you how I'll make it happen. If you like my ideas, we'll move forward. If you don't, your goon boy can kill me already. What do you think?"

Godwin's button eyes narrow to slits. "I hate you."

"Good." I narrow-eye right back at him. "I hate you more."

Hypothesis: that's the least mature conversation between two scientists, ever.

For a fraction of a moment, an amused grin rounds Thorne's mouth. *There.* I'm definitely breaking through to him. It's that, or Thorne's on some pain meds for his limp and the high is kicking in.

Either way, I'll take it. A blank-faced Thorne is a creepy Thorne.

"Follow me," announces Godwin.

In this moment, it's a challenge for me not to cheer. I'm one step closer to figuring out how to take down Godwin, save the undesirables, and get my shapely butt out of this prison.

Yay me.

"The bond between transcendents presses up from the quantum level, is driven by multiple universes and dimensions, and compounds through both force and memory." – Empress Ophelia, *The Lost Book of Transcendents*

GODWIN LEADS Meimi down the main corridor. I keep a safe distance behind them, on alert for any sign of threats or danger.

Meanwhile, every corner of my soul wants me to pull my girl into a hug and congratulate her on a job well done. Those tests were impossible, and she aced each one. Plus, Godwin is a sadistic scumbag. No food or water? Who does that? Even so, Meimi kept pushing the doctor's buttons. More than once, I almost burst out laughing. Fortunately, my body's still healing from the fight with Cole. Nothing like pain to help you keep a straight face.

At the end of the cement hallway, there stands a small silver door. Like everywhere down here, the security is minimal. It takes about a dozen checkpoints to reach ninety-some levels underground. No one is down here who doesn't belong.

Stepping across the threshold, we enter the control chamber for the Simulacrum. Basically, this is a massive concrete box of a room. It's empty as well. There are no chairs or tables, only a small podium in the center of the floor which serves as a small control tower.

Godwin pauses before the podium. After cracking his knuckles, he taps instructions onto the plat panel display atop the console.

"Come here," orders Godwin. "Both of you."

Meimi and I step closer, pausing behind Godwin. He gestures around him. "This is the Simulacrum. You can think of it as my *play room* for testing different scientific theories and scenarios."

"Do I have to?" asks Meimi.

Godwin doesn't answer, but his head vein starts pulsing again. It's getting harder not to laugh.

"I've spent many hours here," continues Godwin. "My plans for the Liberation Celebration are all loaded into the Simulacrum as a detailed hologram. You two will be the first to see the scheme in full." He shoots me a sly look. "Not that *some of us* will understand it all."

In Godwin's mind, I'm nothing but muscle. *Which is hilarious.* Back on my home planet, I'm considered more of a bookworm than a warrior. It's said that I can recount a quote for any occasion. Maybe I can.

Godwin taps the control console once more. The surface of the podium transforms. Before, the control panel looked sleek and dark. Now the structure melts and twists. Within seconds, it becomes a series of delicate cords that gently shift and writhe.

A jolt of shock moves up y spine. I know that tech.

Filaments.

It's Umbran technology.

As the royal family, we often visit other worlds. But we're forbidden to leave any instruments behind, especially filament tech. It's an important rule; leaving filaments behind could derail a society's natural development.

So how did filaments end up here?

My mind spins through possibilities. Years ago, my father contacted Rose and Truman Archer for help. Both of them worked here at ECHO Academy. Maybe my father left this console behind. It's odd, but possible.

"Did you create this?" I ask. *Because Umbran filaments took our sentient millions of years to develop.*

Godwin lifts his chin. "Who else could have done it?"

Which isn't saying that he created the filaments. Even so, the implication is clear. *This is my invention.* Godwin so desperately wants to be a genius. But after spending a few weeks with the guy, I've only seen him display gifts for cruelty and lies, in that order.

Godwin gestures to the control panel before him. The filaments still twist and sway in a gentle rhythm. "This is also the master containment system for the Lacerator."

That gets my attention.

Everyone's heard of the Lacerator. It's Godwin's most famous attack animal. Although it isn't *really* an animal. Since I'm Umbran, I know the Lacerator's what we call a *sentient swarm*. Those are unique groups of particles that operate as a hive mind. They often roam the omniverse.

That said, I've never heard of a swarm getting trapped before.

Reaching into the writhing filaments, Godwin pulls out a long rectangular container from the console's center. Turns out, the box he removes is also made from the same shifting filaments. Sentient swarms often rest in containers like these; we call them nests. Somehow Godwin got his hands on the Lacerator's home. *Strange.*

A memory appears. Before Meimi's memory was wiped, she told me about an encounter with the Lacerator at a place called RCM1. That sentient swarm should have killed her on sight. It didn't. *Interesting.* I set the thought aside to contemplate later on.

The doctor holds up the moving container. "The Lacerator is in here, can you believe it?"

Meimi frowns. "Did I meet the Lacerator before my memory got wiped? Because none of this seems new to me."

"Your memory wasn't wiped," corrects Godwin. "You fell on Newbury Street."

Meimi snaps her fingers. "Why do I think the Lacerator roams around? Did it get loose or something?"

"It used to roam free and cause damage, but I stopped all that." Godwin nods toward the shifting control console. "Thanks to the filaments I placed in this console, the Lacerator can no longer escape."

An idea hits me. *This console could also explain how my powers are blocked.*

"Your central console," I begin, "is it hooked up outside the Simulacrum as well?"

"Yes, I linked it directly into the Boston Dome." Godwin lowers his voice to a conspiratorial tone. "You see, we used to have issues with the Lacerator escaping. Now, we have two layers of security, namely this console as well as the dome itself. My little beastie stays put these days."

Godwin places the Lacerator's container back inside the console tower. After the container is reset, Godwin again taps the top control panel. Shifting filaments stop moving. Instead of a writhing surface of cords, the podium becomes a smooth structure once more. I glare at the thing.

This console is my enemy.

It's what's blocking my powers under the dome.

Simply put, I must neutralize it. Good thing there's not a lot of security around here. I'll have to sneak back and spend some quality time with those filaments.

"As you'll soon see, the Lacerator is critical to my plan," states Godwin. "When my scheme is complete, I'll be more than the winner of this competition." Godwin pauses dramatically.

"Okay, I'll bite," says Meimi. "What will you be?"

Godwin puffs out his thin chest. "The new President of the Authority."

A long pause follows. The temperature in the room seems to dip ten degrees. Godwin is unhinged. He can't run the Authority.

It's Meimi who breaks the silence.

"And there's your *mwah-hah-hah* moment," she says. "Honestly, you leading the Authority is a super-bad idea."

"Still the little clown," snarls Godwin. "Wait until you see the rest of my scheme. Then we'll discover where the true humor lies."

At this point, I don't need to see Godwin's entire scheme. I already know that if Godwin runs the Authority, then no one will be safe.

Especially Meimi.

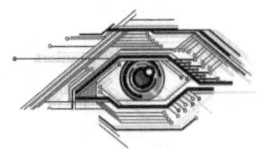

IT'S OFFICIAL. *Godwin is a nutjob.*

Sure, I knew he wanted to win a game of *let's tag people for death*. But taking over the government? That means booting out both President Hope and her brother, General Humboldt.

Not easy.

Godwin presses more buttons on his control console. Around us, tiny blocks of colored light stack up. A hologram builds out across the concrete floor. No question where this is going. We're about to see the Liberation Celebration.

I won't lie. The scientist in me is impressed.

"Next you'll witness my scheme in action." Godwin gestures toward me. "Once I'm done, you can share what's needed to make this happen. Remember, you'll only have two months to finish. Assuming you live to work on this for me, every second will be precious."

"Got it." I'm really happy with how confident those two words sound. Inside, I'm starting to wonder how hard it will be to escape from the Underground.

Pretty hard, probably.

Soon, the walls around us seem to disappear. As the hologram builds out, Godwin remains standing at the podium, tapping on the upper console. Meanwhile, the rest of the space transforms. Before it was a concrete block of a room. Now it looks like the famous Golden Pantheon building of ECHO Academy. It's a fancy dinner theater on steroids. There's a sleek metal stage, an oval floor covered with tables, and a domed ceiling that's lined with—you guessed it—gold.

The real me, Thorne, and Godwin and all stand beside a front row table for the event. Before us, the simulated stage is decorated with a wall of monitors. The many screens combine to show a single video of the Presidential Palace with its white marble columns, wide doors, and curtained windows.

The Liberation Celebration always places a ton of screens onstage. Last year, the displays showed Godwin's new attack animals. This year, the Authority will probably broadcast the undesirables meeting their end. My insides twist.

This is sick beyond words.

All the more reason to appear calm while plotting how to destroy everything.

I risk a look behind me. Sure enough, simulated tables stretch off into the distance. Smiling people in fancy clothes eat their gourmet meals. Camera drones take to the air, signaling the event is about to begin. The audience shouts with joy.

Anxiety rattles my nervous system. Sure, I've seen this event on data feeds. But I always do the same thing: *turn it off*.

A roar erupts from the audience as President Hope steps onstage, followed by General Humboldt. Both are over six feet tall, with brown hair and blue eyes. Their faces and bodies have the same stocky and muscular build, similarities that you'd expect from a brother and sister. President Hope wears a patch to cover the implant in her left eye. Why? She and the Hollow have matching left eyes. Now that the Hollow is in prison, President Hope has covered up her implant.

As the president crosses to center stage, a kind of light exudes from her. Hope thrives under the crowd's attention. Meanwhile her brother Humboldt lurks behind her, tall and sulky.

A moment later, a simulated Godwin slinks out behind them both. Compared to the president and general, the doctor seems small and insignificant: a horsefly that's doomed to be swatted by their thoroughbred tails.

The hologram version of President Hope wears a white suit, high heels, and a dazzling smile. She pauses at center stage. "Welcome to the Liberation Celebration! Every year at this event, we make the continent a little safer and more productive by showing new ways to cleanse undesirables."

The crowd bursts into a fresh round of applause. Not sure how much of that is support or terror, though.

"This year," continues the hologram president, "we held a competition to decide who could tag the most undesirables. But before we present those results, Dr. Godwin would like to make an announcement. I must admit, it's very exciting." She winks at the simulated Godwin. "That is, if he can pull it off."

Stepping to center stage, the hologram Godwin addresses the audience. "Every year, I announce a new attack animal. This time, I have a different creation to add into the mix."

At these words, a large spider bot lurches onstage. *Whoa, I've never seen anything like this.* The machine stands at waist height. Eight hefty metal legs slam onto the stage floor in an odd rhythm.

Scanning the machine, I commit every detail to memory. Chances are, the real Godwin will need me to build this huge bot.

"Behold my new invention," says hologram Godwin. "The Crawler."

Sure, it's your invention. In my mind, I'm already laying out blueprints for how to make this thing work.

"You've heard of mini drift voids," continues the hologram Godwin. "They create a portal between one spot and another on a particular planet."

"Are you going to open a drift void to another world?" asks General Humboldt.

"Maybe next year," replies Godwin.

My brows lift. There's been a ton of theories about opening drift voids to other worlds. How close is Godwin to realizing that? Many scientists think it's impossible to create a gateway to another reality. Maybe it's my old memories seeping through, but I believe there can be drift voids between worlds.

"I've something better," adds Godwin. "This Crawler contains something I like to call an *omnivoid generator*. It creates millions of mini drift voids at once, so this Crawler can visit countless spots on earth ... all at the same time."

My eyes widen. Today during testing, I reviewed parts for building a single mini drift void, meaning a portal between places on the same planet. That's tricky stuff. But an omnivoid? Nothing like that has ever been diagrammed before, let alone built. And Godwin needs one in two months. I nibble my thumbnail.

Yipes.

"And what else awaits inside this Crawler?" Hologram Godwin taps the the metal spider. "The Lacerator, my greatest attack animal."

The crowd lets out a low "oooh."

Hologram Godwin snaps his fingers. Onstage, the wall of screens ceases to show the Presidential Palace. New video appears instead. In it, there's what looks like an abandoned warehouse building. A small box made of shifting fibers sits on the ground before the structure.

My eyes widen with recognition. Godwin showed this same container just moments ago. It's what stores the Lacerator. A word appears in my mind. *Nest.*

Yes, that describes it perfectly. That container is basically the Lacerator's nest.

On the massive screens, the video shows that nest flicking open. A large, dark claw curls out over the side, followed by another. Only this talon isn't solid.

It's made from tiny black particles.

The Lacerator quickly hauls itself out of the nest. A moment later, black particles hover across the video screens. After that, they congeal into a massive beast, only one that's still semitransparent. The Lacerator stands seven feet tall with Stegosaurus-like plates down its back. Gangly legs hold the beast upright. Long arms scrape along the ground. The Lacerator's face is long, with holes for eyes and a wide mouth that's lined with razor-sharp teeth. Leaning back, the creature lets out the mother of all roars.

To my ear, the sound echoes with fear and sorrow. I'm not sure how I can be so certain of those emotions, but I am.

On the other hands, the crowd loves it. A deafening cheer takes over the chamber. Onstage, the video of the Lacerator gets paused mid-roar.

"See that?" asks the real Godwin. "That's the sound of a killer."

"No, it's not," I counter. "That's a being with feelings like ours. You're treating it badly. That's why it lashes out." My voice cracks. "I don't think it wants to hurt anyone. It wants to protect, not kill."

"Silly child." Godwin sniffs. "Save your hearts and flowers. This creature is evil. And if you interrupt me again, you'll be its next victim."

A warm touch grasps my hand. Looking down, I see Thorne has laced our fingers together. Our gazes meet for a moment. Thorne shakes his head while releasing my hand.

He understands.

My heart cracks. I'd thought about the cruelty to all the undesirables. Now, I see that the Lacerator is another victim as well.

Even so, Thorne's touch gives me hope. Maybe I do have an ally after all. And if I do, I can build a real team. I'll need it, too. With every passing minute, it seems my list of goals gets longer.

Save the undesirables? *Check.*

Put Godwin behind bars? *Check.*

Free the Lacerator? *Check.*

Get myself out of here while I'm at it? *Double-check.*

Back on the hologram stage, the virtual version of Godwin raises his arms; the crowd falls silent. With a great flourish, the hologram Godwin pulls a small handheld from his pocket. It's round and red. "Behold! The master mechanism for the entire system. It's been loaded with the exact location of every undesirable on the continent." The latest count of tagging appears on the screen:

Humboldt-Merciless Undesirables Tagged: 1,803,768
Godwin-Horde Undesirables Tagged: 452,337
Total To Be Announced At Liberation Celebration: 2,256,105

The hologram Godwin holds up his arms yet again; the audience falls quiet once more. "Now all President Hope must do is click this red button. Millions of mini drift voids will then open, one for each undesirable. After that, replica Crawlers and Lacerators will emerge through those voids to cleanse the unwanted. With that work done, the Crawlers and Lacerators will return to this very spot, but not as a million separate parts. No, they will become a single entity once more. Together, I call the entire enterprise ... the Engine."

Wait, WHAT?

All the blood seems to drain from my body. Cleansings can take months to complete. After all, the Hollow has been waiting her turn for years. Now Godwin wants me to create a weapon with the power of a nuclear bomb, but with the targeting capability of a sniper rifle. I'll kill millions in an instant.

Back in the simulation, the crowd erupts in the loudest round of applause yet. Sure, this is Godwin's simulation, but I don't think he's wrong.

People will love this thing.

With a great flourish, the hologram Godwin turns to face President Hope, offering her the small red handheld. "Press the button in the center, launch the Engine, and usher us all into a new era of peace and prosperity."

President Hope accepts the mechanism. "This is indeed a great creation. How about we share the success with our viewers?"

The crowd roars with glee. Onstage, the video wall changes to display images of hundreds of faces. Old, young, healthy, ill, pale, dark ... they're all stamped with the word *undesirable* across their faces.

Because they're about to be murdered.

I open my mouth, ready to yell *stop*. Thorne beats me to it.

"Enough," growls Thorne.

Our gazes lock. A realization moves through me. Thorne feels the same as I do. *This is wrong.*

The real Godwin swings his gaze between me and Thorne. His smug look returns with a vengeance. "Let me understand this. Neither of you wants to see the execution? It's the best part."

"I'm with Thorne," I declare. "Besides, you were the one who said *every second is precious*. Stop the simulation. I'm ready to give you my plan."

Of course, the secret version of my plan includes taking Godwin down as well as freeing the undesirables. Not that I'll volunteer that part.

Still smirking, Godwin taps the control console. The simulation disappears, leaving us back in a bare concrete room. "I'm waiting." He nods toward Thorne. "So is he, by the way. If your plan isn't suitably impressive, Thorne will throttle you while I watch."

What a very Godwin thing to say.

"Thanks for the visual." I crack my neck, getting into the zone. It always helps to loosen up when discussing designs. "Here's what you need. First, there's the Crawler. That's got to be heavy duty, able to handle any environment. Inside the Crawler, we must fit a tiny omnivoid generator ... once I figure out how to build one, that is. Which brings me to the cleansing part. Have you tested other killing devices besides the Lacerator?"

"Yes." Godwin lets out a long-suffering sigh. "Those tests were the only thing my previous scientists did, as a matter of fact. If you place anything other than the Lacerator into a drift void, then the target's properties change in unpredictable ways."

I bob my head, thinking. "That makes sense. We don't know much about what creates drift voids. In some ways, we're lucky the Lacerator goes through unscathed."

In a shocking turn of events, Godwin smirks once more. "In case you're wondering, when the last team failed me, I had to kill them."

"No, I wasn't wondering," I say dryly. Inside, I want to scream and run.

But I can't.

Here's the thing about a guy like Godwin. Let him think he gets to you, and he'll steamroll you more by the minute.

"Moving on," I announce. "The Lacerator is the means of cleansing. We'll need some chemical agents to keep it focused on its actual prey versus going out and perforating everyone nearby."

"Agreed," states Godwin. "What else?"

"We must have a real master mechanism in addition to the fake one you'll *pretend to give* President Hope."

A satisfied grin rounds Godwin's mouth. "Quite right."

Thorne rounds on me. "Can you do all this in two months?"

"I can, but I need help. I've got the drift science covered, so the omnivoid generator should be fine. But there's a ton more to do." I glance around the room, making silent calculations. "The way I see it, I need a master chemist, an expert engineer, and someone who can source black market stuff."

Godwin waves his hand dismissively. "I have people I can bring in."

"That would be negatory on that concept," I counter. "I want my own team. Give me twenty-four hours to recruit some folks." I point to Thorne. "Laughing boy here can help me."

Names echo through my mind. *Chloe, Zoe, Fritz, and the Hollow.* Somehow, I know that's who I need to contact. Yes, it's another odd realization, like what happened with knowing the Lacerator's emotions. That said, it's all I've got.

I'm running with it. Chloe, Zoe, Fritz, and the Hollow.

"Ridiculous." Godwin's thin mouth twists into a frown. "You'll leverage my scientists."

"Not a chance," I counter. "This is a huge ask in two months of work. No one's ever created an omnivoid generator before." I march over to Thorne, stopping only when we're face to face. "Go on," I urge. "Let me recruit a team or throttle me now."

But Thorne doesn't move.

Neither does Godwin.

Guess I have to push this one. Grabbing Thorne's wrists, I set his palms against my throat. His touch is warm and solid. And am I imagining this, or are Thorne's hands trembling slightly?

"End this," I whisper.

He doesn't.

Godwin rolls his eyes. "Cease these silly theatrics. Thorne and I will talk and see what we can arrange."

Thorne drops his hands from my neck, and I immediately miss the touch.

Which is weird.

Godwin acts supremely interested in his control console. I haven't known the guy for long, but I can tell one thing: he's scheming. "We're through here," declares Godwin. He waves absently to Thorne. "Take her to her dorm."

Guess that's Godwin's way of saying I passed the tests and have the project. Whoa.

I open my mouth, ready to push for a solid 'yes' on having twenty four hours to find my team, but Thorne takes my hand again. We share a long look. Somehow, I know the request hidden in Thorne's eyes.

Give me a chance to chat with Godwin.

I shrug. It's my way of saying, *give it a try.*

As I'm led out of the Simulacrum, I can't decide if I want to cheer or scream. I survived the tests. *Cheering* would work because I want to bring down Godwin and save the undesirables as well as the Lacerator. *Screaming* is a good idea because there are just too many ways this can go wrong.

In the end, I stay silent as Thorne walks me back to my cell. This time, I'm able to notice more of my surroundings along the way. The Underground is basically a loop of concrete corridors lined with mostly identical doors. I'm guessing the majority are bedrooms, like mine. Every so often, a set of double-doors breaks up the monotony. I notice one that's marked *Simulacrum* while another says *Laboratory*. My pulse speeds.

A lab? Yes, please!

I point to the door in question. "How about we check out the lab?"

"Godwin sent you to your room."

Once again, I'm left wondering if I imagined all his winks, touches, and soft glances. And what was that hand-trembling thing from before? I got the distinct feeling Thorne would never want to hurt me, but then again, this is how Stockholm syndrome starts, isn't it?

We reach my door.

Thorne's face is unreadable as I step inside my cell. My guard quickly closes the door and snaps the lock.

What a creep.

I'm tempted to scream nasty phrases at the closed door when I notice it. There's a small desk in the corner, complete with a data pad. In all the drama with the Simulacrum, I'd forgotten about that part of my room. *Things are looking up.* With a live workstation, I can build out my plan.

My real one.

So I get to work.

"Love and transcendence should be treated with the utmost care. Despite the promise of eternity, they can easily be destroyed in an instant." – Empress Ophelia, *The Lost Book of Transcendents*

AFTER I DROP OFF MEIMI, I trudge back to the Simulacrum. Godwin is still there, fiddling with the control console. He looks up as I enter.

"Is she sleeping?" asks the doctor. No question who *she* is in this scenario. Meimi.

"Doubtful. My guess is that she's at her workstation."

Godwin stops typing and turns to face me. "Why would you say that?"

"Call it a hunch."

In truth, the more time I spend with Meimi, the more I can anticipate her actions. It must be a benefit of her being my transcendent. I wish we could share thoughts and visions again, but that will take some time to return.

If it happens again at all.

There's no way I'm activating our bond again any time soon. It means placing Meimi and my brothers at risk. Not that I have much choice anyway. My powers are still nil so long as we're in the Boston Dome.

Godwin adjusts his small glasses as he eyes me carefully. "You've a natural affinity for my new patient, don't you?"

"As much as anyone."

"Don't be shy. This is a good thing. I *want* you to seduce her."

With everything in me, I wish to punch Godwin's face off. Instead, I merely ask a question. "Why?"

"She made more progress today on the Engine than my own team of twenty scientists did after years of research. The idea of a second controller? Brilliant."

"All the more reason not to have her distracted."

"She's headstrong and foolish. I've seen her type before. High-minded. Principled. She says she'll build my Engine, but when it comes to the last mile, she won't have the guts for a cleansing." Godwin narrows his eyes. "Or am I mistaken?"

There's no point lying here. I'll only seem like a fool. "It's obvious the girl has strong convictions about what she will and will not do. Threatening violence doesn't seem to affect her."

"Precisely. Which is my I need more hooks into her." Godwin types onto the control console. A few yards ahead of us, a hologram of Meimi now stands on the concrete floor of the Simulacrum. "First, there's the science." Godwin reaches for the control panel again.

Tap. A lifelike hologram of the Crawler appears beside Meimi.

"Clearly, this girl likes to build things. The tech will keep her interested for a while. But that won't be enough to finish the job. You must take control of her heart."

Tap. A hologram version of me now stands next to Meimi.

"Then," continues Godwin. "There's her past. The girl will find her memories powerful, even if she can't access them. I'll bring back Luci and Josiah."

Tap. Luci and Josiah stand behind Meimi.

I remember those two from the hospital ... and the day they helped take Meimi away. Luci is actually Meimi's older sister. But that's in DNA only. In reality, Luci took the lead in betraying her own blood.

"Those two?" I frown. "Are you certain that's necessary?"

"Positive," states Godwin. "When it comes to cleansings, you're another one who's too squeamish. Luci and Josiah have no such limitations."

"I've done my share of killing. Fact is, those two already chatted up Meimi at the hospital. They failed."

"It's true that Luci and Josiah didn't immediately form a strong bond. That doesn't mean they're useless, though. With my guiding hand behind the scenes, I think Luci could be a critical agent."

Worry rattles through my limbs. Luci and Josiah? Not sure I want them back in Meimi's life. Over the last few weeks, I researched them both. Small-time criminals, the pair of them.

"What are your plans for those two?" I ask.

"Nothing that needs to concern you. Instead, *this* is where I want you to focus." Godwin returns to the control console once more.

Tap. Holograms of Chloe, Zoe, and Fritz appear. Chloe is seventeen, tall and slim in overalls and pigtails. Zoe, her twin sister, wears a sleek trench coat. Fritz is a middle-aged mountain of a man with spiked-up white hair.

I make sure to frown, as if I've never seen these folks before. Godwin doesn't know I met Meimi before he erased her memories. Back then, my girl told me all about Zoe, Chloe, and Fritz. And yes, I spent the last few weeks researching them even more.

All of which is why when I next speak, I make sure to act like I don't know the histories, motivations, and even shoe sizes of all these people.

"Who are Chloe, Zoe, and Fritz?" I ask.

"Who I want you to recruit for the team. They're all from our girl's previous life. Chloe is an expert in engineering, Zoe knows chemistry, and Fritz is an underworld thug who can acquire hard-to-obtain parts. Chloe and Zoe work in a garage. 1430 Lexington Avenue, Winter's Run, Massachusetts. Fritz hides in a secret lair outside town. He and I have done business before, but he refuses to get involved in the Engine. It's your job to convince him. He's expecting your visit."

"No street address for Fritz?"

"Only if you consider an underground sewer a street. I'll message you how to get there, as well as the specific date and time for your meeting."

"What about Chloe and Zoe? Don't you worry they'll help her regain her past?"

"If that were going to happen, it would've taken place with Luci in the hospital." Godwin shakes his head. "Before I wiped out her memories, our girl was positively obsessed with Luci. Thought her older sister was some kind of saint." He winks. "That's why I'm certain you can wheedle your way into Wisteria's heart. Seducing someone that weak-minded shouldn't prove too much of a challenge."

My hands ball into fists again. The urge to pummel this guy is almost overwhelming. "You're not the one who's seducing."

"Good thing you know the Berkshire Resort, then, eh?"

It takes me a few seconds to realize what Godwin is really saying.

He knows about my fake rendezvous.

I'd deny that I go the Berkshires, but it's all part of my cover-up when I visit my brothers. Now more than ever, Godwin needs to believe that when I leave the Boston Dome, it's to meet up with ladies. Even so, I'm surprised the doctor's been tracking me so closely. Godwin's trickier than I thought.

The doctor chuckles. "No need to respond, I know you keep a love nest. Take Wisteria there. Do what you need to do. Return in twenty-four hours."

The idea sends a pang of worry across my chest. Meimi deserves to be courted slowly, not dragged off to a hotel. After all, I'm an alien. She'll need tons of time to readjust to that reality alone.

"Twenty-four hours." I shake my head. "That's not a lot of time, sir."

"Which is why you should go now." Godwin raises his pointer finger. "And when you return, be sure to bring the team with you." He gestures to the door in a way that says, *I'm done talking*.

"Yes, sir."

As I leave the Simulacrum, I try to tamp down the tsunami of emotions inside me.

Rage.

Worry.

Affection.

Once we're outside the Boston Dome, this will mark the first time Meimi and I will really be alone since her operation. Finally, I can reveal who I truly am.

An alien.

Even better, I can back up my claims with actual displays of sentient power. Before Meimi lost her memory, she knew I was an alien. Maybe she'll accept it again.

Or perhaps she'll turn catatonic with fear.

There's only one option here. For a discussion this huge, Meimi needs some time to mentally prepare.

But how can I give her a heads-up?

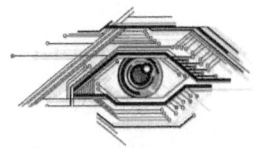

Time flies when you're plotting how to take down psychopathic doctors. First, I had to crack open my data pad and remove any trackers—no way does Godwin get access to my work—but I got that done in short order. Since then, I've drafted both my official plans for Godwin, and my real plans for me. Everything is organized in neat little rows of to-dos using a spreadsheet program.

I do love spreadsheets.

My next step? Find a team to make all those to-dos happen. Those names appear in my mind once more. *Chloe, Zoe, Fritz and the Hollow.*

I'm so engrossed, I don't even hear Thorne come into my room. Before I know it, he's standing beside my desk. Having him so close by, my stomach starts doing flip flops.

Stupid internal organs.

"We're good," says Thorne.

"With Godwin? What did he say?"

"He'll give us twenty-four hours." Thorne steps toward the door, pauses, and then turns around. "Are you coming?"

"As in now?" *And just us two?*

Thorne nods. His eyes are doing that large, blue and soulful thing again. It's making my flip flops even worse. I clear my throat and try to refocus on the mission.

Going on a trip with Thorne. I can do this.

"Sure thing." I scoop my data pad from the desk and take off toward the exit.

Just as we pass the threshold, Thorne grips my shoulders, presses me against the wall, and says, "Shhh."

There's a moment that lasts forever where I feel the hard planes of his body against mine. His breath fans out against my neck. And I know this isn't a good thing, really. I should scream or something. But there's some terrible-yet-unavoidable part of me that's perfectly happy right now. It's like when I set Thorne's hands against my throat, only far more intense.

I'm really losing it.

Thorne leans in until his mouth almost touches my ear. "This is a blank spot for cameras and audio."

"Oh," I say.

This is awesome, I think.

Maybe Thorne and I can set up a little meeting spot on this stretch of wall. I could put up curtains. Bring snacks. All of a sudden, this is the comfiest I've felt since I woke up in the hospital.

Maybe part of me likes Thorne. *A little.*

Or perhaps more of me is going insane. *A lot.*

"I need to give you a heads-up. There are things we must discuss. About me. Once we're outside the Boston Dome."

For some reason, I really have to force myself not to wind my arms around this guy's neck. *More insanity.*

"Sure," I whisper. "That'll be great."

Thorne takes in a long breath. Did he just sniff me? I think he might have sniffed me. I can't decide if that's good or bad.

Probably bad.

I haven't showered in a while, after all. Although, the nurses may have washed me before they put me in this onesie.

Huh. That's an even weirder thought.

I make a mental note to add *take a shower* to my checklist of to-dos. Level of importance: URGENT.

"Good," says Thorne at last.

With that, he steps away from me. Instantly, it's like the interaction never happened. Thorne is back to being Mr. Stonyface as he marches toward the elevator bank. I walk beside him, thinking one question over and over.

What just happened, exactly?

"The sentient decide which universe is the prime or central version. That said, the branch or parallel worlds can be far more pleasant to visit." – Beauregard the Great, *Instructions for Visiting Parallel Worlds*

IN ALL HONESTY, this version of Earth is not my favorite. It has a crap atmosphere. Awful government. Lame tech. Still, this world has two perks. The first is Meimi, of course. Although she's more of a miracle than a perk. The second comes with being an adjunct to the Star Council.

I get access to their motor pool.

For today's trip, I've selected a Land Rustler Hover-All 5000, military edition. Part SUV, part sports car, all power. Nothing compares.

Meimi isn't too impressed with the hovercar, though. As we tool through downtown, she's more amazed by the view. Her gaze stays locked out the window as we tour the city streets. Every glass and concrete skyscraper leaves her gasping in awe. My girl's never been under the Boston Dome.

Well, not while she was awake, anyway.

The dashboard's clock reads 2:03 p.m. as we reach Checkpoint Seven, the exclusive lane for Star Council members, and it's manned by my favorite guy.

Captain Vargas.

The Merciless warrior strolls up to the SUV with his attack animal Marro at his side. Meimi remembers Vargas from his visit to the hospital; she twists the metal cuff on her wrist. That sets off my instinct to shield Meimi at all costs. Already, I'm picturing my sentient forming body armor. They can't appear yet, but that won't stop me from fighting the old fashioned way, if necessary.

After all, I never did get to take down Vargas last time.

Vargas strolls over to the car window. "Hello, Thorne." He makes a point of slowly looking over Meimi. Twice.

Protective energy courses through me. When I speak, my voice is tight. "What is it this time, Vargas?"

He nods toward Meimi. "Is this your slice when you leave the city?"

"Stop it."

Vargas addresses Meimi anyway. "Is he taking you to the Berkshire Resort? That's where Thorne meets all his ladies."

Meimi's face turns pink. This is not how I wanted her to find out about my fake alibi for meeting my brothers. Now how is my big speech going to sound? *Hey, I'm not sneaking out to meet girls. I'm actually an alien from planet Umbra.*

I pinch the bridge of my nose. *What a disaster.*

Just because Meimi is my transcendent, it doesn't mean that Vargas can't screw things up for us.

White-hot rage heats my bloodstream. Before I know it, I've pushed the hovercar door open, stepped out onto the cement, and nailed Vargas in the face with a right hook. I follow it up with a round of speed-hits to his torso. The guy's body armor cracks like an eggshell. He falls over to the ground, unconscious.

"I warned you," I say.

Next Marro gets into the act. Spreading out its wings, Marro screeches and dives toward my face. Meimi comes out of nowhere, grips the animal, and pulls off its golden collar. It hops from her arms and mews.

"That's all right. Run. Go." Meimi makes shoo-fingers at Marro. "He can't make you do anything anymore." She tries to snap the collar in two, but the metal is thick.

"May I?" I ask.

"Sure." She hands over the collar and I crush it in my fist.

Marro mews once more. After that, the little creature skips off into a nearby line of trees. "You may have just started a new race of domesticated cat-snake-bats."

"About time," says Meimi. "Someone needed to."

I can't help but grin. *This girl.*

Vargas groans from the ground. "He's waking up," I say. "We should take off."

Once Meimi and I are back in the hovercar, I realize something important.

After taking down Vargas, Godwin will get an alert within two minutes tops. Plus, I know how the doctor thinks. Godwin will suspect I'm getting even more attached to Meimi than is necessary. Which could be a problem.

Even so, I don't care.

Punching Vargas was worth it.

Now that I'm back in the driver's seat, I pull out through the dome's archway. All the while, Meimi stares at me, pale and wide-eyed. No doubt, now that the excitement with Marro is over, she's focusing on Vargas's revelations about my so-called love nest.

The moment we're outside the dome, both the car and my smart watch start lighting up. Godwin is calling.

"Thorne, should you get that?"

"Right." I hit *accept* on my smart watch.

Godwin's voice sounds through the dashboard. Great. Now Meimi can hear his every word.

"Is this alert correct?" asks Godwin. "Did you just punch out Vargas?"

"He insulted Wisteria," I state.

"Look, I told you to seduce her, but don't go overboard."

If you'd asked me a minute ago, I'd have said there was no way Meimi could look more pale or wide-eyed.

I was wrong.

At the mention of the words *I told you to seduce her*, she reaches an entirely new level of shock.

Damn you, Godwin.

"Sir, I'm running across some magnetic interference out here." To create said magnetic interference, I summon my battle sentient to rise up from my skin and enter the inner workings of both my smart watch and hovercar. Unless you were looking carefully, it would seem like a little grit hovering in the air above my skin.

It isn't.

A moment later, a loud hissing sound takes over the audio connection. "It's getting worse, sir. I'll be back in touch as soon as I can. No later than twenty-four hours, as we agreed."

I picture my sentient cutting off all contact with Godwin, and that's exactly what they do. The line goes dead. A poof of smoke rises up from the dashboard.

"The audio and video tracking system in the car just short-circuited," I say.

"You think?"

"We can speak freely now." *Assuming you ever want to talk to me again.*

Some of the color returns to Meimi's face. "Are we going to that Berkshire hotel?"

"I promised myself I'd never lie to you."

"So that's a yes."

"It is. We must check in by midnight. Godwin will need to confirm that we're together. And since we've lost all other comms, I can't risk failing to check in. If we go totally off grid, Godwin will put a Merciless squad on our tail."

Across the front seat, Meimi holds her data pad so hard, I worry that she'll snap it in two.

I nod toward the device. "You might want to release your grip. You put a lot of work on that thing."

Meimi softens her hold a little. But now she focuses all that angry energy into glaring daggers of chilly hatred in my direction. "Back at the Simulacrum, you said you wanted to tell me something."

"That's right."

"Is that what you wanted to tell me? You were taking me to a hotel?"

"No."

"Then what is it?"

"I never visit a hotel to meet girls. That's all a cover. I leave the Boston Dome so I can contact my brothers. I'm an alien."

"As in ... from another continent or a different planet?"

Here goes.

"Different planet. I'm from Umbra." I quickly scan her face. Normally, I'm the one who's all stony features. Now it's Meimi's face that gives away nothing. "Did that explanation help?"

I risk another look in her direction. What greets me are more ice daggers from Meimi's eyes.

Nope. That didn't help at all.

"Listen to me," says Meimi. "I saw *Beauty and the Beast*. I understand Stockholm syndrome. This is all *mind game* stuff. Next you'll be showing me magic tricks and saying it's your alien powers. You might even say you sabotaged that call with Godwin with your alien mojo."

"I *did* sabotage that call with my alien mojo."

Meimi keeps right on staring, but some of the chill has left her gaze. Maybe she has an affinity for aliens on an unconscious level? I can only hope.

Adjusting her seat, Meimi turns to face me. "Let me make a few things totally clear. You are my guard. You play hot and cold. This evil Vargas guy says you plan to take me to a hotel, and whoa, that's where we're going. There are actual haddock in the ocean that are less fishy than you in this moment."

"I don't blame you." I huff out a breath. "It does look terrible." I lock her eyes with my most serious gaze. "Even so, what I told you is true."

"You have nice eyes and you're my only possible ally. Those are the only reasons I'm still talking to you."

I nod. "Logical."

"And I don't think I've ever stayed in a nice hotel before, so I'm okay with going there. But *you* sleep in the hallway."

"That was always the plan." My sentient shoot me the image of a deer stepping closer for a handful of nuts. Or whatever it is that deer eat. I get the idea. I need to play it cool here.

"Plus," adds Meimi. "I get first dibs on the shower."

"Fair enough." There's a lot more I want to say—like *hello, you're my transcendent!*—but this moment isn't the time.

"Glad that's all settled." Meimi leans back into her seat. "Where are we going before the hotel?"

"To meet some people from your past life."

"Let me guess. Chloe, Zoe, and Fritz?"

Interesting. On one level, it's obvious how Meimi guessed those names. She actually knows these three people far better than I do. That said, I'm curious how she was able to access such specific memories after everything Godwin did to her.

"We'll see Chloe and Zoe first. How did you know?"

"You're not the only one with a fishy side to their personality. I saw those names in a dream."

That piques my interest. "My people place a lot of import on dreams."

"Your alien people. Right." Leaning forward, Meimi turns the radio to an ear-splitting volume.

I get the message.

She's done talking.

For now.

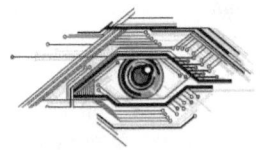

FORGET GENETICALLY ENHANCED ATTACK BEASTS. If you want to torture someone, play government-created ballads at top volume for a few hours. It's awful.

Now, I could certainly turn the radio down or change the station. But the way Thorne keeps wincing? I'm pretty sure he's suffering as much as I am. And that works fine for me.

Hotel reservations?

I'm an alien from outer space?

Please.

I am not falling into his mind traps, period.

That said, my own sanity isn't looking too solid. Why? When I glance out the car window, I see a reflected version of myself that's just like me.

Only blue.

I know, not great.

And Blue Me has a lot of opinions, too. When she speaks, I hear her voice inside my head. And the overly loud ballads drown her out a little, but not all the way.

These are what you call *red flags for ongoing sanity.*

"*You should give him a chance,*" says Blue Me in my mind. "*After all, you know drift science. There are tons of other worlds running parallel to this one. Who's to say he isn't from one of them?*"

"*I'm ignoring you,*" I reply mentally.

Blue Me keeps right on going. "*Just think about Vargas. What a scum-*

bag. Thorne totally pounded that Merciless guy into mush, just for getting all leery at us."

"Maybe that was a little cool."

Okay, it was a LOT cool.

"And Godwin? That creep wants to control you. If Thorne's your ally, wouldn't Godwin want to sabotage him? Couldn't that be why he's saying stuff about seducing you? You could be falling into Godwin's whole trash-talking trap."

I purse my lips. Blue Me just made a few good points there.

"And has Thorne ever done anything to make you feel unsafe?" asks Blue Me.

"He's rude."

"That's not the same thing."

"It's not pleasant. The guy's like ice."

"Only when Godwin is around. Plus, if Thorne were all supportive of you in front of Godwin, then where would you be? With another guard."

I scrunch my lips to one side of my face. This only happens when I'm thinking very seriously about something. In this case, it's how Blue Me made yet another really good point.

Something jabs me in the shoulder.

Oops, it's Thorne poking me.

I scooch away from him. "What?"

"We're at Zoe and Chloe's garage. I've been asking you if you're ready to see them."

All of a sudden, I wish the car floor would open up so I could hide somewhere deep in the earth. "Let me guess. You've been trying to talk to me for a while?"

"Five minutes. The shoulder poke was a last resort."

"I got a little distracted."

And instead of giving me guff, Thorne fixes me with his big blue eyes and smiles. "It's fine. You were plotting and scheming something. I like watching your mind at work."

In this moment, I'd love to have a witty comeback, but all I can manage is a single sound. "Oh."

A warm and mushy sensation expands across my insides. It must be something I ate. No way am I getting gooey feelings about my sketchy guard.

Thorne opens his door and speed-walks toward my side of the

vehicle. No question what his goal is here; he wants to get my door. For some reason, it seems a little relationship-y for him to do that. Like we're on a date versus a quasi-kidnapping. Moving even faster, I slip out my door and pause before the garage.

It's a run-down building, but then again, everything outside the dome is a ruin. The place a long, single-story structure made from cement blocks. A pair of roll-up garage doors lines the front façade. A faded wooden sign reads *Leon's Deluxe Garage*.

Something about this spot feels so familiar, yet I just can't place it.

Curse you, amnesia.

Thorne moves to stand beside me. Even with all the strangeness between us, I have to admit it. I'm glad he's here. There's a certain stony *I can kick ass* vibe he has, which I totally appreciate.

"Before you go in, there are some things we should cover," says Thorne.

"Shoot."

"You knew Chloe and Zoe from before your procedure."

I give him the side-eye. "You're not going to say *accident*?"

"I won't because it wasn't. Godwin targeted you for your science skills. He wiped your memory. That's what this is all about."

"Right." I hug my elbows.

"Sorry." Thorne's voice turns gentle. "I didn't mean for that to surprise you."

"It wasn't a surprise. Not really. I mean, I suspected it all along. It's just different to hear someone say the truth out loud."

Thorne moves to stand in front of me. All of a sudden, only a few inches separate our bodies. "You may not believe this, but I'd never lie or say anything that hurt you. Unless, you know..." He grins and dang, the guy has dimples.

"What?"

"Unless Godwin's around and lying makes your life easier."

"Thank you." We're still so close and, Stockholm syndrome aside, I'm enjoying the liquid feeling that now runs through my insides.

Thorne is yummy.

Someone clears their throat. Looking over, I see a girl standing in the main doorway of the garage. She's tall and wiry, dressed in overalls, and has her hair pulled into matching ponytails on either side of her head.

"Meimi," she gasps. "Is it you?"

Thorne turns around, stopping so his body half blocks the path between me and the new girl. Like the building itself, she seems so familiar. Plus, this chick acts super excited to see me. We must have been good friends.

An ache fills my soul. *How I wish I could remember.*

"This is Meimi," states Thorne. "But the Authority wiped out her memories. She's here because she needs your help."

Another girl pops her head out from behind the first. They look identical, except the second has her blonde hair in straight tresses and wears the perfect amount of make-up. And is that a cashmere sweater? I didn't even know those existed anymore.

The second girl waves in my direction. "I heard what he said. You don't remember me either, but I'm Zoe."

"And I'm Chloe," says the first. "We're twins."

Turning to her sister, Chloe starts talking away as if we weren't here. "Do you think that's *the* Thorne? Miss Edith talked about a hot guy by that name who was really into Meimi." She pulls a red handkerchief from her pocket and rubs her neck, but it only serves to leave a grease stain behind.

"Obviously, he's *the Thorne*," counters Zoe. "But we can't have that conversation with them in the driveway, now can we?" Zoe waves to me and my guard. "Come on inside."

The twins disappear into the garage. Thorne turns to me. "You still want to do this?"

For the first time since I awoke in the hospital, I feel so happy I could smile my face off. Seeing Chloe and Zoe is like finding a lost part of my soul.

"Absolutely," I reply. "Let's go."

"An emperor or empress cannot merely rule their subjects. They must inspire them." – Empress Janais, *The Fifth Age of Umbra*

MEIMI and I step inside the run-down garage. The scent of engine grease and mothballs fills the air. One side of the interior is piled high with beakers and vats of questionable chemicals. The opposite part is crammed with gears, wires, and all things electronic. A kind of no-man's land lies between the two halves, a space that's filled with old rags and dust.

I instantly recognize the layout. My brothers and I have multiple rooms like this. We're like magpies, finding and piling up our junk. Battle gear for Justice. Fortune-telling tools for Slate. And stacks of books for me. We like to think of ourselves as having an organized mess.

Mostly, we just have a mess.

Chloe and Zoe stand in the empty space between their piles of supplies. Both seem wide-eyed and curious. Chloe's the first to speak. "Do you remember anything about us?"

The way Meimi clasps her data pad to her chest, you'd think the thing was a security blanket more than an electronic device. "What did you call me before?"

"Meimi," replies Zoe. "That's your name."

"I like that better than Wisteria," says Meimi.

Chloe sniffs. "That's because Wisteria was your alias when you were stealing stuff."

Meimi pales. "I'm a thief?"

"Not really," adds Zoe smoothly. "How do I put this?" She taps her cheek. "Ah, I have it. You needed to build things without the government knowing. That sometimes required taking stuff from warehouses and leaving anonymous payment."

"So, I'm a nice thief."

"Precisely," says Zoe.

Meimi turns to me. "And I knew you from before?" Her big ebony eyes take on a look that can only be described as hopeful. In this moment, I know one thing.

She wants to trust me. Knowing that, I feel about ten feet tall.

"Yes, you knew me." I can't help myself; I reach up and cup her cheek with my hand. It's grounding to feel her skin under mine. "After you were taken, I found Godwin and convinced him to make me your guard. I've been watching over you, Meimi."

Chloe sniffs. "That is so damn sweet. Holy sh—"

"Language," interrupts Zoe. "What my sister means to say is that this is a sweet scene and all, but you said something else before. You need help?"

I lower my hand from Meimi's skin. Losing the connection hurts, but Zoe's right. We have other things to discuss here.

Meimi twists her hands at her waist. "Where do I begin?"

Chloe raises her arm. "Can I guess?"

Meimi shrugs. "Sure."

"You're working on another hella kickass science gig and you finally want us to participate," says Chloe.

Meimi's mouth falls open with shock. I have to admit, I'm a little surprised myself. I figured Meimi would have to do some fancy talking to get the twins to accept the idea of helping out.

"How did you guess?" asks Meimi.

"Wishful thinking," says Zoe with a grin. "For years, we've begged you to let us in on your schemes. It was about time our luck changed."

Chloe holds out her palm. "Specs. Here. Now."

"Okay." Meimi hands over the data pad. "There are official requirements for Dr. Godwin. And then there's a secret plan for us."

Chloe scans the data pad and gasps. "Fuuu—"

"Language," interrupts Zoe.

"Oh, fudge," says Chloe sarcastically. "Dr. Godwin wants to murder millions of people with his Crawler toy."

Zoe taps the screen. "But we're going to ruin his plans, make him a fool, free the undesirables, and get out of this garage for once."

Chloe brightens. "Day-um. That's awesome."

I've run tons of rescue missions on other planets. Recruiting local help is never this easy. Frowning, I rub my chin. I checked out Chloe and Zoe before. They definitely have the skills to help out Meimi, but I'm not sure they're fully understanding what's at stake here.

I turn to Meimi. "They're not getting it."

"Agreed." Meimi focuses on the twins. "Look, this project is super dangerous."

"But the chemistry specs are awesome." Zoe lets out a low whistle. "My part will be so fun."

"My engineering stuff isn't as cool," sighs Chloe. "A Crawler is basically a fat spider bot. Meh."

"It's not that bad," says Zoe. "It's more of a fat spider bot with an omnivoid generator inside."

"Guys," calls Meimi. "Both of you must be one hundred percent clear. You'll be locked in an underground bunker for two months building something that could help kill millions of people while empowering Godwin to take down the government. If we fail, we'll all be killed. "

"Officially, that's the scheme," says Chloe. "But your secret plan is amazeballs. No one's going to kill anybody. Well, maybe Godwin will have a terrible accident once he hits jail, but that's it."

"Right?" asks Zoe. "Godwin got so many cool people arrested. Now, they're all waiting for him in jail with knives that are made from tin cans and stuff."

I share a long look with Meimi. Without saying a word, we have a quick chat. Sure, Zoe understands prison justice. But this particular mission? Not so much.

Meimi addresses her friends once more. "I still don't think you two get it. This is a huge deal. No one has done anything like this before. We might fail."

"What?" Zoe sniffs. "Of course, we are *not* going to fail. Think positively, for crying out loud."

"Can I swear now?" asks Chloe. "*For crying out loud* really doesn't capture enough emotion here."

"Absolutely not," counters Zoe.

Meimi turns to me. "Help?"

Clearly, Zoe and Chloe aren't registering the risk related to building the Engine. Time for a different angle. If they aren't worried about the Engine, maybe the twins will get concerned about me.

"Look," I say. "There's more going on here than you know."

"Oh?" ask Chloe and Zoe together.

"I'm an alien."

"Really?" This time, it's just Zoe who asks.

"He's kidding," says Meimi. "I think."

"An alien. Holy crap." Chloe tilts her head. "Like from another continent or a different planet?"

Meimi grins. "Wow. That's exactly what I asked him."

"You and Chloe always thought alike," explains Zoe. The three of them then launch into a conversation about other words that trip them up, beyond the whole *alien* thing.

Like nails. As in *ow, I hurt my thumb*, or *I need one for this thing I'm building*?

Jam. *Do I want it on my bread* or *am I enjoying this song*?

Bolt. *Of lightning* or *time to escape*?

This could go on all day.

I rub my temples with my fingertips. Not sure what I expected in recruiting Chloe and Zoe. This definitely wasn't it.

"Ladies," I say.

They launch into a discussion of squash, *the food* versus *what you do to a bug*.

"Ladies!"

Meimi does a double-take in my direction, as if she's noticing me for the first time. "What, Thorne?"

"To answer Chloe's question, I'm from another planet. Umbra."

Zoe frowns. "Are you *really* an alien?"

"Maybe," replies Meimi. "He might be trying to do the *Beauty and the Beast* thing, luring me into his strange enchanted reality so he can control my science skills."

For a moment, I debate the merits of turning blue or using my powers to levitate the entire garage, but I decide that would only cause more delays. If they can talk this long after just saying the word *alien*, I don't want to know what will happen if I take things to the next level.

"Let's try this again." I gesture toward Chloe and Zoe. "Am I correct to assume you want to help Meimi?"

Chloe flips through the data pad. "This outlines an Engine program, both a secret version and the official Godwin version. Is there anything else you need help with?"

Meimi tilts her head. "I'm not sure what you mean."

"How do I state this?" Zoe taps her lips. "Before, you had a short list of topics you were rather obsessed with. Saving broad numbers of people wasn't on the list."

"Still not following," says Meimi.

"Luci," clarifies Chloe. "We're talking about Luci."

"My sponsor mother?" Meimi takes a half step backward. "Why would I be obsessed with her?"

Zoe and Chloe exchange a look. I can almost see the invisible conversation between them. There's no need to wonder what that chat is about. Godwin made the same point. Back when Meimi had her memories, she thought Luci was a saint. Clearly, Chloe and Zoe knew what Luci's really about.

"No reason," says Chloe. "In fact, maybe it's good you lost memories of some stuff."

Meimi rubs her forehead. All this talk about Luci is confusing her. I need to keep things moving, so I focus on the twins. At this point, I think they understand the danger. The twins just don't care.

"How soon can you both be ready to go?" I ask.

They stare at each other for another long second. This time, Zoe answers. "We'll be ready in the morning."

That's good. "Do you need anyone's permission to leave?"

One advantage of being an adjunct to the Star Council: I get access to government records. According to their file, Chloe and Zoe have a very overprotective mother. Or at least, that's how their mother *used to* act. After all, their father is ill. People change when loved ones get sick.

"No," replies Zoe. "We only need to pack."

"I gotta bring my tools," says Chloe. She looks protectively at a nearby pile of gears and soldering irons.

"Same here," says Zoe. "I also need some decent clothes." Zoe turns to Meimi. "I can get outfits for you, too."

Meimi grins. "Thank you. So. Much."

Interesting. I didn't realize Meimi wanted other things to wear. I set that little fact aside for later.

"Oh," says Zoe. "I have the cutest fitted lab coat. It's my fave thing to wear while inventing."

The three launch then into a conversation about what they most love to wear while creating new stuff. Chloe favors coveralls, which are those zip-front onesies made famous at gas stations everywhere. Meimi likes jeans and a T-shirt. Any sense of urgency flies out the window. This is like herding cats. Only I'm thinking about the cats on Umbra, which are often big as a cougar and slower than a glacier.

"Getting back to the project," I state. "Are you two certain you don't need to explain anything to *anyone*? We can't have a posse storming the city to look for you."

Chloe jams her hands deeply into the pockets of her blue coveralls. "Dad just passed away. Mom's taken it pretty hard. In her grief she's, um, gotten radicalized."

"Radicalized," I repeat. Turning to Meimi, I give her a confused look that says, *I'm not connecting the dots on how that means "no permission."*

Thankfully, Meimi steps in to clarify. "Look, this is a huge deal. You guys are going to disappear for months. Maybe we should talk to your mom. Together."

Zoe pulls out her phone. "Fine. We can call her."

Chloe does the same. "I'll do it." Lowering her tone, she sidespeaks to me and Meimi. "I put a translation overlay on my phone. It bleeps over all of Mom's swears because, you know, *Zoe*."

Zoe shakes her head. "You *so* got your potty mouth from Mom."

Chloe sticks her finger in her ear as she dials. "Hello? Mom? I'm putting you on speaker."

An older woman's voice sounds through the speaker. "Hi, honey."

Zoe steps closer to the phone and speaks in a loud voice. "So, Mom. We want to go off with Meimi and take down the government."

"Great! Those BLEEPERS BLEEPING BLEEPED treatment for your father's cancer. I BLEEPING BLEEP BLEEP BLEEP! When will you be back?"

"End of summer."

"Fine. Just call me regularly with updates, that's all. And Meimi?"

Chloe gestures toward Meimi, who steps closer to the phone as well. "Hello, I'm here."

"Hi, Meimi. So nice you turned up. We were worried about you. Go BLEEPING BLEEP them."

And the line goes dead.

So that went well. If strangely.

"Do you need to tell anyone else?" I ask. "Teachers?"

"Nah," replies Chloe. "Meimi totally erased our school. Long story."

Meimi pales. "I did?"

"Don't worry," retorts Zoe. "It was a good thing."

"And I erased a school." Meimi goes back to looking wide-eyed and pale. "I had quite the interesting life."

"You think?" asks Chloe. "Why do you think we want to sneak off with you?"

Zoe slowly turns around, examining the room with an expert eye. "We have so much packing to do."

Chloe gestures toward the door. "You two don't mind showing yourself out, do you? Just haul your butts back here and get us in the morning. Seven a.m."

Zoe gasps. "What? No, nine a.m."

The pair are still arguing as Meimi and I leave the garage and get back into the hovercar. This time, Meimi lets me open the door for her. That makes me smile.

Once we settle onto our seats, I say, "What the hell was that?"

At the same time, Meimi asks, "Aren't they so awesome?"

We both pause, stare, and then burst out laughing. Invisible cords of energy and connection wind between us. I decide not to say another word as we drive away.

Some moments are perfect, just as they are.

"The art of seduction is a topic we historians should never write about. Therefore, I shall segue to the subject of plant life." – Hammurabi the Seventh, *Law of Sentient*

IT FEELS good to laugh with Meimi. Afterward, she puts on music that doesn't make me want to claw my ears off, so that's another improvement. Driving across state with her is soothing, even if the scenery is a little depressing. After all, I thought the Boston Dome was awful since it was all faked up. Now, I'm not sure what's worse: false beauty or real ruins.

Hours later, I pull up to the Berkshire Resort. As one of the most expensive spots on the continent, it even has its own mini-dome.

Unfortunately, it also brings back all the bad memories from this morning's encounter with Godwin and Vargas. As we pull up to the roundabout drop-off, there's a decidedly icy vibe coming from the *Meimi side* of the car.

The chill continues as we enter the fancy hotel itself. Not sure why, but this place is filled with fountains. Water cascades from the ceiling into basins on the floor. Walkways are surrounded by still pools filled with overlarge goldfish. Gurgling fountains even line the walls themselves.

I've been on water planets that were more subtle.

And as always, there's security everywhere. No doubt, Godwin is watching a feed from the spider bots roaming the lobby floor.

Supposedly, surveillance isn't slowed in the rooms themselves. Not sure I believe that, though. Once we get to our suite, I'll use my sentient to check for bugs. Godwin will just have to be satisfied with his lobby video feed and that's it.

Most of the spider bots are new models with blue metal bodies. I suppose it fits with the water theme. As we check in, an older bot wobbles by on spindly legs. Both Meimi and I watch it pass with interest. Those legacy models are far easier to hack into. Right now, I can access all the Authority data feeds I need. But once we get back to the Underground? I'm locked out. It would be handy to have a repurposed bot.

I grab our key cards and sigh. My first priority is ensuring Meimi feels comfortable here. If there's time later, I can go bot hunting. As well as hit some other errands.

We reach the suite. The place has multiple bedrooms and a kitchenette. Setting my hand against the wall, I summon my sentient to check for surveillance. There are a few audio jacks set in to the ceiling. I short-circuit the systems and then go check on Meimi.

She's chosen her bedroom, evidently.

My girl is passed out on the bed, lying atop the covers, and still wearing her gray coveralls. I find a blanket, drape it over her, and go off in search of a bot to steal. My mission is purely professional.

That said, if I find a gift shop, I could pick up a nice dress for her. And if the resort has a fancy place to take Meimi for a meal, then sure, I might make a reservation.

And if there's a good dance club, then I could check that out, too.

So, my mission's *mostly* purely professional.

A few hours later, I head back to the suite. My bot mission was a total failure. Not sure where the old model went, but all the new ones seemed great on the outside, but were stripped down within. None of them could hook directly into the Authority data feed. Total bust.

I lean against the doorjamb, watching Meimi sleep. As she rolls over onto her side, my girl's eyes flutter open. My heart pitches against my rib cage. Those ebony eyes of hers kill me.

A crease forms between her brows. "Can't you wait out in the hall?"

I suppress the urge to grin. *Awake and sassy. She's perfect.*

"Technically, I have one foot in the hall."

Meimi's face is deliciously sleepy as she yawns. "I had some strange dreams. Talked to a blue girl."

I step closer. For my people, dreams are critical. And a blue girl could mean the blue sentient I used on Meimi. "What did she say?"

"I don't remember."

Meimi smacks her lips, and I can't help but I wonder if that's something my transcendent always does when she wakes up. Imagination kicks in. *I picture myself curled beside her. We both awaken. Meimi smacks her lips; I do the same back at her. We laugh.*

I shake my head. *Daydreaming gets you nowhere, Thorne. Focus.*

"What time is it?" asks Meimi.

"A little past nine p.m.," I reply. "Need food or anything?"

Meimi slides out of bed, careful to keep the blanket around her shoulders like a tent. "I'm going to take a shower now." She lowers her voice. "This is the part where you leave." She winks.

Is she trying to flirt with me?

A blush colors Meimi's face.

Oh, yes. She's definitely trying to flirt with me.

My heart swells with pride. I should have expected this. The flirting is part of a scheme; Meimi's clearly got a plan. Wouldn't expect anything else.

Meimi walks sideways across the floor, making a beeline for the bathroom. She's so blushy and cute, I hardly notice what she's done.

Somehow, Meimi got her hands on that janky old spider bot. One of its spindly legs sticks out from under her blanket.

Meimi's plan comes into focus. She's taking the spider bot into the bathroom so she can hack into the thing.

And she's being flirty to distract me.

That's my girl.

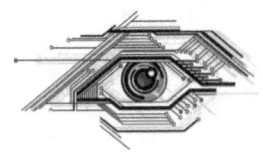

I'M HALFWAY to the bathroom.

With my spider bot.

And my plan to hack into it.

This is an older model. S-Bot A3-4000. The thing is built with a security matrix that a four-year-old could crack. Sure, I could tell Thorne about it, but honestly? I'm not one hundred percent sure I can trust him.

A secret spider bot is a safer spider bot.

As I step along, I try distracting Thorne with some flirty chatter. Not sure how that part of the plan's going, but my face is definitely wicked pink.

And he's not trying to stop me, so there's that.

Thorne tilts his head. "You mentioned dreams before."

"Yup," I say. "There was a blue girl."

Step.

Step.

"Are you certain you don't remember anything she said?" he asks.

For the record, it's hard to sidestep to a bathroom, grip your blanket in a teepee shape, hide a wiggly spider bot, and hold a conversation. Somehow, I manage.

Step.

Step.

"Meimi?"

"My dreams of the blue girl, right. I don't recall a thing. Honestly." I did sleep a little bit before I went on my spider bot search. Come to think of it, I'm not sure what Thorne's been up to. He wasn't around when I snuck off, and at the time, that was all I cared about. "What about you? What have you been up to?"

A flicker of a smile rounds Thorne's full mouth. "Roaming around."

"So you didn't sleep."

"Me?" Thorne shrugs. "Not a wink."

Step.

Step.

I'm so close.

I grip my blanket together even more tightly. "Okay, I'll just take my shower now."

He arches his right brow and doesn't reply. *Dang, that shouldn't look cute, but it is.*

I hiss in a breath through my teeth. *What am I doing?* This is my questionable guard who arguably vowed to seduce me in this hotel. I should not go Stockholm syndrome on him.

Even so, I'm feeling rather flirty.

But that's just to hide the spider bot.

Maybe.

Finally, I reach the bathroom. Kicking the door open, I sidestep into the room. The moment I'm inside the chamber, I drop the bot, close the door, and crank on the hot water in the shower. While the bathroom fills with crazy amounts of steam, I check for any hacker tools.

Cotton balls? Useless.

Soap and shampoo? Also won't work.

No razors either. Which isn't surprising. Although, it would be nice to have a weapon.

Tapping my foot, I scan the bathroom one more time. There must be something in here that can help.

Picking up the box of cotton balls, I dig through the container, looking for anything I might have missed.

And yes! I find the perfect device.

Tweezers.

While I've been searching, the steam has become so thick, it's hard to see more than a few inches before my face. Perfect. Grabbing a white towel, I set the tweezers in my mouth.

Then I stalk toward the spider bot.

My little wobbly buddy is facing toward the white wall. Just what I want. In one swift move, I toss the towel over the bot and cover the video lens. It's always best to cover vid feeds when you're hacking. Otherwise, strange things can—and do—get into the camera's line of vision.

People can get alerted.

Life could get ugly.

Long story short, it's best to cover the screen.

With the bot's video blocked, I sit down, set the device in my lap, and get to work. First, I pop the bot's round hood with my tweezers. Inside, there's a familiar tangle of wires and buttons. I reconnect a few lines, clip off a few more, and then press a button or two.

"Begin voice recognition," I whisper. "Accept Wisteria—" I pause. That name doesn't feel right anymore. "Accept *Meimi* as your new controller."

"Accepted," replies the bot.

I glance at the shower. Is the noise loud enough to drown out our voices? For a long moment, I stare at the door. Thorne doesn't knock or speak, so I figure I'm good to go.

"Meimi says, follow me," I continue.

"Accepted." The bot has a cute, chirpy voice.

"Access data feeds," I command.

"Download in process," says the bot. With that command, the inside of the bot's hood lights up, becoming an activated screen that displays results. That's just what I need. It's like hacker Christmas.

I exhale. The bot is now downloading a full and official feed from the Authority. The complete data set will take time, but I'll get a little info soon. Nothing confidential, but you never know what could be useful. And once we're back in the Underground, who knows what this little guy can do?

"You're my arachnid now." After closing the hood, I tap my bot's "head." "I'm calling you Rakkie."

Knock ... knock ...

Surprise jolts through my nervous system. "Yes?"

Thorne's voice sounds through the door. "If you're showering, you may want to change into different clothes. I picked up some stuff in the gift shop."

Dropping Rakkie, I open the door a crack. Steam flows out the opening. "What kind of clothes?"

Thorne steps closer to the door. His huge blue eyes lock with mine. Unlike the first time I met him, there's nothing but warmth in his gaze. My skin prickles over with awareness.

Gulp.

Thorne reaches forward, wrapping a strand of my hair around his finger. "Your hair isn't wet."

"I'm having a sauna moment before the shower."

"Ah." Thorne half smiles and whoa, there are those dimples again. "Sauna moment."

All of a sudden, I realize that I'm talking about showering. With Thorne. Well, not with Thorne as in we're both under the water, but close enough to be really uncomfortable.

"You have clothes for me?" In my mind, the question is really smooth. In reality, my words come out about two octaves too high. I sound like a chipmunk.

Thorne holds out a pile of garments topped with a black dress. "I make no claims about the fit. I described you to the woman in the gift shop and she did the rest."

I grasp the pile of stuff. The dress is simple and classic. There's a nice wrap, too. And the underthings are both cute and my size. My eyes get all stingy. I have the sneaking suspicion this is the nicest outfit I've ever owned. I sniff.

Thorne drops his hand. "Are you all right?"

"Oh, fine. Just ready to get dressed. Thanks." In a move of supreme smoothness, I slam the door right in his face. After the door is closed, I realize this is a *let's go out* kind of outfit.

Maybe it's even a *let's seduce Meimi* outfit.

I hold the dress against me. It's got a sweet and swishy bottom. Who cares what Thorne thinks he's going to do? I'll get dressed up and have a massive meal that's charged to Godwin. In fact, the more I think about it, the more it would be a crime NOT to wear this dress and have some fun.

An update light blinks atop Rakkie's head, interrupting my thoughts.

Huh, my little guy already downloaded something useful.

Using my tweezers again, I pop open the bot's hood. This time, inside of the bot's cap, the screen's lit up with data. The good news is that I'm getting an info stream specifically for Godwin and his staff entitled *Liberation Celebration*. I scan the names.

Eleanor Gertz – tagged for cleansing – cancer
Zachary Legion – tagged for cleansing – no employment
Miss Edith Smalltown – tagged for cleansing – over 70 years old

The last name makes my stomach lurch. Didn't Chloe and Zoe mention a Miss Edith before? I shake my head. What am I thinking? There are tons of names on the master list. Chances are, I know lots of folks who've been tagged. I glance at my wrist cuff once more.

Star Council Level Access: Godwin
Humboldt-Merciless Undesirables Tagged: 1,938,142
Godwin-Horde Undesirables Tagged: 481,003
Total To Be Announced At Liberation Celebration: 2,419,145

Last time, the total was just over two million. Now the number is closing on two and a half. My body feels numb. This can't be real. How can I be all that stands between so many people and death?

Rising, I turn to the mirror and wipe off the layer of steam with my forearm. Looking up, I catch my own reflection. I look like I always have, save for one difference.

My skin is blue.

In the mirror, Blue Me speaks. "Remember what I said. You're free from your past now—embrace that. Focus on your plan. You're already missing stuff."

"What do you mean?" My data pad is in perfect order, and absolutely hidden from Thorne.

"It's what we talked about before. You need Chloe, Zoe, Fritz, and *the Hollow*. You forgot about her."

"The Hollow, right."

Some small part of me knows I should be shocked by all this. For whatever reason, I'm not. By this point, chatting up a blue version of myself feels natural. A moment later, the illusion is gone. In the mirror, my skin is back to its regular shade.

As I step into the shower, I repeat the name in my mind.

The Hollow.

Somehow, I must recruit her as well. And fast.

"Every world has its own beauty. If you're fortunate, you'll find time to uncover it." – Beauregard the Great, *Instructions for Visiting Parallel Worlds*

I PACE the plush carpet of the suite's living room, excitement zinging through my veins. Plans for tonight keep spinning through my mind.

The resort has a romantic place for dinner. Everything is oak tables and candlelight. Afterward, they have a laid-back dance club that plays classic jazz. I already changed my sentient into a dark suit for the occasion. Now I'm waiting for Meimi.

"Ready!" she calls from her chamber.

My heart soars. When I reply, it takes all my warrior training to keep my voice level. "Good news."

A door swings open, revealing the most beautiful girl I've ever seen.

The black dress fits her in all the right places. Meimi has curves and I love it. The silk wrap hangs lightly around her shoulders. She isn't wearing any make-up, but my girl doesn't need it. She's stunning with just her ebony eyes and long brown hair.

My transcendent.

This time when I speak, my voice comes out a little rough. "You look stunning."

"Thank you." A gentle blush colors her cheeks. "What's the plan for tonight?"

"Are you certain you want to waste an evening with me?"

"Positive. I've decided I'll seduce you and then lock you out in the hallway."

"Really?" I can't help but laugh. *My girl and her plans.* "I love that idea." I can't help myself. Crossing the room, I set my hands at her waist and begin swaying from side to side. "As long you're near, that's all I need."

Meimi giggles. "What are we doing now?"

"A practice dance as I review our schedule for the evening."

Meimi loops her arms around my neck and leans against me. Together, we slowly move from foot to foot. She nuzzles my neck. "About that schedule?"

"Right." I tighten my grip on her waist. "We'll begin with dinner."

"Good."

"And then go dancing."

"Even better."

Taking her hand in mine, I guide her into a twirl. There's no need for us to speak; the movement is natural. As she spins around, the dress flares to show off more of her legs.

With that, it's official. Every inch of Meimi is beautiful.

"This is the perfect dress for a twirl," I add. "We'll have to do that multiple times tonight."

She leans in against me and we slow dance again. "I can't believe this is happening. It's like a dream."

"Do you want to stop?"

"No, I want to live this moment to its fullest." She stops and pulls away. The loss of her body against mine is almost painful.

"What's wrong?" I ask.

"Before we go, there's something I need to tell you about my plans for the Engine. We must recruit the Hollow. Maybe Fritz will know how."

"That's a tall order, even for him." I guide her against me once more. "Yet when you look this lovely, I think anything is possible."

Beep, beep.

"What's that?" asks Meimi.

"My smart watch." I guide her into another twirl. "No reason to stop dancing."

Beep, beep.

"Is it Godwin?"

"No, I blocked Godwin."

Meimi stops dancing and steps back. "Shouldn't you check it?"

"Yes." I glance down at my wrist. "It's Fritz."

Normally, I would simply have my sentient create an earpiece in order to take the call. That said, everything is going so nicely this evening. I'm not sure Meimi is ready for that kind of display of my alien powers.

And in all honesty, I'm not ready to review them either. We're having another perfect moment, and I just want to enjoy it. No deep reveals of my alienness.

Which means there's only one way left to take the call.

"Do you mind if I take this as a vid feed?" I ask.

"Not a problem." I can't help but notice that Meimi takes another step away from me, though. "After all, Fritz is our best bet to find the Hollow."

I tap my smart watch. A tiny beam of light pours out from the edge of the device, creating a hologram on the other side of the room. The semi-transparent image shows a barrel-chested man in green denim overalls, the type popular with farmers: complete with a bib-style front and shoulder straps. He has heavy limbs and short, spiked-up hair.

Meimi walks up to the hologram-Fritz and steps around the simulation. She knew the guy before her memory was erased. In fact, Fritz was the part of the group who betrayed her to Godwin. Although technically, it was Fritz's boss, the Scythe, who did most of the betraying. Fritz negotiated that she'd get wiped instead of killed.

"Hello," I begin.

"Turn your vid on," orders Fritz. "I want to see you."

Every smart watch comes with a minicamera to project video to your caller. It would be easy enough to activate that for Fritz. But I won't. If Meimi wants him to know she's here, that will be her choice to speak up.

And, if I'm being honest, I'm angry that Fritz interrupted our dance. He doesn't deserve to see Meimi.

"No video," I declare. "Why are you calling?"

A muscle twitches on Fritz's thick neck. "I am not meeting you."

"That's not what Godwin told me."

"Tough. I'm heading out of town for an extended vacation. You want someone to help Godwin with another one of his schemes? Look someplace else."

"No," I counter. "Stay put. I'm on my way now."

"Good luck with that. By the time you get here, I'll be gone."

A million calculations flash through my mind. Fritz is more than one of the last black market suppliers left standing. He's also got a history with Meimi, and not all of it is bad. I checked into past dealings. Fritz may act tough, but he fights for Meimi. Getting her more credits for her jobs. Making sure she got her memory wiped instead of ending up dead. I want him on the team. He'll help protect my girl.

"No," I say solemnly. "When I mean now, it's now."

A pang of regret tightens my chest. Tonight was going to be special. I'd purposely avoided any displays of my powers, and it was working. Meimi and I were getting to know each other as people.

More than that.

As transcendents.

Now Fritz and his negative attitude are screwing everything up.

I stiffen my spine. In this moment, keeping Meimi safe is more important than her happiness.

Holding up my hand, I summon my sentient.

In my mind, I picture a drift void forming. At the same time, I envision my dark suit transforming into battle armor. A loop of black particles appears nearby. Within seconds, the swirl thickens into a dark plate that hangs in midair. My clothing changes as well.

Meimi stands there, her lips parted in shock.

In the hologram, Fritz frowns. "There's a dark circle in my office. Did you put this here? What's going on?"

Fritz can wait for his answers. All I can do in this moment is focus on Meimi. There are a million things I want to explain. That I wasn't lying; I'm really an alien. How I crossed multiple universes to protect her. And the fact that she's my transcendent.

Sadly, there isn't time for any of that.

I just stick to the basics. "This is a mini drift void that connects to Fritz's office. Do you want to come with me? I understand if you don't."

"No." Meimi hugs her elbows. "I'll stay here."

I nod. "Be back as soon as I can."

There isn't time for a long transition to Fritz, so I punch my fist through the center of the void. Broken shards of the dark plate tumble to the floor, revealing an opening directly into Fritz's small office. I step through the new portal, leaving behind the fancy hotel.

A moment later, I stand inside a small concrete room that's decorated with a table, a few chairs, and not much else. Fritz stands before me. As my portal vanishes, every muscle in Fritz's face falls slack with shock.

"What the hell?" he asks.

I fold my arms over my chest. "Let's just say I have access to tech you don't."

"I told you I didn't want to meet."

"Why aren't you helping Meimi?"

Fritz huffs out a breath. "Look, it's not my call. My boss, the Scythe, has to approve any help for her. He thinks we've done enough already."

Tilting my head, I scan Fritz carefully. The guy's ice-blue eyes are wide with worry. Fritz wants to help my girl.

He just needs some extra motivation.

"Fine." I plunk myself down into a nearby chair. "I'll wait until the Scythe can talk to me."

"I've already sent him six comms, asking for an exception. The Scythe is dead set against this. He won't even open a chat." Fritz steps around his desk and takes a seat as well. "Getting him to call me back may take a while, if ever."

I send out my sentient to scan the room. They shoot me images of the tech wired into Fritz's desk. It's a flat-top panel that's sending out a live data feed to the Scythe.

Fritz's boss is already here and listening to every word.

"That's fine." I kick my legs out and get comfortable. "For Meimi, I've got the time."

Hours pass. Fritz keeps buzzing the Scythe from the data panel embedded into his desk. His boss keeps not answering.

It's all a show, of course.

A lie.

As Fritz and I wait in his office, the Scythe is already listening to everything we do. Research is one of my top priorities. I already looked into Fritz and his boss, just in case they could be helpful to Meimi. The Scythe loves mind games. In this case, he wants to see who'll give in and speak first.

It won't be me.

There's one major downside to waiting, beyond the obvious fact that I'm missing my date with Meimi. Sitting around gives me way too much time to think about what I've just done. My family is in charge of guarding and gardening the omniverse. Sentient send us to planets. We fix things that could cause inter-dimensional problems. That's it. We're not supposed to go around flashing our powers, and for good reason. To begin with, it could throw off a planet's development to know that so-called aliens exist. Also, seeing our tech can give bad people worse ideas.

When I visit a planet, the sentient will mark an item as red, and that's all I'm supposed touch or change. Sometimes it's as small as moving a butterfly around. Other times, I must save someone's life.

Bottom line: what I'm doing now for Meimi could get me in deep trouble. Little stuff like surveillance is one thing; opening drift voids is another. And since I first met Meimi, I've been doing a lot of both. Even we royals have to answer to Umbra's security tribunal. That could get ugly.

In this moment, I don't care. Meimi's safety is all that matters.

Finally, a refined voice echoes through the room. "Hello, Thorne."

I don't bother hiding my smile. That was a competition of wills, and I just won. "Scythe."

"Tell me why I should help you."

"You're not helping me. This is for Meimi."

"Either way," comes the Scythe's smooth reply. "Give me a reason. Godwin already shared his scheme with me. When built, his Engine will precision-kill anyone in the world. Meimi is the only one who can create it. Helping her means painting a target on my own back. Why would I do this?"

"Because it doesn't change the power Godwin has, only the speed with which it can take place. I'm sure you've noticed you're of the few ... what do you call yourselves again?"

"Black market entrepreneurs," offers Fritz.

"One of *those* left standing," I continue. "Your days are numbered."

"Still not convinced," intones the Scythe.

I rub my hands over my face. It's a risk to share Meimi's true plans, but I don't have much choice. There's no reason for him to help us otherwise. Sure, I could micromanage him with my powers, but I'm not outside the dome that often. And even if I *could* get outside the dome more, I've already broken too many rules in how I've been using my abilities on this planet.

Taking in a deep breath, I drop the verbal bomb. "Meimi plans to do more than build the Engine."

When the Scythe next speaks, there's no missing the smile in his voice. "I do so love Meimi's scheming."

"I know," I add. "Her science projects made you rich."

"This could be good for us, boss," adds Fritz.

"Let me put it to you this way," I state. "For the plan to succeed, we need the Hollow."

"President Hope never wanted her favorite advisor arrested," says the Scythe. "Could Meimi's scheme also clear the Hollow's name?"

"Absolutely."

"In that case, I'm interested. Tell me more."

"You can ask Meimi yourself."

I've already pushed things to even let Fritz and the Scythe know that her secret plans exist. If Meimi wants to hand over more details, that's her call.

Fritz's thin mouth quirks with a smile. He likes the idea of seeing Meimi. "And how will that work?" asks Fritz.

"Meet us in the Underground two days from now. Simulacrum level. Eight a.m."

"Agreed," states the Scythe.

"One last thing," I add. "If you fail her, I will track you down no matter where you hide."

Rising up, I open another drift void in Fritz's office. Within seconds, a loop of black particles turns into a portal that leads directly to the hotel. I must say, Fritz looks suitably shocked. That's exactly the effect I was looking for.

"Wow," whispers Fritz.

"Remember what I said about failing Meimi." I meet his eyes and deliver my iciest glare. "Because I know what you did to her before, and you've no idea what I'm capable of."

For emphasis, I punch through the void. Stepping through the new opening, I once again enter the main room of our hotel suite. Meimi's curled up on the couch, fast asleep. Her new little spider bot buddy crawls back and forth before her. It's automatically gone into guard mode.

I slip closer. The bot stops, rounds on me, and raises two of its pincer legs as weapons. That's sweet.

Anyone who guards Meimi is a friend of mine. I hold my arms up, palms forward, a sign the bot should read as surrender. "I'm not going to hurt her. She just got out of the hospital. Meimi needs to rest in a proper bed."

The bot lowers its pincers and moves back.

"Thanks, buddy," I whisper.

Scooping Meimi into my arms, I carry her back into her room. As we move along, she looks up dreamily into my eyes.

"Did we have a good time?" she asks.

"The best."

Meimi smacks her lips and closes her eyes once more. "That's nice."

Stepping into her room, I tuck my girl under the covers. The spider bot follows us inside. Once Meimi is set, the bot takes up its patrol routine again, this time pacing around the bed. For her part, Meimi doesn't so much as flinch, she's so out of it.

My poor transcendent. She definitely needs more sleep.

And she's not the only one. I could use a bit of rest myself.

With that thought, I head off to catch some snooze. There's no way I'll be able to sleep in another room, though. Someone could open a drift void in Meimi's chamber and attack.

Someone? Who am I kidding?

When it comes to Meimi's safety and drift voids, it's my father I need to worry about. There's no way I can be too far from her, so I grab some blankets and set up a makeshift bed on the other side of her closed door. That way, if anything happens, I'll be the first to know.

And with that thought, I drift off to a peaceful sleep.

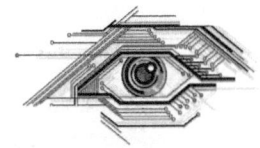

OPENING MY EYES, I wake up to find myself not in a hospital bed or uncomfortable cot, but in a fancy hotel. I peep under the covers. I'm still wearing my black dress from last night.

Oh, sweet mother of science.

Last night.

A memory appears. *Thorne raises his hand, black particles lift from his skin, and he opens a drift void in our hotel suite.* There are no monoliths involved. No software. Zip. Thorne just—whoosh—opens a drift void. And here's the frightening thing.

The sight wasn't all that scary.

If anything, it seemed natural.

Thorne even asked me if I wanted to join him in a little jaunt through the mini drift void to go yell at Fritz.

What the ever-loving WHAT?

Now, I've learned one fact about this memory-loss thing. If something doesn't surprise me, then it was probably part of my life before Godwin monkeyed with my head.

Did Thorne and I go traipsing through drift voids together?

And that question leads to the other startling revelation. Thorne really is an alien. And not only that, but at one time, I must have known he was from a different planet. Because I'm oddly cool with this whole thing.

By now, I know how my memories knock around my unconscious.

Whenever they direct me that someone is good, that's what they've proven to be. And right now, my memories say Thorne is okay.

Even so, the idea of trusting Thorne feels like lightning bolt to my already over-zapped internal power grid.

Case in point: last night after Thorne left, I just passed out on the couch.

Now it's the next morning, and I'm still in a state of shock.

My head stays fuzzy as I get ready to leave the hotel. Thorne gives me more clothes. In this case, it's jeans and a long-sleeved T-shirt. Both fit and are cute. He tries to chat a few times. Every time he asks a question, I give a one-word answer.

At least I have my project to distract me. And my spider bot Rakkie.

Every so often, I review plans on my data pad. At some point, Thorne and I get into the hovercar. I sleepwalk through picking up Chloe and Zoe. Thorne spends a ton of time loading their stuff into the back. Rakkie decides that's a good nesting spot, and hangs out atop their pile of supplies.

Eventually, we hit the checkpoint to reenter the Boston Dome. Vargas is there, as always. Can't say he looks great, though. He isn't wearing his helmet this time, probably because his face is all bandaged up. Thorne really did a number on the guy.

Sorry not sorry.

Vargas scans me, Chloe, and Zoe carefully while Thorne idles the hovercar.

"Three girls now, eh?" asks Vargas.

"You want another broken nose?" asks Thorne.

Ignoring that comment, Vargas points to Chloe. "What's your name?"

"Bite me," says Chloe.

Vargas winks, which looks especially weird on a black eye. "Maybe when you're done with Thorne here, you can—"

"Stop it." Thorne kills the engine and opens the door a crack. "You want part two, keep right on talking."

Vargas lifts his chin. "They need wrist cuffs. Humboldt's rules." He hands Thorne the silver loops of metal. I explain the situation to Chloe and Zoe, who put the cuffs on their left wrists.

With that done, Vargas steps back from the hovercar. "You're free to go."

The incident with Vargas perked me up a little, but not too much. I barely notice the ride through Boston Dome and ECHO campus. There's no missing the excitement from the back seat, though. Chloe and Zoe have never been in the city before. They comment on every building, hovercar, and drone.

We park in a concrete bunker at ECHO Academy. There's a long elevator ride down to the Underground, with Chloe and Zoe chatting the entire time. We then pass through multiple security checkpoints and reach our dorm floor. Chloe and Zoe declare that the place looks like a prison.

I counter that I need another nap.

The sisters go off to check out the laboratory. Normally, that would be like catnip to my inner scientist-feline. But all I can think is that I misjudged Thorne ... and this entire situation. If there are outer space characters in this scheme, how does that affect everything?

If I'm being honest, a big part of that *everything* is my heart.

I'm already falling for Thorne. Romance and science don't often go together, even when aliens aren't involved.

As Zoe and Chloe hit the lab, I slog back into my little concrete room, curl onto the bed, and try to sleep.

I barely notice Thorne and Godwin walking off together. The doctor asks my guard rapid-fire questions. Thorne appears calm as he answers each one. I can't hear what they're saying, but in all honesty? I'm not sure I could process their words, even if I could hear them.

Everything has suddenly turned upside-down, and I don't know how to right it again.

"Never trust those who say they are your friends. Rely only on those who show it." – Empress Janais, *The Fifth Age of Umbra*

THE MORNING STARTS off badly and goes directly to hell. It's clear from the get-go that Meimi is overwhelmed. Not that I blame her. In fact, it's amazing she's stayed focused through all this.

So that was the *bad* part.

The *directly to hell* stuff happens the minute I walk off the elevators with Chloe, Zoe, and Meimi. Because Godwin grabs my arm. "We need to talk."

"Yes, sir."

In truth, I'd rather ensure that Meimi settles in. Although it's understandable she's out of it, I still worry. The more time I spend with her, the more deeply I sense her moods. It's not like the mental connection we shared when we first met. Still, it's enough to put my senses on alert.

Godwin marches off to the Simulacrum. He spent so much time in that place, building out his plan, I suppose he feels like it's his home base. Once we're inside, he claps his hand on my shoulder.

"The two new scientists seem happy. How did they handle their first meeting with our little patient?"

I shrug. "Chloe and Zoe idolize Meimi. They've always wanted to team up with her on something. The twins know Meimi's lost her memory, but they're rolling with it."

That's the best explanation I can give Godwin. He'd never understand something like loyalty or friendship coming into play.

"Perfect," says Godwin. "You did well."

"Thank you."

"The Scythe wants to visit here next week. He'd like an official review of his plans with Meimi. Says you made quite an impression on his minion, Fritz."

"Good to know."

What I don't add is that the unofficial review of Meimi's plans takes place in a few days. We'll need to hide that from Godwin, of course. Now that we have Meimi's spider bot, that process will be a lot easier.

Godwin jams his hands into the pockets of his lab coat. "I'm moving forward with my schemes regarding Luci."

"And what are those?" I ask.

"Still in process. You'll know when they're final." He asks a ton of questions about the trip. Why did the comms short out? Where did we go? How did Zoe and Chloe react to joining the team? What was my trick to convincing Fritz and the Scythe?

I answer all his questions with as few words as possible. An electrical problem messed with the comms. We went to the resort and the garage, as requested. Chloe and Zoe are excited to work on top tech. And the Scythe isn't convinced yet. He needs to see the full plan first.

Once Godwin's questions die down, I decide to approach another key topic. "There's another team member we need to bring in."

"More than Chloe, Zoe, and the Scythe?"

"Yes. We need the Hollow."

"What?" Godwin frowns. "Why?"

"The highlight of your Engine is the cleansing. People need to see that happen on live video feed. But no one's done that before. How do we choose the best cleansings to show? Can we broadcast all of them at once? Perception is reality, Godwin."

"I fail to see how this relates to the Hollow."

"She's forgotten more about how to manipulate Authority info feeds than anyone else knows."

Godwin rocks on his heels for a moment. "Perhaps she'd be minimally useful. But I can't get her for you." He shrugs. "I put her in jail, after all."

That's when it hits me. Godwin's so casual about the so-called treason from the Hollow. That can only mean one thing. "The Hollow is innocent, isn't she?"

Godwin rolls his beady eyes. "The Hollow is one of those brilliant minds without the sense to look out for herself. Always trying to help President Hope. Never looking over her shoulder for who might be an enemy."

"If she's innocent, and you set her up, what makes you think she'll help Meimi?"

"We're calling her Meimi, now?"

"That's what she decided."

"Once the Hollow realizes that Meimi will die without her help, she'll step in and do everything she can. Her kind is predictable in their idiocy." He wags his finger at me. "That doesn't mean I can spring her from prison. Even I don't have that kind of pull."

"The Scythe has it."

Godwin steeples his fingers under his chin. For the record, the doctor totally has the power to bring in the Hollow, he just doesn't want to waste his juice. But making the Scythe do it? It's clear that might be interesting.

"Yes," says Godwin slowly. "The Scythe could do it."

"Right," I say. "We just need to convince him when he arrives for the review."

"Agreed," states Godwin. "Also, I checked the vid feeds. Meimi came in wearing an outfit that was *not* an approved coverall."

A pang of resentment moves up my spine. I loathe the idea of Godwin peeping in on Meimi. "Your coverall attracted unwanted attention outside the dome." *Not true, but plausible.*

"Fine," says Godwin. "Why don't you tell Meimi that you got me to allow her and her friends to wear whatever they want? That will help you build closer bonds with her."

"All the ladies would like that option. Thank you."

"And?" Godwin bobs his brows.

"Not sure I understand what you mean." Although with the brow-bobbing routine, it's pretty obvious what Godwin wants to know.

"How did your seduction fare? Successful?"

"What else?" It's a non-answer answer, but I hope Godwin accepts it.

"Perfect. I'm putting you into the cell that adjoins hers. That will keep things nice and cozy. You can even turn off the recording capabilities in both rooms, if you like. Or not." He bobs his brows again.

Rage boils inside me. Godwin is disgusting, pure and simple.

"That's all for today." Godwin waves his hand airily. "I have more meetings with the president now. I'll be back in touch when I can."

"Excellent, sir."

As the doctor speeds out the door, I make a silent vow.

No matter what, Godwin will get what's coming to him.

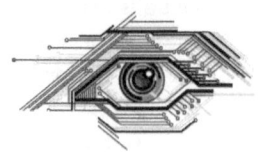

ANY MINUTE NOW, Fritz will arrive for our secret review of my plans. As I pace around the laboratory, two thoughts strike me:

This lab was awesome.

And then, we "fixed" it.

Here's the situation. While the rest of the floor is modeled after a Turkish prison, the Authority built our lab to be all things metallic and cool. Picture a spaceship interior from an old Earth movie, and that's the idea. All the surfaces are sleek. Burnished glass and steel decorate each workstation, fancy gizmo, and storage locker. And the entire place is long as a city block. Gorgeous.

Then Chloe, Zoe, and I did our thing.

It began when the sisters entered the lab. I let them divide up every Bunsen burner, glass beaker, or stick of furniture into either *chemistry* or *engineering*. Zoe's chemistry stuff got dragged to the left-hand side of the room, while Chloe's engineering supplies became stacked on the right. Now the lab looks like a cross between a spaceship and the twin's old garage, with one key difference.

I've set up a table in the middle. *Neutral territory.*

Although Chloe and Zoe are sisters, they're used to working alongside each other, not teaming up on things. My hope is that if I sit between them, I can help them get along.

We'll see.

Tweet, tweet!

Rakkie lets out a few short electronic beeps. No question what that means. Fritz has entered the building. I speak into my smart watch, which I've hooked up to the lab's speaker system.

"Chloe and Zoe," I announce. "I need you at the conversation pit." This is another one of my additions to the room. Thorne found us a few couches from other places in ECHO Academy. Our hope is that we can hang out here and brainstorm.

Thorne. Just thinking his name makes my pulse go berserk.

I haven't been purposely avoiding my guard. The other day, when he approached me with some way to replace the Lacerator with another alien, I said, *sure.* And that's just for starters. Recently I've also said *yes, no,* and *soup* to him. Although, I wouldn't have said *soup* if the other choice for dinner hadn't been tacos.

Never eat the Authority's spicy food.

Plus, I really have been busy.

Zoe, Chloe, and I only got here two days ago. Ever since then, it's been nothing but a whirl of activity. I've been revising my plans. Chloe and Zoe have been settling into the laboratory. Thorne's been off doing guard things, like working with Rakkie. Now our spider bot can short-circuit all the tracking feeds on our floor. Whenever one of us wants privacy, we just tell Rakkie. The bot then loops videos of us typing away at our workstations or whatever. Handy.

I stare at the door. Will Thorne walk through soon? Or will he fly in using his alien jetpack while shooting laser beams out of his eyes? For some reason, I've segued off the whole *whoa, he's an alien* thing and *wow, he can replace the Lacerator* to nonsensical brainstorming about what his otherworldly powers are really like.

Turns out, I can spend hours imagining alien powers. It's not healthy.

Shaking my head, I refocus on the task at hand. Thinking about Thorne is still not a great use of my time. It only leads to more alien jetpack scenarios.

The door swings open. Both Fritz and Thorne step inside.

Thorne looks tall and swoony in his black body armor. Per usual, he has his Mr. Unreadable face on. I try not to obsess about what he's thinking. That vow lasts about two seconds before I start to wonder anyway.

Is Thorne frustrated? Could he be acting standoffish to give me space? Both?

Move on, Meimi.

For his part, Fritz looks like a mountain of a man in his denim overalls, spikey white hair, and ice-blue eyes. He marches precisely two steps inside the door, stops, and folds his arms over his hefty chest.

"I'm here," Fritz announces with a frown. "Give me your plans."

Tilting my head, I look the man over. Fritz was definitely part of my life before my memory wipe. Chloe and Zoe confirmed it. But standing before this guy now? I feel nothing, unless you count the fact that I'm annoyed.

I'm here. Give me your plans.

Whatever happened to saying hello?

"Chloe and Zoe are on their way," I explain. "We can start when they get here."

"Why aren't they present now?" asks Fritz.

"They are," I say slowly. "Just in different parts of the lab." I snap my fingers as if an idea is forming. "I've got it. While we're waiting, you could practice saying *hello* to me. Like a person."

Out of the corner of my eye, I catch Thorne smiling. He loves it when I'm sassy. Maybe that's part of his alien DNA. After all, he could consume emotions like I eat tacos. Well, not Authority-made tacos, but you get the idea.

I shake my head again.

Focus.

"Fine," grumbles Fritz. "Hello, Meimi."

"Hello, Fritz." I look to Thorne. "Hi, you."

His smile deepens and dang, there are those dimples again. "Meimi."

Chloe and Zoe march in from different directions. Today Chloe's in another set of gas-station-style coveralls. She makes that look work. Meanwhile, Zoe's in a fitted white coat and matching boots that say, *this look goes from laboratory to conservatory.*

Zoe pauses to my left; Chloe's on my right.

"So, you're that dickhead," snaps Chloe.

"What?" Fritz shifts his weight from foot to foot. "I didn't do anything. It was all the Scythe."

Zoe looks down her nose at Fritz. "You worked Meimi half to death on all your little projects and paid her next to nothing. She should have been able to afford her own country for the money she earned you."

I step forward. "As interesting as this is, we have to get to *the plan*." Although I've only hung out with the twins for a few days, I've already learned that they are queens of getting conversations derailed. Sadly, I've also been doing a good job of distracting myself with brainstorming details about Thorne's alien status. If I don't take charge here, we'll never finish.

Chloe raises her hand. "I'll get our data pads."

"Thanks." I gesture toward the couches. "Do you want to hang out in our conversation pit?"

"No," snaps Fritz. "We stand here."

Chloe hands out the data pads and I launch right into things. Sort of.

"Okay, we'll just stand here awkwardly by the door then." I lift up my data pad. "As you can see, there are two sets of plans. One is the scheme for Godwin's official Engine."

Fritz looks up from his data pad. "Is this place secure?"

"No, I'm broadcasting this to President Hope. Of course this place is secure." Fritz is really getting on my nerves. "As I was saying, Godwin wants to launch his so-called Engine at the Liberation Celebration. It's a massive spider bot called a Crawler that will be loaded with an omnivoid generator, which is a device that can send multiple versions of the same Crawler to many places at once. Make sense so far?"

"Umph," says Fritz.

"I've got it," says Zoe.

"Me, too," adds Chloe.

Thorne meets my gaze and winks. In this moment, all my worry about his alien status melts away. He's here and winking. That helps. *I can do this.*

All of a sudden, I realize Thorne and I have been looking at each other for an overly long period of time. *Oops.*

I clear my throat. "So that was Godwin's scheme. My plan is that we get to the Crawler first and swap out the Lacerator with a replacement. That not-a-Lacerator will then go to the many millions of undesirables, but instead of killing them, it will heal them."

"What if they're just poor?" asks Fritz. "Many people get ranked as undesirable after losing their job."

"We have a list of everyone and why they're undesirable. We'll set up logic for each fix. Most cases, it's just as simple as erasing their unemployed status from the master database."

"And you're sure a not-a-Lacerator can do this?" asks Fritz.

"The correct term is knowledge sentient swarm," states Thorne. "And yes, that's exactly how they work."

"But you don't have this swarm thing," counters Fritz. "Do you?"

"I will," says Thorne. And the way he says those two words, Fritz knows one thing. If he continues pushing, Fritz will end up with some free tooth extraction courtesy of Thorne's fist.

So Fritz flips through screens on his data pad instead. "How will you get this replacement Lacerator into the actual Crawler?"

"That's all in section 92," I point out. "The celebration schedule calls for a puff of smoke to roll out before the Crawler goes onstage. Zoe will develop a mega-smoke thingy that goes backstage as well. I'll use that as cover while I swap out the Lacerator for our replacement."

Zoe raises her hand. "Although, I'm working on a hallucinogen too. That was in the original plan and it's much cooler from a chem perspective."

I do a double take. *Huh.* I thought I'd talked Zoe off the hallucinogen option.

"Either way," I continue, "the Authority will broadcast the event from the Golden Pantheon at ECHO Academy. We'll need you to get Zoe's smokescreen chemical in there."

The more we speak, the deeper Fritz frowns. We're not convincing him, and there's a still whole list of semi-illegal supplies we need from his organization. Worry corkscrews up my spine.

"Look," I continue. "My goal here is *not* to kill millions of people, but to *help* them. And if we can take down Godwin at the same time? That's a bonus."

"Sure," says Fritz. "And how do you see things ending at the Liberation Celebration?"

"It's like this," I reply. "Godwin already confessed that he set up the Hollow and wants to overthrow the government. By the end of the celebration, we'll expose that. The good doctor will end up in a bad jail cell. The Hollow will be free. The undesirables will be alive. Everybody's happy."

For the record, I also wanted to squeeze in overthrowing the government into this scheme. But as it turns out, that's a tall order. Not something that I can do in two months. Still, it's on the list.

"There's more to your scheme than that." Fritz finally looks up from his data pad. "Let me get this straight. In front of millions of people, you're going to set off his Crawler ... but turn it into a tool to help the undesirables instead of killing them ... expose Godwin as trying to set up a coup against President Hope ... all while keeping your names out of it, clearing the Hollow of wrongdoing, and freeing the Lacerator."

"That's it," I say. "We'd also like to attend ECHO Academy in September, but that's more of a bonus thingy."

"Oh," adds Chloe. "We also-*also* want a big board to track everything. Like a monitor we suspend from the ceiling. So we can see how things are going."

"That's the only part of this plan that's reasonable," says Fritz. "The rest is impossible! A complete fantasy!"

Thorne has mostly been quiet this whole time. Now he steps forward, stopping when his body is directly between me and Fritz. It's a very Thorne thing to do. He's so protective, and in this moment, I totally appreciate it.

"Explain," states Thorne. "What's so impossible about Meimi's plan?"

"First, Godwin's got some third party company developing his Crawler. It's under huge security. You want me to get you access to wherever they are storing it backstage so you can swap out Lacerators. That won't be easy."

"You used the word impossible," says Thorne.

"Because you'll only have a matter of seconds while the smokescreen rolls out. That's not enough time to break in, open the Crawler, swap out Lacerators, and get to safety. And your whole plan for making that happen is a puff of smoke? Like I said, impossible."

I lift my chin. "It's all in the plan."

Fritz shakes his head. "Plus, there's just too much stuff that you're making for the first time with only two months to do it. Meimi must invent an omnivoid generator. That's never been done. And how do you know what this Lacerator replacement can really accomplish? Maybe you can save these undesirables one day, but they'll be dead the next. It's a waste of time."

Thorne steps closer to Fritz. "I saw the same specs, and I think Meimi's plan is brilliant. If you're too scared to get us information on how to access the Crawler, admit it. But don't go after Meimi and her team."

"Team?" asks Fritz. "That's the worst part of all. These three are not a team. Chloe and Zoe are building up their own parts of lab. Meimi is more traffic cop than leader."

Before, Fritz was just mildly irritating. Now his bad attitude is making me see red. Mostly because he does have a point.

"Are you done?" I ask.

"No," replies Fritz. "One final problem. You have all of this controlled by a simple master mechanism."

"Three master mechanisms," says Chloe. "The official one for President Hope, the secret-but-fake one for Godwin, and the real one for us."

"Here's the thing," says Fritz. "The mechanism will never work. You'll need to calibrate millions of sets of data at the same time, all in tandem with drift voids."

"I thought of that," I state. "If it gets too complex, that's just another reason to have the Hollow on the team. She's got information-processing implants that should make all that work easy. Plus, she's already slated to be executed at the Liberation Celebration. We just need to free her early and get her to hook her into the Crawler's systems."

"And that all comes back to you, Meimi. Now you're running around backstage, accessing the Crawler, swapping out the new Lacerator, and freeing the Hollow ... all in a matter of seconds."

"It's tight, I know." With each round of pushback from Fritz, I feel like I'm shrinking. "But Godwin already has Thorne and I on standby backstage. I won't be doing this solo. And if you get us the information we need, there's enough time to both alter the Crawler and get the Hollow loose. Not a ton of time, I'll admit. But it's possible. I've run every scenario."

"No," says Fritz. "Just no."

Thorne pokes Fritz in the center of his chest. "Stop playing games. I was there with Meimi when you had her build a drift void generator that fit inside a suitcase. She got the job done in less than twenty-four hours. And that was her working alone. Now she's got me, Chloe, and Zoe to help. We will do this, whether you're in or not. The only question is, do you want to be on Godwin's side when this is over?"

I step closer to Fritz as well. As I get nearer, there's no missing the shimmer of light around his skin. I've seen that particular look before at the Simulacrum.

"Wait a second," I say slowly. "That's not Fritz."

"I know," adds Thorne. "You want to come out and play, Scythe?"

A burst of light surrounds Fritz's body. A moment later, the Scythe stands in his place. I've only met the guy a few times, but the ultimate crime lord looks unchanged. His dark suit is perfectly matched to his black hair, olive skin, and strong bone structure. The guy could be a model from an old Earth magazine, if it weren't for the fact that his eyes look right through you. That part's unsettling.

"This is one of my newer technologies," says the Scythe. "A mini hologram projector. I'd prefer it if you'd keep it under wraps."

"We'll keep your secret," I say. "But I want an answer. Will you do this? You've said it's impossible, but you haven't said *no* to helping us."

"I haven't, have I?" The Scythe sets his hands in the pockets of his dress pants. "So I have two parts in this plan. One, I ensure you can get access to the Crawler. Two, I get the Hollow moved to this floor so you can work together."

"And three," I add, "there's a list of supplies we need. Screen 7 on your data pad."

"And our list includes that tracker monitor," says Chloe. She's already told me twice how she can't wait to set it up. I guess as an engineer, this is like playtime for her.

"Understood." The Scythe goes back to scanning the data pad. A long silence follows. *Has the Scythe made his decision?*

"Well?" I ask.

"Your friend Thorne is right," says the Scythe. "I'd rather bet *on* you than *against* you. I'm in."

My shoulders slump with relief. "That's great news."

"But I have my price."

An icy feeling crawls up my spine. Somehow, I suspect that I've had this particular *price conversation* with the Scythe before. "What do you want?"

"A favor," replies the Scythe. "To be called in when I want it. That's all."

Thorne shakes his head. "Not a chance. Let me owe you. Leave Meimi alone."

"Not a deal." The Scythe glares at Thorne. "I'd bet against you in a heartbeat."

"It's fine," I say quickly. "I agree to the terms."

The Scythe pulls a small data chip from his pocket. "Place this in your spider bot. It will enable us to stay in touch without so much fuss."

Thorne swipes the black chip from the Scythe's fingers. "I'll take care of it."

A predatory gleam shines in the Scythe's dark eyes. "Protective of her, aren't you?"

"I *am* her guard." Thorne opens the lab door. "I'll see you out." The words are there, if unspoken:

If you screw over Meimi, you'll regret it.

As Thorne leads the Scythe away, I can't help but smile. This may be impossible, but don't some of the best things start off seeming that way?

Even relationships.

As I turn that thought over, I drag Zoe and Chloe over to our conversation pit.

There's so much let to do.

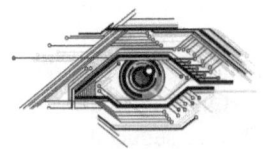

NOT SURE HOW long I spend in the lab. It's hard to track clocks in the Underground. Time also gets slippery when you're trying to keep Zoe and Chloe loaded onto a single train of thought.

And yes, I keep staring at the lab door.

Thorne still hasn't returned from escorting the Scythe out of the building. Whenever that was.

By the time we decide to quit the lab, it's close to midnight. As I approach my dorm room, I notice a light gleaming from under the door. My pulse speeds up. Maybe Thorne has come back at last.

After the talk in the lab, he and I have tons to discuss, starting with the fact that I've adjusted to the idea of him being an alien. I'm smiling when I pull open my door. What I see inside isn't Thorne, though.

It's Godwin, Luci, and Josiah.

A jolt of worry moves through my insides. Before I can stop them, words fall from my lips. "What are you three doing here?"

"Why, we've stopped by to congratulate you," says Godwin. "You've done well. Your recruits look capable. The lab is a bit unorganized, but you'll soon put that right, eh?"

"Sure." I keep staring at Luci and Josiah. They haven't said anything, and Godwin hasn't mentioned them either. So why are they here?

"I can call you Meimi now, I assume?" asks Godwin.

"Sure." I really string out the word *sure*. There's another shoe coming and I really want it to drop already.

"Before I forget," says Godwin. "I put Thorne in the room next to yours two days ago. But when I came in here, the adjoining door wasn't open. Now, why would that be?"

My tired mind tries to catch up with this news. I didn't realize Thorne had moved in next to me. In fact, he hasn't touched that adjoining door. He didn't even tell me he'd moved nearby.

Of course, the truth won't help me here. The doctor thinks Thorne seduced me on the trip to the Berkshires. I suppose that means I'm easier to control, by his scummy standards.

"Well?" prompts Godwin.

"I'm a neatnik," I lie. "I like to keep it closed when we're not using it."

"Ah," says Godwin. There's that smug look of his again. It's like he knows every secret I have and can't wait to ruin my life.

And sadly enough, that might be true.

"And you brought Luci and Josiah?" I ask.

"Yes," answers Godwin. "I thought you may want some company. My treat. Consider it a reward for a job well done."

Josiah eyes me from head to toe. Once again, there's that disgusting *leer* of his. "Yeah, lots of rewards," he says slowly.

No way do I want to know what that means.

I make a great show of yawning. "Hoo-wee! I am so, so, sooooo tired. I'd love to visit, but I must snooze."

Josiah steps toward me, that disgusting leer still stuck on his face. "Sure, babe."

I hold up my hand, palm forward. "I rest alone. As in, all of you must be far away from me. Just to be one hundred percent clear."

Luci strolls up to my side and links her arm with mine. "Why don't you guys go on ahead and we'll have some girl time?"

Josiah frowns.

Godwin shrugs.

I grab my chance to get rid of them both.

Crossing the room, I reopen the door. "I love Luci's idea! Run along now." I make sure to give Godwin my very best impression of a grateful puppy. "Thank you so much."

The doctor chucks me on the chin. "Keep up the good work."

"I will."

It seems to take forever, but eventually the doctor and the Leer Master cross the room and step out the door. I close it behind them and sigh.

"Apologies about Josiah," says Luci. "He means well. It's just that he gets overly excited."

"That's one way to put it." I lean against the closed door. "So, what do you want to talk about?"

Luci rushes across the room and takes my hands in hers. "You don't remember this, but I'm your sister."

"Sister." Memories tickle at the back of my head, followed by an onslaught of ugly feelings.

A weight of shame.

The burn of betrayal.

An ache of loneliness.

"To show his appreciation, Godwin asked me to give you some good news." Luci pulls a data chip from her pocket. The Scythe handed one like this over to Thorne. Only while the Scythe's chip was black, this one is red. "Do you know what this is?"

"Sure. A data chip."

"Obviously." Luci giggles, but it seems more forced than real. "This contains a computer virus. It can only work one time and then —poof—the data disappears. It can set free any one undesirable. Permanently."

"I understand how one-time viruses work. It's linked to the instance of the chip. One chip, one virus, one use."

My thoughts race through Luci's words. I must admit, the *permanent* part is enticing. I've figured out how to wipe someone's slate clean from undesirability. But setting a person aside as untouchable in the system? That's something I don't know how to do. Yet.

It takes an act of will not to make grabby hands at that chip.

"If you succeed," continues Luci "then Godwin has approved me to give this chip to Mom."

All the air seems to get sucked out of my lungs. "Mom?" Fresh emotions pour through me.

A jolt of fear.

The warmth of love.

A cut of anguish.

"You know Godwin took you away to have your memory wiped, right?" asks Luci.

"Yes." The word comes out as barely a whisper.

"There's a reason why that happened. You and Mom were playing scientist in some run-down factory and you flipped the place into two-dimensional space-time. The Authority thought you'd set off a nuclear bomb. That's a major science crime. You got Mom marked as an undesirable and slapped in prison. Because of you, our mother could be killed."

Something about Luci's speech feels like a lie, but I can't tell what. And it does feel true that Mom is at risk. Anxiety tightens around my throat. Just when I was feeling stable again, Luci drops this bombshell. I reach for the chip. "Can I have that now?"

Luci sets it into her pocket. "Sorry, dear sister. Once the Liberation Celebration is a success, then gGodwin says I can give this to Mom. I know it might be tempting to you to focus on all those undesirables being cleansed. Now you don't have to. You can focus on saving our mother." Luci holds up the chip. "Without this, she's doomed. No matter what."

A weighty realization settles into my bones. This is all another way of Godwin trying to control me. Sending me off with Thorne for a lovers' getaway. Now he's tempting me to finish his Engine so my own mother will live. This guy will not give up. Do I really think I can outsmart him?

Luci gives me a sympathetic smile. "Just do what Godwin wants, okay? That way, some good can come out of this for both of us."

"Why don't you give the chip to Mom now?"

Luci inhales a shaky breath. "If I did that, then I'd end up dead, too. You don't want that, do you?"

"No." That's the word I say, but in reality? I have no idea what I want when it comes to Luci.

She motions to the door. "Now, if you don't mind, I'll let you get that sleep you talked about."

Stepping aside, I allow Luci to leave. The woman who calls herself my sister smiles as she strolls away. Once she's gone, I get ready for bed, but it takes ages for me to fall asleep.

And when I do, I have another one of those super-strange dreams.

In my dream, I return to the ruined kitchen at the Ozymandias Chemical Factory. I'm not alone, either. The blue version of me waits there as well. We don't say any hellos or talk about what happened with Chloe, Zoe, Fritz, and the Hollow. Somehow, I'm certain she already knows.

"Go on," says Blue Me. "Ask the question."

"What question?" In all honesty, I didn't realize I had one.

"About Luci."

Oh. That question.

"Is Luci really my sister?" I ask.

"Yes."

I press my palms against my eyes. "The last time we met here, you said that it would help me to *not remember* certain things. Was Luci one of those things?"

Blue Me nods. "You idolized her. She handed you over to Godwin. Fritz and the Scythe helped as well, but it wouldn't have happened without Luci."

I hug my elbows. "So that story about how I got to Godwin? The accident on Newbury Street?"

"Another lie. You did flip the factory into two-dimensional space-time, though. That said, the Scythe could have hidden it. He chose not to. There was too much money to be made in handing you—I mean *us*—over to the government."

"You said it was good I don't remember things. Now I'm not so sure. It isn't easy to be blindsided like this. I'd rather know it all."

"If you want your memories back, then maybe you should ask Thorne."

"What can he do?"

Like last time, Blue Me's body begins to turn transparent. "I don't have much time. And sadly, I don't remember everything either."

An electric shock of realization hits me. "Wait, don't go! I forgot to ask you about my mother. Where is she?"

Suddenly, Blue Me disappears. The room reforms. It's not destroyed anymore. There's now a clean table set with mismatched napkins. A large chair sits by the window. A voice echoes in from nearby.

"Meimi, where are you?"

I'd know that tone anywhere. "Mom?"

SMASH!

A hoverdigger careens through the kitchen wall. Its serrated nose-cone chews through everything: brick, wood, and tile. Merciless soldiers march through the new hole in the wall. Their black armor gleams in the hoverdigger's headlights.

"Meimi!" calls Mom.

One Merciless isn't wearing his helmet: Captain Vargas. He points right at me. "Get her!"

My heart thuds so hard, my pulse beats in my throat. On reflex, I take off through the right-hand door and step onto the factory floor.

"Meimi! Meimi!" Mom's voice grows more faint.

"I'm coming!"

My body knows where to go as I race up a metal spiral staircase. At the top, there's a half-opened door.

That's Mom's room.

I burst through the door, but there's no sign of my mother. Blood pools on the floor. Footfalls sound on the metal staircase outside. The Merciless are closing in.

"Kill her!" cries Vargas.

I can't focus on the Merciless, though. I keep tearing through sheets and shelves, looking for any sign of my mother. Everything seems covered in blood.

"MOM!"

That's when I wake up screaming.

"The bond between transcendents is a cry between souls." – Empress Ophelia, *The Lost Book of Transcendents*

ONE ADVANTAGE of having the room next to Meimi's: I can sleep by her door without anyone being the wiser. Before, I had to pretend I was spending all night patrolling the halls. Now, I just curl up with my blanket by the connecting doors, and I'm fine.

"MOM!"

Meimi's cry cuts through the night. Her voice quakes with terror. Every muscle in my body goes on alert.

Rising to my feet, I kick my blankets aside. "Meimi, are you all right?"

No response.

Using all my strength, I slam my shoulder against the connecting door. It shatters as it falls in. I rush to her bed.

"MOM!"

Sitting beside her, I take her hand in mine. "Meimi, wake up. It's me, Thorne."

Her eyes flutter open. "Thorne!"

She reaches for me. It's the most natural thing in the world to pull her onto my lap. My left hand stays clasped around her palm. My right fingertips gently play with the hair at the nape of her neck.

"Shhh," I whisper. "You're safe now."

Minutes pass. Meimi's breathing slows. My heart rate goes back to something like normal as well. When I'm certain she's calm, I speak again.

"Can you tell me what happened?" I ask.

"It was just a dream."

"My people put a lot of weight on dreams, remember?"

"I went back to this factory where I used to live."

"Ozymandias Chemical."

Meimi leans back until I can see her brown eyes gleaming in the dim light. "At first, it didn't bother me that I couldn't remember things. Now, it hurts."

"I understand. What happened in the factory?"

"I saw a version of me, only ..." Meimi shakes her head. "It's too strange."

"Any detail can be important." Leaning in, I set my forehead against hers. "Please tell me."

"The other me was ... blue."

I suck in a shocked breath. Blue? Only Umbrans dream about themselves as blue. Although I suppose humans could do it as well. Also, what's known about Umbrans and transcendents is zero. *Nothing to worry about then.*

"And after that?" I ask.

"The Merciless broke into the factory. I tried to find my mother. I got to her room but she was gone. Everything was covered in blood."

"Your mother is safe. When Godwin came to get you, I put her in hiding. She's on my home planet."

"Umbra?" Meimi sits up a little straighter. "So she wouldn't be slated to be killed after the Liberation Celebration?"

"Not a chance. Who told you that?"

"Luci. Godwin had her stop by. She claims she's my sister. Is that true?"

"It is."

"That's what I'm afraid of. There are all these hidden facts about my past. It was okay for a few days. I'd just woken up. And then, I only wanted to focus on my plan. But now, I want my life back. According to the blue version of me, you can return my memories."

I've faced my share of surprise battles. Being a royal isn't easy. But this request from Meimi makes my entire body freezes with shock. I hadn't thought she'd remember that I could return her memories.

Plus, Meimi was having enough trouble accepting I was an alien without anything extra getting added into the mix. Honestly, I hadn't thought about it much. Mostly because kissing Meimi would bring Cole after her. Not an option.

"You're an alien, Thorne. I accept that. You must have extra abilities. Special powers. Can you get me my memory back?"

"Yes and no."

Meimi scooches off my lap. Can't say I blame her.

She narrows her eyes. "What do you mean?"

"If you thought my ability to open drift voids was a lot to handle, then what I'm about to tell you? This is a ton more. Do you really want the truth right now?"

Meimi worries her lower lip with her teeth for a moment before replying. "I do."

"Before Godwin took you, I kissed you. It wasn't an ordinary kiss. You remember the particles I used to open the drift void at the hotel?"

Meimi nods.

"Those are called sentient. There are different types that do various things. What we call *second sight sentient* are blue particles. They can show you other places in your current world or visions of the future. When I kissed you, I set your memories into the future where Godwin can't get at them."

"But in my dreams, that blue version of me could remember some things. Not everything, but she's told me a lot of stuff."

"You and I"—I gesture between us—"we aren't a typical pair. We love each other in so many parallel worlds, our feelings bleed over to this reality. Before I split out your memory, we could share thoughts and emotions. My people have a name for it. You're my transcendent. It means the rules might not apply to us, an din a lot of ways."

Meimi runs her fingertips over her lips as she soaks all this in. "When I had my memory, did I accept you as—*what did you call it again?*—my transcendent?"

When I speak, my voice comes out low and husky. "You did."

"Can you kiss me again? I want to remember."

"I can't. My father is Emperor of the Omniverse, the universe of universes. His body contains a special set of particles called Crown Sentient. He's convinced that a transcendent pair will kill him and take the crown. He sensed when we kissed. He tried to come here and kill you. I had to fight him."

"Oh, Thorne." Reaching forward, she takes her hands in mine. Her brown eyes glisten with sympathy. "Was that the day you were limping?"

"It was." My heart almost bursts with affection for her. "I'm the one that should apologize, though. If I kiss you again—if I return your memories—then my father will come back here and finish you off. Even worse, he's convinced that you're the transcendent for my brother Justice. Cole would kill you both."

"Cole?"

"When my father gets in a rage, my brothers and I call him Cole."

"I see." Meimi is clear-eyed and calm. *Ever the scientist.*

"There's more. I can't access my powers under the Boston Dome. The Lacerator is what we call a sentient swarm. As long as Godwin blocks the Lacerator, he blocks my powers as well. I can only access my abilities outside the city."

Meimi gives me a sad smile. "Not a lot of happy news for either of us, is there?"

"There is one good thing," I say. "The Lacerator is made up of battle sentient; that's why it kills. But we could replace the Lacerator with a swarm that's knowledge sentient. That way, they'd be ideal for the Hollow to command. My brother Slate can help us find the best swarm."

"Slate?" She grins. "How many brothers do you have?"

"Two. Justice is older; Slate is younger."

"And you're all in line to become Emperors of the Omniverse?"

"That's Justice's destiny. I'm not strong enough in sentient."

Meimi rolls her eyes. "Are you kidding? What I saw in the hotel was amazing."

"Wait until you meet my brothers. Then you'll see what sentient and their hosts can really do."

"About that." She worries her lower lip with her teeth again. "I'd like to meet them. Go to Umbra. Be with my mother. Escape this whole mess. If we leave the dome, you can do that, can't you?"

I eye her carefully. "Is that what you really want?"

"Yes." She nibbles on her thumbnail. "No. I don't know."

"Can I give you an opinion?"

"Please."

"If you left here—and if Godwin killed all those people—then you'd hate yourself forever. You want to finish this."

Meimi sighs. "But you heard what the Scythe said. My plan is impossible. Things might be better if we go outside the city and you open some drift voids, flush Godwin into another dimension, and—BOOM—problem solved."

I slide across the bed, stopping when our hips touch. For this part of the conversation, I want to feel her near. "Listen to me." I lace her fingers with mine once more. "Your plan is brilliant. Maybe I could create drift voids and punch holes in this universe. That might get rid of Godwin. But it won't repair the ruined fabric of this society. They need your plan. Free the undesirables. Expose Godwin for who he is. That's how to rebuild this world."

Meimi looks away and doesn't respond. She's not convinced.

"May I tell you something else?" I ask.

"Sure."

"All this while, I've only been concerned for your safety. My family, we destroy whole universes sometimes. It's never easy. That said, it's always for the greater good. But every moment I spend with Godwin, I see him take the idea of the greater good and twist it into something evil. I want to fix this, too." Unlacing our fingers, I set my knuckle under her chin, guiding her gaze until our eyes lock. "I believe in you, Meimi."

Little by little, her lips curve into a grin. "Well, if we're going to do this, I need that sentient swarm of yours."

I meet her smile with one of my own. It's great to have Meimi back in planning mode. "Absolutely. I see my brothers tomorrow morning. With any luck, I'll have good news for you when I return."

"The Scythe is delivering that tracking board tomorrow. By the time you get back, the twins and I should have it all set up. Then you can see our master schedule."

"Can't wait," I say. "How about we celebrate with an early breakfast? I specifically requested Godwin send us edible food. No more Authority tacos."

Meimi chuckles. "I like the sound of that."

Together, Meimi and I step off for a rousing breakfast of granola bars and freeze-dried yogurt. It feels natural, which is somehow strange. I just told her about my complex alien world, and if anything, she seems more at peace with the idea, not less. I start to worry about that fact, but then Justice's words come back to me instead.

You're a lucky man.

I am, indeed. So I set my concerns aside and simply enjoy some time with my transcendent.

"War is always best fought with *brothers, not* between *them."* – Wu Zhao Zetain, *The Art of Sentient War*

A FEW HOURS LATER, Justice, Slate and I stand in the ruined lobby of a different apartment building. After the fight with Cole, that last building had too many bad memories. Not that this place looks much different. Smashed-up reception desk. Fetid furniture. That said, the windows here are mostly cracked and boarded over, so that's a change.

My brothers have just stepped through the drift void; we haven't even said our greetings yet. Once again, their outfits remind me of a cowboy and preacher from the Old West. I'm about to start my hellos when in a surprise move, Slate is first to speak.

As always, younger brother says one word: "Picture."

I pull on my ear. It's a reflex reaction, since I can't believe what I'm hearing. "Do you want to see a picture of Meimi?"

"I'd like to see that too," adds Justice.

"Sure." I glance around the ruined lobby, like a painting of her will be pasted on the wall. Then it hits me.

My smart watch.

"I've got it." I start fiddling with the device on my wrist. "Meimi is setting up her tracking board today."

"What's that?" asks Justice.

"It's so she can stay on target with her big project. We got a little spider bot the other day, and I asked Meimi to keep the bot's video tracked on her. That way I can check in." I adjust a few more controls. Finally, the image comes in on the tiny screen: Meimi strolling across the laboratory floor. I lift my wrist. "It's small, but there you go."

Justice and Slate step closer. My sentient send me another mental image. This time they send me the picture of not one, but two deer approaching me carefully. I smile at their humor. The whole idea of a transcendent is overwhelming to my brothers.

"My stars," says Justice. "She's something."

"Transcendent," adds Slate. His voice is low with awe.

Looking down, I see the camera feed has already changed. Rakkie is no longer projecting video of Meimi. Now the picture shows Zoe and Chloe.

Justice taps the image of Zoe. "That's what you call a real angel right there."

Slate does the same, but to the picture of Chloe. "Beautiful."

I almost fall back on my butt, I'm so shocked. I've never heard the word *angel* from Justice before. And Slate? I didn't even know he found anything beautiful, let alone a girl.

And these are Meimi's two best friends.

This could get very complicated.

The camera picks up Meimi once more. Now it's my turn to tap the screen. "No, guys. *This* is Meimi. Those other two were Chloe and Zoe, her friends."

With that, my brothers launch into a long game of Twenty Questions—or in Slate's case, Twenty Words—about Zoe and Chloe. Are they twins? Where did Meimi meet them? Why are they in the laboratory? What exactly are their roles in Meimi's master plan? At first, the whole thing is a big smile. After all, these are the two most eligible bachelors on all of Umbra. They have their choice of sentient-carrying women to choose from. And I happen to know both like to play the field.

Even so, I've never heard either of them show this much interest in any woman. It must be some kind of halo effect from the fact that Meimi and I are transcendents. Maybe that makes Earth women more interesting?

Whatever their motivations, there are other reasons why my brothers and I all trekked to this spot. It's not romance.

"Guys," I say at last. "I'd love to keep answering your questions, but there are things we need to discuss."

"Of course," says Justice. Those are the words my brother says, but I can't help noticing how his gaze stays locked on my smart watch. I decide to shove my hand in my pocket and remove temptation.

I turn to Slate. "Last time we met, you were researching how to free up my powers. I still can't access sentient under the Boston Dome."

"Closer," replies my younger brother.

In Slate-talk that means he's almost got a solution for me, but not quite yet. "Thanks for keeping at it," I say.

"He'll figure it out," states Justice. "You'll know it's fixed because I'll call you again."

I chuckle. Justice is notorious for sending me summons to speak at any time, and across multiple dimensions. "I look forward to your comm."

Justice adjusts his white Stetson. It's his move when he's trying to charm someone into doing something. In this case, the "charmee" would be me.

"Brother," begins Justice, "I was thinking again about that video you showed of Zoe."

"No way am I bringing out my smart watch again."

"What an idea." Justice rubs his stubbled jaw. "I wasn't going to suggest that, but since you bring it up, how about one more peek?"

"Chloe," adds Slate.

This is unbelievable. "How about this? We finish catching up on non-girl stuff, and the next time I see you, I'll bring Chloe and Zoe in person."

"Right." Justice rubs his hefty palms together. "Go on."

"Dr. Godwin's plan is to send a battle sentient swarm around to kill millions of people."

"No," states Slate.

"We agree. Here's Meimi's plan. What if we replace the battle swarm with one made of knowledge sentient?"

"That would work," says Justice. "The swarm would have to come willingly, though."

I turn to Slate. "Think you can find a volunteer?"

"Try," replies Slate.

"That's all I ask," I say.

"Hey, I've got an idea," says Justice. "Since you're bringing those lovely ladies with you next time, how about I take it on myself to help Slate in his search?"

"Thank you." I smile. "I was hoping you'd say that."

"Not a worry," declares Justice. "After all, it's the least I can do, considering how I know you're going to keep your word to us and all."

I hold my hands up in mock surrender. "I'll bring them. I swear."

"Good," declares Slate.

Now that we're done with the pleasant topics, it's time for painful stuff. "How is Father?"

"Cole," states Slate.

I know what that means. Dad has returned to being unhinged. "I'm sorry to hear that."

"He's getting sneaky, too," adds Justice. "Spends all day locked up in his lab, working on something big. Even Mom doesn't know what he's up to."

"Assassination," adds Slate.

It's one word, but there are hours of discussions behind it. Mother believes it would be kindest for the three of us to team up and assassinate Cole. Every emperor or empress who takes in Crown Sentient is doomed to the same fate: they all go insane. Janais thinks it's kinder to have the killing blow come early.

"I'm not ready for that," I say. "Last time, Cole shared that he knew about transcendents. That changes everything, in my opinion. If you two can find Umbran transcendents to share your powers, then you could face Cole, remove his Crown Sentient, and keep him alive. I've been thinking about it, and since I found my transcendent, I think that's a sign. You guys will find yours next. There is hope for Dad."

"I like where you're going with that," says Justice. "Trouble is, Cole's still Cole while we're out a-looking. How about this? We put

Cole on his own planet and seal him off there with red sentient. An exile void."

I shake my head. "That's a nice idea, but only emperors can do that, and I'm assuming Cole would never do it to himself." Which Justice knows already. This is his way of trying to lighten the mood.

Justice snaps his fingers in pretend disappointment. "Aw, shucks. Back to the drawing board."

A tingling sensation moves up my spine. I hate leaving Meimi this long. Today, Godwin was visiting Humboldt. Those get-togethers tend to end fast. I can't risk him getting back to the Underground and not finding me there.

"I better be on my way," I say.

"Look," declares Slate.

No question what he wants to look at, either. *Chloe.* Plus, there's so much seriousness in Slate's gray eyes that it's hard to say no. And with the block on our sentient powers, it's not like my brothers can easily sneak into the Boston Dome and pay a visit.

Of course, it's a small movement to reveal my watch. But that's not the point. I've been trying to keep my brothers focused and the images on this device are distracting. That said, both my brothers look so interested, I lift my wrist anyway.

"Sure. You can have one last look before I go."

Both Justice and Slate look for so long, I start to lose blood flow to my hand.

"My lady doesn't seem too happy, does she?" asks Justice.

Looking down, I see that Meimi, Zoe, and Chloe are standing in a circle, gesturing wildly. There's no audio, but I don't need that to know they're yelling at each other.

And is that smoke coming from somewhere in the back of the lab? Bands of worry tighten across my chest.

"Go," orders Slate.

He doesn't need to tell me twice. "Bye, brothers." I hop on my hoverbike and speed back toward the city.

I can only hope I arrive in time.

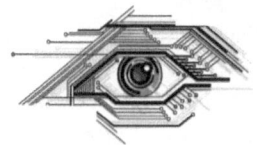

I STAND in the Underground lab alongside Chloe, Zoe, and Rakkie. Above our heads hangs the big board, which is the monitor where Chloe wanted to track stuff. Of course, we're using fake names for all the milestones. Godwin is on a need-to-know basis and, turns out, he doesn't need to know much. We've been disagreeing about how those milestones should be listed.

And we've been doing that for an hour now.

"It should go alphabetically," declares Chloe. "The deadlines for my work should be listed first, then Meimi, and then Zoe."

Zoe, as it turns out, has a real problem with being last. Why? Her name starts with a Z. Seems she always got last in line at school or whatever. And it also seems that if I had my memory back, I'd recall all this myself and wouldn't need to be reminded.

More and more, I want my memories. Badly.

It's a super frustrating conversation. Even Rakkie has given up. The little bot is lying on his spider back, waving his spindly legs in the air. It's a very clear pantomime for how he feels about our conversation. *Dead on arrival.*

Fact: back at the hotel, I uploaded some artificial intelligence protocols into the little guy. I think he's getting an attitude.

Smack!

The door bursts open; Thorne rushes in. He speeds across the lab and pulls me into his arms.

Not going to lie.

I have no idea what's going on, but the hugging is nice.

Okay, more than nice.

Leaning back, he cups my face in his hands. "Are you okay?"

"Beyond the fact that we *still don't have a goals sign*"—I make sure to glare at Chloe and Zoe for the last part—"I'm fine."

"But I saw smoke in the vid feed from Rakkie. I thought there was a fire." He looks over at Rakkie on the floor. "And is that bot all right?"

"Fine," I reply. "Just displaying the finer points of physical sarcasm."

At these words, Rakkie hops back to his feet and skitters around while making little tweeting noises. I'm pretty sure the little thing is laughing at us.

Zoe waves her hand dismissively. "Don't worry about the smoke. It's over now. I was working on a new hallucinogenic; something to fluster the audience while we swap out the Lacerator. My concoction was supposed to make a haze."

Thorne frowns. "But shouldn't you have some way to siphon off the smoke so everyone doesn't choke to death?"

"Well, I *should* have that," says Zoe. "But someone stole that equipment and dragged it to *her* side of the lab."

Chloe lifts her chin. "I need it more than you do."

I lean my head against Thorne's chest. It's a very comfortable spot. Maybe I'll stay here forever.

"Ugh," I sigh. "Getting the lab set up was supposed to be the easy part."

Snick!

Two chains hold the big monitor above our heads. Now, one of those metal strands makes unsettling creaky noises.

"Your board is about to fall," states Thorne.

"No, it's not." Chloe grabs a ladder that is most decidedly on Zoe's side of the lab and jams it under the edge of the board. "Problem solved."

"You took my ladder," warns Zoe. "I want the ventilation system back."

Tweet, tweet!

Rakkie goes berserk. That's a different set of sounds from when the little bot is playing around. That level of noise means only one thing.

The doctor is on his way.

"Stop fighting," I order. And because it's the best plan at this point, I add: "Godwin's coming. Look busy."

Everyone takes their places. I return to my desk. Chloe pretends to sort through a pile of gears. Zoe holds up an empty beaker and examines the nonexistent contents. Thorne leans against a nearby stretch of wall and looks menacing.

Godwin steps through the door; he's not alone. My heart sinks.

The Scythe is with him.

The last time tall, dark, and dangerous was here, the Scythe had stopped by for an unofficial visit. I'd forgotten that he was coming by again. This time, the visit is an *official* inspection, where the Scythe checks out our operation and gives his verdict to Godwin.

Now, it's true that the Scythe already committed to me that he'll help.

But it's also true that he's a crime lord and lying liar.

It's also-*also* true that the lab looks like a total mess. I mean, if I were the Scythe, I'd be tempted to back out. And I'm nowhere near his level of *ethically challenged.*

Godwin spreads his fingers in the universal symbol for excitement. Yup, Godwin made *jazz hands*. "You just saw a hologram of my schemes back at the Simulacrum." The doctor now spreads his arms wide. "Now you can witness the minions who bring my ideas to life."

I'm busy pretending to type the same sentence over and over when I catch the whole *minions* line. What Godwin understands about my official plans to make his Engine is zero. Mostly because I give him fake reports. But even so, he should show the team some respect.

The Scythe slowly steps around the lab. I see the situation through his eyes. Questionable chemical stains on the walls. Concoctions recently smoking away in a corner with no ventilation. A janky monitor that's propped in place with a random ladder. And let's not forget me, who probably looks like I haven't slept in days ... and that I'm about to scream with frustration because, let's face it, that's the truth.

"So, what's your verdict?" asks Godwin. "Does this inspection meet your standards?"

The Scythe pauses, leans on his left leg, and sets his hand in a pocket of his sport jacket. He could be a male model, back in the era when Earth had both fashion and models.

"What can I say?" asks the Scythe. "I'm impressed. Now, let's discuss my price." Turning to Zoe, he gives her the barest of winks.

Hold it right there.

This means two revelations.

One, the Scythe is still in.

And two, the Scythe winked at Zoe.

In response, all the blood drains from Zoe's face.

The Scythe doesn't wink. This isn't good.

"Excellent!" cries Godwin. "We'll return to the Simulacrum to discuss specifics." He shoots a quick glance at Thorne. "The Scythe will requisition that *part* for you, by the way."

By *part*, the doctor means the Hollow. As code words go, it's rude to treat her like a piece of machinery. Still, I can't help but be happy that the data guru is on her way.

Thorne nods. "Thank you, sir."

Godwin and the Scythe stroll from the room. Once they're well and gone, Zoe sets her hands on her throat. "Did the Scythe really wink at me?"

"He *so* winked," says Chloe.

"The man's really handsome," adds Zoe. "But a little scary."

I raise my pointer finger. "Make that a *lot* scary." I turn to Thorne. "Back to business. Godwin said something about a *part*. Does that mean what I think it means?"

Thorne grins. "Yes, the Hollow is coming."

"Wow." Leaning back on my heels, I stare up at the ceiling in a general show of gratitude. "That is great news. Things are looking up."

All of a sudden, the big board creaks, sways, and tumbles off its ladder prop to fall *splat* on the floor. Little bits of glass fly everywhere. Rakkie skitters past, slips on some splinters, and tumbles onto his back again. This time, I'm worried that the little bot might actually be damaged.

A weight of worry settles on my shoulders. We have less than two months to finish this project and more than two million lives riding on the line. And we're still a hot mess.

Sadly, things are actually *not* looking up.

"There is no torture quite like being trapped in a routine mission on a parallel universe of no import." – Beauregard the Great, *Instructions for Visiting Parallel Worlds*

DAYS PASS.

Meimi keeps focusing on our big project.

Not a lot of actual work gets done, though.

I've been on planets with nothing but rocks and fire where more stuff got created in less time.

Leaning against the lab wall, I make a quick mental inventory. Zoe is still developing her hallucinogen and not the smoke screen, which she calls the puff bomb. Chloe keeps complaining that she needs to know *how* to fit an omnivoid generator into the Crawler without being limited by other people's ideas. Too bad Meimi is the one actually designing the omnivoid device. Today, things got pretty heated. Now the twins are in their rooms, supposedly engaging in quiet research.

It's a nice way of saying, *Meimi put them both in a time-out.*

Meimi's a brilliant scientist, but leading a team is way different from building prototypes alone. At the same time, Chloe and Zoe are super talented, but they don't exactly play nicely with others. I step in where I can, but most of my time needs to be focused on Godwin management. If I didn't keep his schedule full, the guy would be down here constantly. So far, I've figured out how to flood his apartment, set up fake meetings with President Hope, and convince his girlfriend, Trixie, that the guy is ready to propose. She's naturally clingy and super skilled at sucking up his time.

Even so, I know Meimi is getting worried. She's not sleeping. Or eating. Or thinking about anything other than the millions who could die if she fails. My girl is running on adrenaline. Take this moment for instance. Right now, Meimi is typing away on her data pad so quickly, you'd think the Liberation Celebration was tomorrow.

That settles it. Meimi needs a break.

Stepping over to her side, I rest my palm on Meimi's shoulder. "May I take you out to lunch?"

She wipes her hands over her face. "I can't leave the building. There's too much to do."

"Ah-ah. I've heard there's a fresh shipment of fake waffles in the kitchenette."

She gives me the side-eye. "Fake waffles?"

"You know, the rubbery ones you hate." I take her hands in mine and haul her to her feet. "Come on. You know you want some synthetic breakfast."

A smile rounds the edges of her mouth. "You know what? I think I do."

I pull her close against me. "You know, we never did finish our dance."

"But now we're in a lab."

"It's a romantic lab."

"No, it's not."

Even so, Meimi's already started swaying from foot to foot. I give her a twirl because my girl is a very good twirler. She steps back into my arms, her chest pressing against my own. Our mouths are only a breath apart. Her heart thuds so hard, I feel it against my ribs.

Damn, do I ever want to press my lips to hers.

There was some reason we weren't supposed to kiss, but in this moment, I can't remember what it was.

Tweet, tweet!

Rakkie goes nutso nearby. At first, I want to punt the little bugger across the room for interrupting our moment. Then, I realize it. That's Rakkie's visitor alarm.

Someone's coming.

"Who's on their way?" asks Meimi. "Please tell me it isn't the Scythe."

I step to a nearby display and scan the news. "No, it's the Hollow."

At those words, Chloe and Zoe race into the room. Both look wide-eyed and breathless. "I was checking the data feeds," they say in unison.

"You first," says Chloe sweetly.

"Oh, no. You begin," counters Zoe. Her tone is even nicer, if that's possible.

Turns out, these two act crazy-nice to each other when they're actually incredibly ticked off.

"The Hollow is coming," announces Chloe. "I can't wait to meet her. She designed her own data access and processing implants. I think she could have some great ideas for squeezing the omnivoid generator inside the Crawler."

"And I want to talk to her about vid feeds," adds Zoe. "Even if I can get my hallucinogen to work, it won't fool the folks at home. The Hollow is an expert at manipulating video. That way, my hallucinogen doesn't have to do everything."

"Drop the hallucinogen," says Meimi in a singsong voice. She's only said this a hundred times today. "Work on the puff bomb."

Zoe ignores those words instead of starting yet another yelling match. Is that progress? Whatever it is, it's quiet. I'll take it.

Chloe bobs on the balls of her feet. "When is she getting here?"

Footfalls sound in the outer hallway. Godwin only wears dress shoes, and he's the sole guy who can march around here without an invite.

"She's arriving now," I announce.

But the Hollow isn't the one who stomps through the lab door. It's Vargas.

I stifle the urge to groan. Of course, the Hollow wouldn't be sent here without a military escort. And Humboldt would never miss the chance to send his favorite spy into Godwin HQ.

Vargas stomps along for a few yards and stops. He pulls off his skull-helmet. Now, I see something I never thought I'd witness. Vargas's face is slack. A look of genuine surprise lights his eyes.

Vargas is stunned.

"I saw you girls in Thorne's hovercar," stammers Vargas. "Why are you here?"

Chloe shoots him an impolite finger gesture. "Because we're scientists, shithead."

Zoe lifts her pointer finger. "I'm going to let that language pass." She glares at Vargas. "You really had that coming."

Vargas leans in closer to Chloe. "You're feisty." He licks his lips. "I like that. I'm Captain Vargas of the Merciless."

"I'm Chloe of the *you don't have a shot* people."

"We'll see." Vargas turns toward the door. "Ah, the rest of my command is here."

More Merciless warriors file into the lab. My protective instincts go into overdrive. Without my powers, it won't be easy to keep Meimi and her friends safe against so many.

Then again, it might also be fun.

A woman stands in the middle of the group. She's as tall and lithe as a dancer. Her skin is deep ebony, which contrasts with her short white hair. Silver implants gleam in her eyes and on her fingertips. She wears simple white trousers and a matching cotton tunic.

The Hollow.

"Stop," orders Vargas.

Everyone halts.

A snide grin curls Vargas's mouth. "I think the Hollow disobeyed that order."

My hands curl into fists. I've seen Vargas's type before. He's making up a reason to hurt the Hollow. No doubt he thinks it will impress Chloe.

He couldn't be more wrong.

For her part, the Hollow stands perfectly still.

Sure enough, Vargas turns to Chloe. "We've implanted a blood-borne virus into the prisoner. Makes it easier for us to control her." Vargas holds up a small handheld that's little more than a flat square with a raised button. "Only the best criminals get an *agony switch* like this one." He presses the button with his thumb.

Hunching over, the Hollow hisses in a pained breath.

"She'll scream soon," declares Vargas excitedly. "Just give her a minute."

That's not happening.

Crossing the floor, I rip the handheld from Vargas's grip. Exhaling, the Hollow stands up straight once more.

She's no longer in pain. *Good.*

"Your delivery has been made," I tell Vargas. "You can go."

Vargas cuts his gaze toward Chloe. "I hope to see you again soon."

"And I hope you drop dead from the new plague," counters Chloe.

Vargas grins. "I do like mine feisty."

I point to the exit. "Door. You. Now."

A flash of worry comes over Vargas's face, but he hides it quickly enough. That's satisfying. The guy hasn't forgotten how I pummeled him at the Boston checkpoint.

"I'll take my leave with pleasure." Vargas plucks the switch from my hand. "But just try to control her without this, if you think you're so clever."

I stifle a groan. Only a sicko like Vargas would think he's raining on my parade by taking away something called an agony switch.

With that, the Merciless march away. This time, I trail them to ensure everyone leaves the Underground. It would be just like Vargas to pretend he got lost and cause problems.

Once I'm certain they're totally gone, I head back to the lab.

It doesn't seem like anything changed since Vargas departed. The Hollow stands in the same spot as before. Meimi, Chloe, and Zoe wait nearby. I take up my classic spot leaning against a wall. If Godwin does a drop-by, I must look distant and official.

"Is this room secure?" asks the Hollow. She has a faint French accent.

"Yes," replies Meimi.

"Then why am I here?" asks the Hollow.

Meimi hands her a data pad. "This is everything you need to know. Once we get your retinal scans, we can get you full access to the stuff we didn't even show Fritz."

Gripping the data pad in her left hand, the Hollow rests her right fingertips on the screen. A moment later, the metal attachments on her fingertips glow with white light. Then the Hollow's silver eyes flash with tiny letters and numbers, images, and data.

"This is a strong plan," says the Hollow. "But you're missing the whole celebration side of this."

"Meaning?" I ask.

"The logistics of the actual event," says the Hollow. "If you want to place something inside the Crawler, it's important to know more than just a slice of the evening's schedule. You must understand every aspect. There's no knowing what could be important."

Meimi nods. "My bot downloaded some info, but I haven't had time to analyze it." She steps closer to the Hollow. "Do you know about the Liberation Celebration?"

"It's where I'll be executed," says the Hollow. "I've taken an interest."

"But I thought you were in prison," states Meimi. "How did you get this info?"

The Hollow grins a white-toothed smile. "Oh, they've no idea what I'm capable of. I can still take data in; it's getting it out that's a challenge. If you remove that blood-borne virus out of my system, you'll be amazed what I can share ... particularly about Godwin."

Zoe and Chloe gasp. "Cool," they say in unison.

The Hollow lowers the data pad. The light from her fingers vanishes. No letters or numbers shine in her metal eyes. "I've assessed your plan. I'm not part of this team."

I kick off the wall and stalk closer. "You don't mean that."

"Let me clarify," says the Hollow. "I'm not part of this team because *no one is*." She turns to Meimi. "You need to fix this. Stop looking at this as three people. We are one team with a single plan. This isn't four separate timelines, it must be a single decision tree."

I do a double-take. In a matter of seconds, the Hollow pinpointed what was wrong with the project and how to fix it. I'm impressed.

Meimi gasps. "You're right." She speeds over to her workstation, fires up her computer, and gets to work. "I should have used Gantt charts all along."

The Hollow turns to Chloe and Zoe. "Do you have anything to eat around here?"

"Oh, yes," they say in unison.

"I'd love a tour," says the Hollow.

As Chloe, Zoe, and the Hollow trudge off to the kitchenette, I pull up a chair beside Meimi's workstation. I've spent years learning battle tactics and how to rule. It doesn't matter that I won't be emperor one day; learning is its own reward. And now, all that's important is how my skills might help Meimi. As for Godwin? I'm done babysitting that guy. If he shows up, I'll deal with it.

Nothing will stop me from helping my girl retool her master plan.

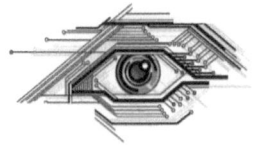

I SIT in the lab's conversation pit. The couches are fake leather and stick to my legs. *Ouch.* I really shouldn't have worn a skirt today. But I was trying to feel grown up, and a skirt suit seemed to fit the bill. Now I'll have heat rash.

Although, the rash could also be my nerves.

Thorne, Chloe, Zoe, and the Hollow all sit nearby. Everyone has data pads with the new plan. Chloe and Zoe flip through screens as they soak in all the changes. The Hollow sets her fingers on the data pad while her eyes light up. It's been a week or so since she arrived. Although honestly, it's hard to know. Living without sunlight will do that to you.

All this time, I've been locked up with Thorne and working on revised plans. It's not as fun as it sounds. Thorne already met my alter egos, Sarcastic Meimi and Sleepy Meimi. Over the past days, he's met even more sides of me, namely Bossy Meimi, Stinky Meimi, Furry Meimi (I still haven't gotten my hands on a razor; Godwin is a freak about that), and my favorite, Hangry Meimi. For some reason, he still likes me.

And I like him more every day, too.

Thorne and I haven't had more dances or heart-to-heart chats, but I've gotten to know more of his sides, too. There's Protective Thorne, and his alter ego, Hyper-Protective-and-in-a-Murderous-Rage Thorne. There's Challenging Thorne, who debates the finer points of plans until I can't decide if I want to poke his eyes out or kiss him. There's Romantic Thorne, who I sadly must still avoid.

There's been no kissing, obviously. We can't risk attack by Thorne's evil omniverse-ruling father. That said, the No-Kiss Rule is a real bummer.

And then there's Sweet Thorne, who makes sure I eat and get some sleep. I knew this side of him a little before, but I've gotten to know it a lot more.

I like all the Thornes.

He likes all the Meimis.

So far, so good.

Only now, we're showing the team all that our multi-selves have done, and that's a little terrifying. Zoe, Chloe, and the Hollow all sit nearby, scanning the new plans. Silently. I don't know how they'll take it.

Finally, Zoe looks up. "You changed my hallucinogen into a big puff of smoke?"

"I did that a long time ago, Zoe."

"Making the drug work is too risky," says Thorne. "It'll be easier to have smoke roll backstage."

"I know you really wanted to develop that drug," I add quickly. "But it will work better as a puff and a *ta-da* moment in the show. Plus, it will be way less suspicious afterward."

Zoe purses her lips. "Okay, I get that."

Thorne and I share a long look. I mouth three words: *she gets that.*

He arches his right eyebrow, becoming I-Told-You-So Thorne. This version always gets me to smile. Now is no exception.

"Besides," says Zoe. "Now I have plenty to keep me busy with figuring out how to neutralize the Hollow's blood-borne virus."

"Most appreciated," says the Hollow.

Chloe shoots me a worried glance. "You're doing a ton of running around the day of the event."

"I'm supposed to be monitoring things for Godwin. That makes me the natural for legwork."

The Hollow's fingertips flash more brightly as she runs them over the data pad's screen. "This version is so much better."

"Thank you," I say. "Thorne and I teamed up on everything." He and I share a quiet look that warms me to my toes.

"So." Thorne scans the group. "What's the verdict?"

"The first thing we have to do is rearrange the lab." Chloe rises. Evidently, she's ready to start working right now.

Whoa.

Zoe rises. "I'll help."

A chill of surprise prickles across my skin. I was waiting for a long fight on this. But they're all ready to go. I turn to the Hollow. "How about you?"

"My first task is to learn how to handle the new version of the Lacerator. I'll set up some scenarios in the Simulacrum."

"You know how to use that?" I ask.

The Hollow winks. "Absolutely."

"Great." I stand up and wipe my sweaty palms on my skirt. "In that case, I'll set up the new monitor." I turn to Thorne. "Want to help me?"

He laces his fingers with mine. "Always."

The Hollow leaves for the Simulacrum. Zoe and Chloe move to the other side of the lab, where they begin dragging ventilation equipment around. The moment becomes one for just me and Thorne.

We did it.

We fixed the plan.

Together, we may even have saved millions of lives.

From the deepest corner of my soul, I want to wrap my arms around his neck and kiss his face off. Why is it that when you can't do something—like kiss a guy—then that becomes the number one thing your obsessive mind focuses on?

I don't know the answer, but I can say this.

If the situation ever changes, I won't miss my chance for a kiss.

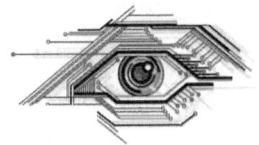

THORNE and I approach the lab door. For the first time since reworking the plan, we're getting together to chat up where things stand for the Liberation Celebration. As we close in on the lab, low voices echo into the hallway around us.

"I think she's coming," says Chloe.

"I hope she likes my new chem dart launcher," adds Zoe. "That way, the puffs of smoke will start from multiple spots."

Not sure why these chats always make my stomach woozy, but they do. Thorne gently rests his hand on the center of my back. That's calming. Together, we walk into the laboratory and park ourselves around the conversation pit. All the while, Thorne smiles and nods at folks like a pro.

A thought hits me. Thorne is part of the royal family back on his home planet. Perhaps he's marched into tons of places while touching the backs of Umbran women. Like maybe at a ceremony for dedicating new spaceships. That would be cool. Perhaps they also have an annual ball, like Cinderella only in space. That would be fun, too.

Although I'd have to kill his space Cinderella date.

And all that raises another question. Did Thorne date anyone? I mean, I'm his transcendent, but maybe that's not exclusive. Could Thorne be keeping tons of transcendents back at his home planet? Like a transcendent harem or something? What do I know? It's possible.

My blood pressure spikes. I've been so focused on defeating

Godwin and protecting millions from being cleansed, I really haven't been thinking about what it means be romantically interested in an alien.

Damn, he could be a sophisticated hologram, like the Scythe was to Fritz but even more advanced. I could be alien catfish bait.

This is serious stuff.

Chloe clears her throat. Shaking my head, I forcibly snap myself out of my thoughts about Thorne.

And I realize that everyone is sitting around the conversation pit, staring at me like I've grown a second nose. I might even have been muttering to myself again. That's been happening more and more lately.

Sweet mother of science.

And *this* is why I don't let my imagination explore Thorne's alienness. It never ends well. Mostly for me. And with this Liberation Celebration coming up, I need to focus on my projects, not work myself into a frenzy over Thorne.

After all, assuming I live through this, there should be plenty of time to worry about the alien side of Thorne later on. For now, I can simply return to hanging out with my new mental friends, *forced ignorance* and *denial*.

"So," I begin. "How are we doing this week?"

One big thing Thorne and I changed in our revised plan was to talk about *stuff we needed to get done* instead of *who owns what*. It's been working pretty well.

And yay, denial! I can focus again!

Chloe leans forward. "About the master mechanisms. These are the fake ones for Godwin and President Hope." She opens her hands, showing some small square devices. "We modeled them after old Earth remote controls."

I try to keep my features level. "Really?"

Zoe straightens the lapels of her fashion lab coat. "I told you she'd make that face."

"What face?" I ask. "I'm not making a face."

"Yes, you are," sighs Chloe. "It's your look that says, *oh sh—*"

"Language," interrupts Zoe.

"Fine," huffs Chloe. "Her looks says, *oh shhhhhhh-ugar plum fairies, we're all going to fail and die. Gee. Darn. Drat.*"

Zoe nods. "That works."

The Hollow leans back onto the couch. She's changed her loose white pants and tunic for the same look, only in silver. "Giving them a simple, old-fashioned remote control is a good idea," says the Hollow. "My data shows neither of them can handle sophisticated tech. Buttons that say *on, off*, and *kill* are about their speed."

Thorne frowns. "I thought Godwin was more of a techie than that. After all, he built out that whole mock-up of his master scheme in the Simulacrum."

The Hollow picks a bit of lint off the back of the couch. "The last team of scientists did all that. All Godwin knows is how to steal other people's work."

"Which brings us to *the real controller* for the Hollow." Chloe pulls what looks like a thin square of paper from the bib pocket of her coveralls. The tiny sheet gleams with transistor patterns.

That's no ordinary paper there.

Chloe hands the sheet to the Hollow, who slips it under her wrist cuff. The device's embedded screen immediately changes from green to blue.

My jaw just about hits the floor, I'm so impressed.

"The real Controller will be the Hollow's hacked wrist cuff?" I ask. "That's brilliant!"

"It's not done yet, but yes." Chloe beams.

My mind takes a snapshot of this moment. Not too long ago, we weren't a team. We were a crazy mess. Now, everyone's working together. We're actually making progress on things. On reflex, I gaze down at my wrist.

Star Council Level Access: Godwin
Humboldt-Merciless Undesirables Tagged: 2,136,904
Godwin-Horde Undesirables Tagged: 478,162
Total To Be Announced At Liberation Celebration: 2,615,066

My chest tightens with sorrow and worry.

More than two and a half million now.

When I look up, Zoe brushes her fingers across her wrist cuff as well. "I checked the feed from Rakkie. They tagged a bunch of kids from our high school last week."

Our group began this chat with what we've gotten done lately. Now, a chill cools the air as our conversation becomes something else entirely.

"President Hope never wanted the job," states the Hollow. "But you should have seen the creeps Humboldt wanted to put in. Believe me, whatever she approves, there's a long list of much worse stuff she's talked the Star Council out of. Together, we were trying and change things. Then Godwin framed me. And the worst part? The look of betrayal in Hope's eyes. In some ways, that's worse than being on that undesirables list. I lost who I was. A good person."

Zoe leans forward, resting her hand atop the Hollow's. "Chloe and I hid off-grid so the Authority wouldn't mark our dad as undesirable." Her voice cracks. "He died anyway, though. We couldn't source the cancer treatments he needed. And what hurts *us* the most?" A tear slowly rolls down Zoe's cheek. "All this time, the government had the tech to save him, he just didn't make enough money to be considered worth it."

"Then after we lost Dad, Mom turned unhinged." Chloe shivers. "She reached out to the Sister Rage rebellion. It's not a real group, more of a trap by the government to find undesirables. She got caught." Chloe stacks her hand onto Zoe's and the Hollow's. "They tagged her last week."

I twist at my cuff, remembering the upbeat voice in the phone, telling me to BLEEPING BLEEP. Suddenly, Chloe's and Zoe's short tempers make more sense.

"You didn't tell me," I say.

"You've had a lot on your mind without that," replies Zoe. "There will be plenty of time for tears. Later."

I don't know what to say to such a selfless act, so I decide to share some of my heart as well.

"When I first saw the download of names, I didn't recognize many of them. But then I saw Miss Edith. I've been thinking about her ever since. She must have been special to me. I can't stand by while she's cleansed." I set my palm atop everyone else's.

Thorne rests his elbows on his knees. "I'm honored to be here with you all. You inspire me." He rests his hand on the stack.

There's a long moment where we just sit there, connected. We're all working together as a team. But now? We're also on a mission. Somehow, that's important.

"We better get back to it," I say at length. Everyone lowers their arms, and I sense the ties forming between each of us.

This caper is more than a project.

It's the adventure of our lives.

"There's work, and there's purpose. Always combine them." – Empress Janais,
The Fifth Age of Umbra

I RUB my neck and think through what just happened. These
four ladies have faced down some serious stuff, and yet they've
chosen to stay locked the Underground, trying to make things
better.

Our talk continues, only now, we refocus on the Liberation Celebration. Zoe shares how she plans to neutralize the Hollow's blood
virus. Chloe explains how Fritz came through with Captain Fran-
cisco, the custom builder who's making the Crawler. The captain
wants specs.

"but we don't have those yet," explain Meimi.

"Why not?" asks the Hollow.

"Two reasons," answers Meimi. "One, I haven't finished building
the omnivoid generator yet, so I'm not sure how big it will be. Two,
we haven't found the replacement for the Lacerator. There's no
knowing if we'll even find a new sentient swarm, let alone what size
container it'll fit in."

"I may have good news there," I say. "My brothers are working on
finding us a different version of the Lacerator."

Chloe's eyes go large. "They are?"

"What can I say?" I ask in reply. "I'm connected."

Everyone nods. Seems my reply covers things enough, at least for now. After all, I am Godwin's goon. For all they know, I have many friends in low places.

"Next time I talk to them," I continue, "they should have details on the replacement, including what kind of container the creature would fit in."

Here it is.

The big ask.

I promised my brothers that I'd bring Chloe and Zoe. In all truth, I have no idea if the twins will want to go. After that passionate speech about saving the people they care about, I feel guilty even asking them to leave the Underground.

"It's like this." I shift my weight on the couch. "I'm supposed to meet my brothers today outside the dome."

Chloe raises her hand. "Can I go? You deactivated the tracking on all our wrist cuffs."

Some of the tension eases from my neck and shoulders. "Absolutely, you're all welcome to come."

The Hollow rises from the couch. "Appreciate the invite, but count me out. Until my blood-borne virus is gone, I can't leave the building without serious pain."

"Understood," I say.

Zoe's blue eyes flash with excitement. "I'm in."

I turn to Meimi. "Will you go as well? I really want you to meet my brothers."

Her face turns a pretty shade of pink. "Sure, I'd love to meet them. When do we leave?"

"How about now?" I ask.

"Do we need to, you know, explain *anything* before we go?" she asks. There's no question what Meimi really means here. *Do we need to cover the whole aliens issue before we take off?*

"No, my brothers are just regular guys. You know." I wink. "On the surface, anyway."

Meimi nods. "Perfect."

And even though I promised my brothers I'd bring Chloe and Zoe, I can't ignore the sense of unease in my stomach. What if the twins figure out my family is from another planet? Suppose they aren't able to find a replacement for the Lacerator? There aren't a lot of ways this could go off the rails.

Even so, there's only one direction. Forward.

"All Umbrans contain sentient within their bodies. What makes a royal is not only holding more sentient than most, but also developing related powers to a new level, whether it be battle, knowledge, second sight, or—in the case of an emperor or empress—detecting danger." – Hammurabi the Seventh, *Law of Sentient*

AN HOUR LATER, I'm driving my favorite hovercar out of the Boston Dome. Meimi rides shotgun while Chloe and Zoe sit in the back, chatting up a storm. We got lucky crossing the checkpoint. There were no long lines, so I didn't have to use the Star Council lane.

Which means I also didn't have to deal with Vargas.

Chloe was especially appreciative.

"I don't know why Vargas glommed on to me," she announces from the back seat. "All the guys usually drool over Zoe. No offense."

"None taken," says Zoe. "But guys drool over you as well. It's just that, Vargas aside, your feisty act generally turns them away. You're like..." She taps her lips. "What are those extinct animals from old Earth again?"

"What?" asks Meimi. "You mean all of them?"

"The ones with the quills," clarifies Zoe.

"Porcupines," I say.

"You're from Umbra," says Meimi. "How do you know that?"

Chloe raises her hand. "What an Umbra?"

I decide to ignore that question and focus on Meimi. "Things were boring before you woke up. I spent a lot of quality time on history databases attached to ECHO Academy."

Chloe leans so far forward from the back seat, her pigtails brush Meimi's shoulder. "I said, what's an Umbra?"

I give Meimi the side-eye. "Should I share?"

Chloe bounces in her seat. "Let me guess! Let me guess! Umbra means you're from..." She scrunches up her mouth to one side of her face, deciding.

"Outer space," deadpans Zoe.

Meimi gasps. "How did you know? His home planet is called Umbra."

"WHAT?" Now Zoe leans forward so her face is between me and Meimi as well. "I was kidding." She looks at me like I've got six eyes or something. "You're from outer space?"

Meimi closes her eyes. "Oops."

Chloe leans back in her chair again. "Oh, I totally suspected it."

Zoe leans back as well. "You did not."

"Did so." Chloe starts counting off things on her fingertips. "First of all, Thorne is always saying things like *your* atmosphere or *your* sun."

Zoe shrugs. "I thought he just wasn't that great with the English language. Like he was from New France or something."

I narrow my eyes, thinking through all my conversations with Chloe. I hadn't noticed that said stuff like *your moon* when really, the moon is for everybody on the planet. Something to watch in the future.

"Second," continues Chloe, "the guy doesn't eat, sleep, or work out, and yet, he's ripped."

"You noticed that?" asks Meimi. There's a jealous edge to her question which I like far more than I should.

"We're locked in a subterranean prison and he's the only guy around so yes, I totally noticed." Chloe rolls her eyes. "It's not like I'm interested. I get he's yours. It's just that I have eyes, you know?"

Meimi scooches so far away from me, she's almost plastered against the passenger side window. "I didn't say we're together. Thorne and I aren't together."

Chloe smacks her lips sarcastically. "Sure, you're *not* together."

At this point, I'm thoroughly enjoying the conversation. It's great that Chloe noticed the bond between me and my transcendent. It's even better that Meimi is blushing up a storm right now.

"Back to your second point," says Zoe. "The food, sleep, and buff-ness could all be good genetics."

"No one has that good of genes," says Chloe. "Not on this planet anyway. Which brings me to the third and final clue."

Zoe folds her hands neatly in her lap. "This'll be good."

"Meimi said Thorne was an alien," explains Zoe.

"I was kidding," offers Meimi.

"I remember when that happened," confirms Zoe. "Thorne didn't sleep for three days and Meimi said that it's because he's an alien. Then she said she was kidding. That totally didn't confirm any alienness."

"Just wait." Chloe gestures toward Meimi. "Say those three words again."

"I was kidding?"

"See. There." Chloe rounds on Zoe. "You had to notice it that time. Meimi said that like it was a question. She did the same thing when she first brought up the *Thorne is an alien* thing. Her *question voice* always means there's a hidden something-something going on."

I raise my hand. As the resident alien here, I feel like my voice needs to be heard. "I remember that day. Chloe's right about the voice thing. It was suspicious." Not sure when I started following along in the semi-nonsensical conversations with Meimi, Chloe, and Zoe ... but I'm one of the girls now.

"So," says Zoe. "What are you?"

I give Meimi another side-eye. These are her friends, after all.

Meimi takes in a deep breath before answering. "He's absolutely an alien from another planet. His brothers are aliens, too."

Chloe and Zoe share a long look, followed by a short shrug. "Oh," they say in unison.

"That's it?" I ask. "Oh?"

"Well, Meimi's a drift science maven," explains Zoe. "That involves opening voids or whatever to other worlds. Chloe and I always said it was a matter of time before she dragged some alien into her life. I just thought he would be *different*, that's all."

This has me interested. I glance at Zoe in the rearview. She's not kidding. Her and Chloe had some idea about what I'd be like. Clearly, I don't match expectations.

"How different?" I ask.

"Oh," sighs Chloe. "Meimi has a wild imagination. She's always wanted to meet the Jell-O men from Pluto, that kind of thing."

Zoe nods. "Or someone with six arms, an extra eye, scales, wings, you get the idea."

Meimi pops her hands over her mouth. "I never said that."

Chloe shoots Meimi a dry look. "Come on. *Who's* the one who can't remember anything about her past ... and *who's* been that person's best friend for YEARS? You have a thing about odd space men. Own it."

All the color seems to drain from Meimi's face. "That explains a lot."

It takes everything in me not to laugh out loud. "Sometimes she does get a little dreamy."

"And mumbly," adds Chloe. "Don't forget that."

Meimi scrunches lower in the seat. We've clearly hit a nerve.

"My guess?" asks Zoe. "When she does that, she's thinking about you having antennae or something."

Meimi scoots even lower in the chair. "Ugh."

"That's enough," I say. "You're embarrassing Meimi." I park the hovercar beside the abandoned apartment building. "And we're at our destination."

Meimi lifts her hands from her mouth. "Are your brothers arriving in a cool spaceship, by chance?"

I grin. My girl does have some imagination. "No, drift voids. And they're already here."

Not for the first time, I wonder about the wisdom of introducing Chloe and Zoe to my brothers. Janais is still screening princess candidates for Justice. She wants someone with extra powers for second sight, so their children will be able to both kick ass and see the future. And she has similar plans for Slate.

If my brothers fall for these humans, things could get even more complex than they already are.

I shake my head. I'm worrying about nothing. My brothers are both happy bachelors. They got interested in Chloe and Zoe because they're friends with my transcendent. By now, they've probably forgotten all about my promise to bring the twins to our next meeting.

I step out of the hovercar. The apartment building only has a few windows that aren't boarded up. Plus, the few that could still be considered "windows" are pretty thick with grime. Even so, I can still see through them a little bit.

My brothers wait inside. Justice wears his best suit. His hair is slicked back and even combed. The guy's permanent five o'clock shadow is gone. And Slate's not in his preacher uniform. Instead, he's wearing human-style jeans, a Henley, and some serious boots.

For my brothers, this level of dressing up is a major deal.

Oh, no.

I turn to Meimi. "Why don't you and I go inside first?"

A little crease forms between Meimi's eyebrows. It's a sign that she suspects something's off. "Sure." She turns to Chloe and Zoe. "You two don't mind waiting a few minutes, do you?"

Zoe and Chloe shake their heads *no*. I'd take that as a good sign, but it's not. They aren't speaking because their gazes are glued to the lobby interior. And my brothers.

My sentient find this situation hilarious, by the way. They start sending me images of hearts, flowers, and little cooing birds. Not sure how I ended up with smart-ass sentient. But I did.

Oh, well. Better get this over with.

With Meimi at my side, I head toward the lobby door.

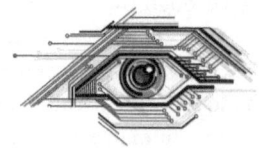

I'M JUST ABOUT to meet some of Thorne's family. Which isn't a big deal. Because we aren't together, no matter what Chloe and Zoe say.

Sure, maybe I tried on about ten different outfits before deciding on dress pants and a sweater, that doesn't mean I care what his brothers think.

Not a chance.

I'm a big bad scientist who's planning to take down none other than Dr. Godwin. Millions of lives depend on my success. With so much to worry about, why would I ever get nervous about meeting my non-boyfriend's alien family?

Thorne and I walk toward the apartment building. As we reach the front door, my stomach feels like I hit zero gravity.

Damn. I'm totally panicking.

Thorne does that awesome move where he sets his hand on my back. It's centering.

He leans in until his mouth almost brushes my ear. "You look beautiful today."

"Thank you." That zero-gravity feeling fades a little. It's like I'm back on solid ground again.

Thorne opens up the front door. We step inside. I don't remember my past, but I do sometimes get feelings about people or places. And this lobby feels totally ordinary to me, even though it's a ruin. I've definitely been in places like this before.

Thorne pulls me closer against his side. "Meimi, this is my older brother Justice." He points to the taller brother, a guy with a rugged face and bulky body who's wearing a corduroy suit.

"Hello, miss." Justice tips his white Stetson.

"Hi, there."

"And this is my baby brother Slate."

Slate looks like a regular teenager, what with his low-hanging jeans and loose Henley, both of which highlight his whip-strong body. Slate's shoulder-length white hair and gray eyes are a definite tip-off that there's something cool happening with this guy. Unlike Justice, Slate doesn't jump into the conversation.

"Hello, Slate. Nice to meet you."

Slate bows his head slightly. "Transcendent."

Thorne gives my waist a squeeze. "Slate isn't much of a talker. What he means to say is that it's very unusual for one of us to find our transcendent."

Slate pulls a small container from his pocket. At first, it looks like an ordinary box. Maybe something small enough to fit some jewelry or something. But it isn't ordinary. This container is made from what look like shifting silver fibers.

Thorne told me we might be able to get a replacement for the Lacerator. And this container is the same size as the one in the Simulacrum.

I gesture to the box. "Is that what I think it is?"

"Yes, this is the sentient swarm I mentioned before." Thorne takes the small box from Slate. "The container is its nest."

"And it's silver," I say.

"The same color as all knowledge sentient." Thorne looks to Slate. "And this swarm chose to help us? I don't want to get dragged in front of the tribunal."

Slate nods. "Volunteer," he says.

Justice keeps glancing toward the window. Slate keeps glancing that way as well.

Huh. Do they know Chloe and Zoe are here? And why would they care?

Justice finally tears his gaze from the window. "We may have a breakthrough in terms of releasing your powers."

That grabs my interest. If Thorne can use his powers in the Underground, he could help us out, big time.

Thorne sets his hands on his hips and stares at the ground. I know that pose. He's glad about the news, but there's still something missing. "Anything else?"

"You might be able to hide your transcendent from Cole," adds Justice.

Now that REALLY grabs my interest. Words start babbling away, seemingly on their own. "Do you mean that Thorne and I could ... you know ..."

Thorne gives me a sly look. "The answer is yes."

I know what that means. *We could kiss.* The fact shouldn't make me as happy as it does.

On second thought, maybe it should.

"Thanks." Thorne nods to Justice. "I look forward to getting your call to confirm things. How do you think you can shield us from Cole's detection?"

Justice doesn't reply. Instead, his gaze is locked on the doorway. Slate's doing the same thing.

I glance over my shoulder. Zoe and Chloe stand on the threshold. Justice keeps staring at Zoe. His mouth hangs open. There may even be a little drool there.

Zoe marches over to Justice and grins. "Hi, I'm Zoe."

"Justice."

"So you're Thorne's brother."

"Yes."

"And you're from another planet."

"Slate."

Zoe frowns. "You want me to talk to Slate?"

"No," answers Justice quickly. "I meant that Slate is from another planet as well. I'm just tongue-tied. That must happen all the time with you."

"Oh." Zoe's eyes sparkle. "Aren't you sweet as sugar?"

"No," says Justice.

"Are we back to one-word answers then?" asks Zoe.

"Maybe." Justice sighs.

Poor guy. I've never seen anyone have it so badly for a girl as Justice does for Zoe. And all she did was stand in a doorway.

I turn to Thorne. "How about we chat with Slate?"

"I love this idea."

Justice tries to grab Thorne's hand, holding him in place, but my guy sidesteps the grab. The comment is there, if unspoken.

Talk to Zoe on our own. You can do it.

Together, Thorne and I step over to Slate. Unlike Zoe and Justice, Chloe and Slate are deep in conversation about something called *cosmic alignment*.

"If you don't mind," says Slate. "We'll be with you in just one moment." He returns his focus to Chloe and keeps chatting away.

I shrug. "Okay."

Thorne pulls me aside. "This is beyond strange. My brother Justice is scheduled to be the next Emperor of the Omniverse. Normally, he can talk to anyone, anywhere, anytime. Usually it's Slate who can't talk."

"Then what *does* Slate do?"

"Sit in a corner doing odd yoga poses and communing with the multiverse. He only gives one-word answers. Always."

I rub my neck. "Everyone seems to be getting along."

Across the room, Zoe slaps Justice's cheek. "Rude!"

I hiss in a breath. "Or not."

Zoe stomps from the lobby; Justice follows her outside.

"Well," I rock on my heels, trying to ignore the sudden awkwardness of the moment. "Since we have the new Lacerator 2.0, maybe we should get back to the Underground."

Thorne nods so fast, I'm surprised he doesn't get whiplash. "I'll get Chloe."

"And I'll check on Zoe."

I walk outside and retake my shotgun spot in the hovercar. In the back seat, Zoe stares out the window, her arms crossed and chin up. You don't need to be an expert in body language to realize one thing. *She's ticked off.* What did Justice do?

Speaking of Justice, he steps up to the window and sets his hand against the glass. Silver particles flow out from his palm, creating a loop on the clear panel.

Justice is opening a drift void.

One moment later, there's a new hole in the glass. Justice leans in and whispers in Zoe's ear. I decide that the windshield is a fascinating place to stare. After all, Zoe deserves her privacy.

Sure enough, the windshield ends up having a much better view. Chloe and Slate march out from the building, chatting up a storm as they go. Thorne follows behind them, his face pale with worry.

Behind me, Zoe breaks out into a low chuckle. There's the stomp of footfalls as Justice walks away.

I still want to give Zoe a little privacy, so I wait for what I consider to be a huge stretch of time before turning around.

3…

2…

Flipping about, I face Zoe. "What happened?"

She smiles from ear to ear. "Nothing." I don't think I've ever seen someone look radiant before, but that term could describe Zoe right now.

Thorne retakes the driver's seat while Chloe slides into the back.

Side note: I really want to drive this hovercar, but unlike a drift void generator, all the controls look totally foreign. I'm guessing that I never learned how to drive before I got my memory wiped. Ah, well. Something to look forward to.

Chloe waves at Slate through the window. If Zoe is radiant, then Chloe and Slate are beaming. Thorne revs up the engine and we pull away.

"Your brother is so cool," exclaims Chloe. "Why didn't you tell me about him before? And did you see that container he brought? It's made from shifting threads and everything. I think it's a polymer. He told me how to fix the Crawler so the Hollow can more easily control everything."

"That's great," I say. *And it is.*

"Somethings this project seems impossible, but today, I'm thinking that maybe, it can happen." Chloe leans against the window, her forehead leaving a heat halo against the glass. "All those people…"

It's been a fun trip, but at Chloe's words, all the happiness seeps from my mood. Pulling up my sleeve, I check my wrist cuff.

Star Council Level Access: Godwin
Humboldt-Merciless Undesirables Tagged: 2,349,838
Godwin-Horde Undesirables Tagged: 535,982
Total To Be Announced At Liberation Celebration: 2,885,820

A weight of worry settles into my bones. Now, the number of undesirables is closing in on three million. The Liberation Celebration takes place in less than a month.

Back to work.

AUGUST 1 – TWO WEEKS BEFORE
LIBERATION CELEBRATION

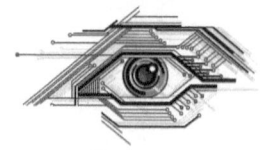

ONE MINUTE, eleven seconds.

That's the countdown blazing on the monitor that hangs above the laboratory floor. It's also how long I have to complete what we're calling my *sneak-around* at the Liberation Celebration.

It isn't going well.

Basically, we turned the laboratory into an obstacle course for me to practice. And by we, I mean me, Thorne, the Hollow, Chloe, and Zoe. We tried to set things up in the Simulacrum, but it turns out, that place isn't easy to program. Plus, the Lacerator started rattling in his cage so much, the room started to shake.

Thorne says I don't remember this, but the Lacerator and I met before. The creature supposedly likes me.

Sure. Likes to have me for dinner.

So the Simulacrum is a no-go. We're using the lab as an obstacle course instead.

And when it comes to practicing my sneak-around, my best time so far has been two minutes and two seconds.

Did I mention the goal time is about one minute?

Ugh.

"Let's try it again," I announce. Or rather, I *try* to use my best announcer-leader voice. It's hard to speak loudly when you're panting.

"You sure?" asks the Hollow. "Maybe a break would be better."

"Nah," I say. Sadly, that word is accented by yet more panting. "Let's do this."

I look to Thorne. "You ready?" He's the first stop on my sneak-around. According to our official schedule, Thorne and I wait in a monitoring room that's just off the main stage. Godwin wants us there in case anything goes wrong. A few guards hang in the room with us.

Key fact: the guards have the Hollow's agony switch.

Step one on my sneak-around is for Thorne to knock the other guards unconscious and take back the switch.

For the record, this is my favorite part.

"So ready," says Thorne. He's always totally calm and not panting. That helps me get a little more centered.

The Hollow has connected herself to the big board, so she's now our official timekeeper. "Starting countdown in three, two, one!"

Zoe stands in the middle of the room. "Poof! My cloud of camouflage smoke goes up and—oh, no—it doesn't just cover the stage as a special effect. It also fills all the rooms behind the stage, too."

Thorne has set up three garbage cans as his fellow guards. After he kicks the bins over—*that's to symbolize knocking them out*—Thorne pulls out an old waffle wrapper from the last trash can. That's supposed to symbolize the Hollow's agony switch. Once I get that switch to the Hollow, she can deactivate her blood-borne virus and then set up the real master mechanism for the Engine. Grabbing the wrapper from his hand, I race from the far right-hand wall to my second stop.

"Call out the steps!" cries the Hollow. "You won't be able to see a thing through Zoe's smoke screen."

"Right."

I always forget to call out the steps.

"And close your eyes," adds the Hollow. "Zoe's smoke screen is built to be impossible for anyone to see through, including you."

"Right again."

Wow. Am I ever bad at this.

Closing my eyes, I talk through my movements to reach the Lacerator. "Five steps from the guardroom to the staircase. Go up fifteen stairs. Turn right. Take twenty more steps. Touch the palm scanner. Open the door. This is the metal container for the Crawler."

For our run-through, Chloe sits on a swivel chair and plays the Crawler. Although I can't see her, I know she's sitting somewhere nearby with her hands up in a high-five motion. That's the height of the top of the Crawler. I need to reach that panel and hit another palm scan in order to open the machine, get the Lacerator out, and swap in the new sentient swarm.

"Six steps to the crawler," I state. I take my six steps, reach out, and...

Son of a bra–ket notation. I'm nowhere near Chloe.

"Keep going," urges Thorne.

I rush over to Chloe, tap her hands, and mime taking out the Lacerator's container. Next I pretend to put the new one inside and pause.

What am I supposed to do again? I got so off track, I'm not sure what's next.

The Hollow guesses my question. "You need to get me that agony switch," she says.

"Right." I slap my palm against my forehead. "The agony switch."

"And call off the steps," urges Zoe.

"Steps, sure, yes." Closing my eyes, I turn around to the imagined door. "Six steps out, turn left, take fifteen steps, and open the first door on my right. March forward twenty paces, and I'm at the Hollow's cage."

I open my eyes a crack. I'm nowhere near the Hollow's cage. I toss the waffle wrapper in her direction because, hey, in real life I could throw her the agony switch. The wrapper floats lazily to the floor, nowhere near the spot where the Hollow is standing.

I bite back a moan. "So let's pretend I got that to the Hollow. Twenty paces out of the room. Another four steps down the hall. Take the staircase down. Another twenty-three steps. Open the door and I'm back in the room with Thorne."

"Time," echoes the Hollow. "That's the end."

Little by little, I lift my gaze to the big board. *Three minutes and twenty-two seconds.* My time on this is getting worse, not better.

That's just not okay.

"Let's try again," I declare.

Zoe yawns. "It's past midnight. You have a few weeks to work on this. Maybe it's better to take a break."

"It can't be after midnight." I check the wall clock. *Yipes, it's definitely after midnight.* "Okay, let's call it quits."

Zoe, Chloe, and the Hollow wave their goodbyes and rush from the room. I get the distinct feeling they think that if they hang out too long, I'll ask them to run the sneak-around again.

And yes, I am tempted to do one last drill.

Thorne steps up behind me. I can sense his body warmth cascading along my back. "You ready for sleep?" His voice has a husky edge. I think it's just because he's tired, but when it comes to Thorne, I'm constantly reading all sorts of sexy intentions into him. It's really unhealthy.

"I won't be able to sleep. I'm too wired."

Which is true.

It's also true that if I go back to my bedroom with Thorne anywhere nearby, I'll kiss his face off, no matter the fact that his homicidal father will pop through dimensions to kill me.

I know that sounds crazy.

Still, if you had to hang around someone like Thorne all day long, you'd be thinking stuff like that as well. The guy's like catnip to my inner kiss-feline.

Thorne leans in. "Why don't you work on your omnivoid generator?" His voice sounds low and growly in my ear.

When he talks like that, I'd agree to anything. Truth is, I *absolutely* need to work on my omnivoid generator, but there are other things to do as well.

"I wish," I grumble. "But I must get those progress reports to Godwin."

"You did that this morning."

"And the video?" We recorded an official dry run before for Godwin. This version didn't include any of my secret sneaking around.

"The doctor loved it." Thorne steps around to stand right before me. "So go work on that omnivoid thing. You know you want to."

You know you want to.

Again, my mind goes dirty places. *Yes, yes. I really do want to do anything with you.* But the chances it would eventually involve kissing are about one hundred percent.

Still, I force an innocent smile. "In that case, I'll get started."

I head over to my corner of the lab, pull out my prototype generator, and get to work. Not much left to do. Sometimes, that's the trickiest part.

Thorne approaches. "Need help?"

"Aren't you supposed to be keeping Godwin busy so he doesn't come back with any fresh plans for us?"

"Battles are triage. You need to finish this first."

"Thanks. As a matter of fact, I'd love some help."

And I love you.

Wait? Where did that thought come from?

I clear my throat. "I mean, some help would be nice. Pull up a rolly chair."

With that, Thorne and I settle in to work. Sometimes with Chloe or Zoe, I feel like we're stepping all over each other. But with Thorne? Working together is like an intricate dance. It feels so natural, as if we've done something similar before.

It gives me hope.

Somehow, Thorne knew I needed that.

And maybe I love him just a little bit for it.

Deep in my soul, something changes. Because this time, thinking that word—love—feels just fine.

"Sentient pull you to alternate universes in order to accomplish a specific task. Get in and out quickly. Never become attached to any parallel worlds. You never know when you may be called back to destroy it." – Beauregard the Great, *Instructions for Visiting Parallel Worlds*

MY PULSE SPEEDS as Meimi rehearses her sneak-around for the big night. She races across the lab floor, counting off steps as she goes. It's been two weeks of back-to-back practice. Tomorrow is the big day. Sometimes, I wonder if these tasks are even *possible* to complete in a little over a minute.

But every time she tries, Meimi gets a few seconds closer.

I cross my fingers.

You can do this.

The big monitor displays the countdown.

3 ... 2 ... 1 ...

"Done!" cries Meimi.

The Hollow jumps up and down. "You nailed it!"

Meimi grins from ear to ear. "That's cause for a celebration."

"How about a party in the kitchenette?" asks Zoe. "There are still some leftover sawdust cookies." The packaging reads *chocolate chip*, but Zoe is right. The stuff really does taste horrible. At least these so-called treats don't leave you sick to your stomach—unlike the Authority's tacos—so they're always a team favorite.

"Great idea," says Meimi. She gathers up the silver swarm box from Chloe and places it into the pocket of her hoodie. Lately, we've been practicing with it, since the container itself is a little slippery so she needs to get used to handling it. Plus, the silver swarm is calmer when Meimi's holding it. Like the Lacerator, it tends to rattle up a storm unless Meimi has it in hand.

Tweet, tweet.

Nearby, Rakkie starts beeping away. My heart sinks. There's only one reason why our small mechanical friend would get this excited.

Godwin is about to show.

I pinch the bridge of my nose. I should have known this would happen. Unless I keep Godwin busy, the man starts scheming. And with these past couple of weeks being so busy, I've given him way too much time on his own.

"You know what that alarm means," announces Meimi. "Look busy."

Everyone hustles over to different desks. My job is to lean against the wall and look threatening, so that's exactly what I do.

A few minutes later, Godwin strolls through the laboratory door. "Greetings, Thorne. How are the girls tonight?"

"Our *team of scientists* are doing well." I probably shouldn't have emphasized the *team of scientists* part as much as I did, but I can't help it. Godwin ticks me off. These four are pulling off what's next to impossible. They shouldn't be addressed like they're hanging around, braiding one another's hair and playing with dolls. Not that there's anything wrong with hair and dolls, but still.

I really hate Godwin.

The doctor steps over to Meimi. "I have some news for you. Lately, I've found myself with free time to generate new ideas."

On reflex, my hands bunch into fists. I know exactly how Godwin got all his free time. I used to micromanage the doctor's life from afar.

Swiveling her chair in Godwin's direction, Meimi looks up from her data pad. "What is it, doctor?"

"First of all," begins Godwin, "I have good news. I spoke to the headmaster and—assuming everything goes well at the Liberation Celebration tomorrow—all of you can attend ECHO Academy in the fall."

"The Hollow, too?" asks Meimi. "I mean, can she go back as a teacher?"

"Not her, obviously." Godwin rolls his eyes. "She'll be dead by this time tomorrow night. But the rest of you. Absolutely."

The Hollow doesn't bother looking up from her data pad. She's known Godwin for longer than we have. She directs her rage into compiling more info.

Godwin holds up an agony switch in his right hand. "Anything to say about that, my short-lived friend?"

The Hollow stops typing, looks up. Her face is deadpan as she speaks one word. "No."

That's the way to handle Godwin, by the way. React with emotion and it's gasoline on the fire of his sadism. Most days, I can keep my cool.

Today isn't one of them.

With the Liberation Celebration tomorrow night, I'm just too cranked up. The last thing I need is quality time with Godwin.

"I have a second gift as well," adds Godwin in a syrupy tone. "And this is just for you, my dear Meimi."

A flicker of unease lights Meimi's brown eyes. The doctor is acting way too nice for this *gift* to be anything good.

The doctor cups his hand by his mouth. "You can come in now."

My back teeth lock with frustration. So Godwin brought reinforcements. Last time, it was the Scythe. The door opens, and two people step through.

Luci and Josiah.

Damn. The doctor mentioned some master plan with these two ages ago. But when that failed to really materialize, I thought the guy had dropped it.

Guess with all his free time, Godwin picked up that idea again.

Luci races across the room to pull Meimi into a one-sided hug. "Great news! You'll be attending the Liberation Celebration with me and Josiah tomorrow night."

All the blood drains from Meimi's face. "I will?"

Josiah strolls up, eyeing Meimi along the way. "Yes, indeed."

"Isn't that a wonderful treat?" asks Godwin. "You can even stay with your sponsor parents tonight."

Luci grasps her fingers together under her chin. "We'll have a lovely evening together. I can even get you ready for the celebration!"

"She's picked out matching dresses for you both," adds Josiah. "Really hot ones, too."

"Show some respect," I snarl.

Godwin laughs, and it's one of those guffaws that are too loud and long for the situation. "Be careful, Josiah. Thorne here has already seduced *that one*." As he says *that one*, Godwin gestures toward Meimi.

I slam my fist into the palm of my free hand. "You hired me to guard her, *sir*. That's what I'm doing."

Godwin's face melts into one of his super-smarmy grins. "And now you're off duty, Thorne. Meimi is moving in with Luci and Josiah, effective from now until the end of time. You'll stay here and guard the other *scientists*."

"What?" asks Meimi. "You can't do that. The event is tomorrow. I need to stay with my team. Do last-minute prep. You know."

"I don't think so," says Godwin. "I have all your paperwork. Everything is more than ready."

Meimi sets her hand on her throat. "But I'll still be in the guard room at the event, right?"

Godwin chuckles. "How can someone so bright be so dull sometimes? You're to sit with Luci and Josiah in the audience, my sweet. Enjoy your reward for a job well done. Dress up in a nice gown and eat a fancy meal with your sponsor parents."

Rage courses through my nervous system. My mind blanks from anything but the urge to protect Meimi. "Listen, Godwin. You're not taking Meimi from me. That's final."

"Really?" Godwin raises the agony switch in his hand and presses the button. Within minutes, the Hollow is screeching with pain. Zoe and Chloe rush to her side, patting her shoulders and offering words of encouragement. It doesn't help. Meimi tries to approach the Hollow, but Luci blocks her path.

"Shall I stop now?" asks Godwin. "Or should I inject all the girls with the same virus?"

"It's fine," says Meimi. "Please stop." She shoots me a pleading look. I know how important this event is to her. To all of them. If they get shot with the virus, there will be no chance for anything. And millions of lives are at stake.

Not to mention Godwin's potential downfall. That's a possible bonus.

"What do you say?" Godwin asks me.

"Meimi goes with Luci and Josiah," I reply.

"Excellent." Godwin presses the button again, and the Hollow exhales. The pain is gone. She collapses forward. Chloe and Zoe catch her before she falls.

After that, things start happening so quickly, it's hard to keep track. Luci and Josiah usher Meimi toward the door. The last thing I notice is Meimi patting the front pocket of her hoodie as she says goodbye. The movement makes my heart crack with grief. Being separated from my transcendent is like having half my soul torn away.

Even so, I have to be strong. There's no question what Meimi means by that movement.

My girl wants to move forward with the plan.

After all, she has the new silver swarm, and that's one key to our success.

Trouble is, it's only one.

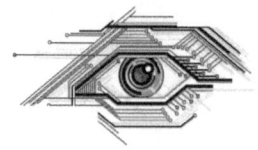

NUMB.

That's how every inch of my body feels as I walk away from my team.

No, we're more than a team.

They're all part of me somehow.

Sure, I knew Chloe and Zoe before, but I still don't remember any of that. Over the last two months, we've become closer in new ways. After all, I never worked with the twins on any science project before, let alone something this big.

And the Hollow? She's supposed to be executed tomorrow night and by none other than the Lacerator. Our plan was to help her claim her freedom while bringing Godwin to Justice. Now, I don't even know if we can keep her alive.

Finally, there's Thorne. I feel his eyes on me as I walk down the hallway, Luci and Josiah on either side of me. The last few months have been like relationship boot camp. I've seen him at his best and worst. He's witnessed the same with me. An empty feeling takes up residence in my soul.

I can't let them see that I'm upset.

I won't cry.

Even so, the tears stream.

Everything I've worked so hard for has been blown apart in a matter of minutes.

Leaving the Underground behind, we reach the Earth's surface. Fake sunshine burns into my eyes. The medicinal scent of scrubbed air fills my lungs. Luci and Josiah have a hoverlimo waiting outside. The way they keep glancing between me and the vehicle, one thing is clear. These two think I'll be impressed.

I'm not.

Once we climb in, Josiah orders the driver to begin a slow tour of the ECHO Academy campus. The buildings look like funky sculptures come to life. The shapes soar, buckle, and stack. A handful of students march across the patchwork of thin roadways that connect the different structures.

"These kids shouldn't block our way," grumbles Josiah. "We're riding in a Star Council official vehicle. Don't they see the logo?"

I crouch lower on my seat. Even though the windows are tinted, I don't want any part of this. The roads are clearly for pedestrians. Josiah's just being a creep.

Josiah knocks on the barrier between the massive back seat and the driver. "Honk at them!" he orders.

The limo driver taps the horn once. *Lightly.* I decide that I like this particular chauffeur, whoever they are.

Josiah pounds on the side windows with the palm of his hand. Seems like he's moved on from bothering the driver to doing the dirty work himself. "Get out of the way!"

At last, the students step off the walk and onto the grass, allowing us to pass by. I sink even lower on my seat.

"See that?" ask Josiah, his Adam's apple bobbing with delight. "This is a Star Council vehicle. They had to move."

I don't answer. For the time being, all my sass is on vacation. Instead, I stare out the window. For so long, I'd wanted to tour the campus, but that wasn't possible. The few times Thorne and I left, we had to rush out of the Boston Dome for one reason or another. Then, there was always the Engine to worry about.

Godwin's Engine.

My Engine.

So many times, I didn't think we would get it all done, but we did.

I rest my hand on my hoodie front pocket. The sliver sentient is still in here.

There's still hope.

Eventually, we pull up before the Blockhouse dormitory. It's a squat building with lots of small square windows. Luci, who's been quiet through the never-ending tour, now turns to me.

"What do you think?" she asks. "Blockhouse is an up-and-coming dorm."

"Meimi thinks it's amazing, obviously," says Josiah. "This is our home base and it's the best dorm on campus. We only sponsor the finest students."

If I thought Josiah's campus tour took a long time, that's nothing compared to how long it takes for the guy to leave the hoverlimo and enter the dormitory proper. He keeps finding people he thinks he recognizes.

Josiah waves down yet another unsuspecting victim. As long as they've gray hair and a nice suit, Josiah will approach them.

"Sam, is that you?" asks Josiah.

The supposed Sam pauses, his gaze locked on the Star Council logo painted on the limo's doors. "Do I know you?"

"Didn't we meet at a Star Council event on campus?"

"No, I'm not an adjunct."

Neither is Josiah, but he doesn't state that. "Oh, my mistake. I was just in my hoverlimo and thought you looked familiar. I'm Josiah DeBurgh and I run this dormitory."

With every person Josiah approaches, my numbness fades a little more.

Anger replaces it.

Josiah pulled me away from my friends so he could show off in a hoverlimo. The guy is foul. There was never a real desire to show me anything on campus, only to parade himself as part of the Star Council. All while Luci and I sit in the car quietly.

Well, I've had it with being just another float in the Josiah Dickhead Parade. I turn to Luci. "I'm going in."

She pales. "Josiah's not done yet."

"Even better," I state.

I leave the car. The moment my feet touch the sidewalk, the driver immediately revs the engine. Luci hops out as well. The hoverlimo takes off so quickly, I'm surprised a few students don't get caught in the grille.

Josiah stops talking up his latest victim and storms over to me. "What gave you the idea to get out of the car? Was Luci behind this?"

"No," I reply. "I come up with ideas all on my own. It's called the cerebral cortex."

"Watch your mouth," snaps Josiah. "I've visited the Simulacrum. Godwin gave me a tour. He thinks I have potential."

"Godwin's only using you to manipulate me."

"Now, Meimi," gasps Luci. "You don't believe that."

"It's what he's done all along. So here's what's going to happen. You'll take me to my room or whatever. You'll leave me alone. End of story."

Luci frowns. "But you have to go with us to the Liberation Celebration tomorrow night. Godwin's orders."

"Couldn't keep me away," I reply. And that's the truth. "Now what's my room number?"

Josiah pulls out a key card from his suit pocket. "812."

"812," I repeat. With that, I swipe the card from his hand and march off into the building. This last-minute move from Godwin threw me off, but I'll get my head back into the game. I only need some quiet to regroup.

Then, I'll figure out something.

"Never stay too long in any one parallel world. It's far too easy to get attached. Always guard your heart." – Beauregard the Great, *Instructions for Visiting Parallel Worlds*

GODWIN and I stand in the Simulacrum. He's showing me different three-dimensional charts of how he'll reform his new government. I'm being offered the chance to—as Godwin calls it—*do the things that must be done.* He calls it *acting as the lieutenant of his secret police.* I nod, listen, and try to look interested.

In my heart, every instinct I have tells me to run after Meimi.

I can't ruin my cover, though.

Godwin still believes that I seduced Meimi on his orders. If he suspected how much I really care for her, I'd be out on my ass. And since I still don't have my powers, I need Godwin. He's my best connection to keeping tabs on Meimi.

I stare at the podium for the hundredth time. How many nights have I snuck in here and tried to deactivate the control panel on my own? Too many to count. Whoever set up that system to block my powers, they're good.

"So, what do you say?" asks Godwin. "Want to run my secret police?"

I force myself to bow slightly at the waist. "It would be my honor."

"Thought so! Consider it your new role, as of this moment. Your first mission is to stay here in the Underground until after the Liberation Celebration. I want those two girls secure."

"You mean Chloe and Zoe?"

"Yes, the mouthy one and her pretty sister. Vargas will be down at some point to take away the Hollow for the event. He's got his eye on one of the twins."

"Chloe."

"Whichever. They're two of the best scientists I have and I don't want Vargas stealing their hearts. If anyone does seducing around here, it's you, am I right?"

This man is so gross.

"Always."

"In that case, I'm off," says Godwin.

I walk him to the exit elevators. Godwin thinks I following along at his side because I admire him so much. He's wrong, of course. I want to be sure Godwin is well and truly gone before I talk to Chloe, Zoe, and the Hollow.

We have big decisions to make.

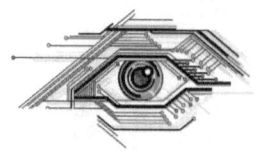

Knock, knock.

Someone's at my dorm room door. The place looks like a nine-year-old girl's fantasy from old Earth. Lots of pink, poufs, and dolls. It's a little weird.

Okay, a lot weird, considering how I'm seventeen.

For hours now, I've been sitting on my pretty princess coverlet, trying to rethink my scheme for the Liberation Celebration. Although the decor here is odd, someone did think to bring up my data pad. I keep going over sections of my plans, trying to make things work again.

Nada.

Here's the trouble. So much centered on the fact that I could move around backstage while Thorne watched the guards. Now, I'm stuck hanging out with Josiah and Luci.

Knock, knock.

There it is again.

"Who is it?" I ask.

"It's Luci. May I come in?"

An idea appears. If I can get some information on tomorrow night—when we're arriving, where we'll be sitting—that might help.

"Sure," I reply.

Luci steps inside. She's wearing a long pink robe that's tied at the waist. I check the clock. Nine p.m. I've been so focused, I haven't noticed how late it's gotten.

"What do you think of the room? I decorated it for you and everything."

"It's ... very bright."

"And did you see the pink gown in your closet? We'll match tomorrow. Just like sisters." Her mouth tightens to a thin line. "Or not." She throws up her hands. "Honestly, I don't know why I got that dress. It's just something I did."

Way to make a special moment there, sis.

"What's happening tomorrow night?" I ask.

"We arrive. We take our seats and watch the show. Pretty basic really."

"It would help to have more details."

"Godwin says to tell you zero. He's sending you to ECHO Academy afterward. Isn't that great? You'll be my sponsor student."

"*Great* isn't the word I'd use."

"You're impossible," huffs Luci. "Why can't you just do what you're told?"

"I'm here, aren't I?'

"But you're scheming. I can tell. And after everything I've shared with you! I told you that if you cooperated, it could save our mother's life. And yet you're still undermining things."

"Mom's safe," I say slowly. "I found out."

"Oh." Luci's face pales.

"Anything else for me?" I ask.

"There are other people at risk," continues Luci. "What about Miss Edith? She's on the undesirables list, too." Luci pulls the red data chip from her pocket. "Once everything goes smoothly tomorrow, I'll give you this. Then you can still save anyone you want. Doesn't that mean anything to you?"

Somewhere in the back of my mind, pieces align. How Luci wants my success, but only to feed her own. They way she decorates rooms like I'm nine but tries to destroy what's most important to me.

"Luci," I begin, "why do you hate me?"

"I don't hate you," she answers in a syrupy-sweet voice.

"I'm serious. You want me to cooperate. So tell me the truth."

Emotions flare across Luci's pretty face. Mock sadness. Despair (also fake). And finally, pure rage. That's the real Luci.

"Come on, give it to me," I order.

"I can't stand you because you're not my sister."

A chill of shock prickles over my skin. "What do you mean?"

"Mom and Dad adopted you. It ruined our lives."

I set my fist against my chest. "That's not right. I'd feel it if it were true."

Luci looks down at me, her features the definition of *disgust*. "I was old enough to know that Mom was never pregnant. All the same, she swore me to secrecy. I hated her for it. You're not my flesh and blood. You mean nothing to me, you never have. She found you through some orphanage near ECHO Academy and after you arrived, you were all she cared about."

It's as if the floor has been pulled out from beneath me. All of a sudden, I have the sensation of tumbling through empty space. "You never mentioned Dad."

"Dad changed after you were born. He wouldn't talk or move." Her eyes glisten with tears. "Mom's obsession with you is what destroyed his mind. Because of you, my father died of a broken heart."

When I next speak, my voice breaks with pain. "But I was a baby. I didn't make Mom do anything."

"Don't pretend. I hate you and *you hate me right back*." Her voice lowers with menace as she says these last five words. This is critical to her.

My hatred matters to her.

And that fact, more than anything else, makes all my feelings of anger melt away. Inside my soul, I touch the little girl who idolized her older sister. That part of me still exists, even if I can't remember it.

"No, I never hated you. You'll always be my sister. And I still love you."

"Only because you don't remember me."

"I've seen enough from you over the last few months to last me a lifetime. Even now, I know you. Love you. Forgive you. And most of all, I'm sorry for you."

As soon as I say the words, I know they're true. I have my friends at the Underground. I have my connection with Thorne. Luci is alone with herself, her resentments, and Josiah. For now, there's nothing more to be done.

Luci stares at me for a long moment, her jaw grinding out silent rebuttals. A look of regret flashes in her ice-blue eyes, but it's gone too quickly to be sure. In the end, Luci only tightens her robe around her waist and leaves.

Once she's gone, I lean against the back of my pretty princess bed. No wonder Luci decorated the room like I was nine. She's still stuck on me as a little kid.

It's so strange.

Why fix up a room with such care for someone you supposedly hate?

"When it comes to completing missions on parallel worlds, unexpected circumstances may block you from your goal. Never despair. Always improvise." – Beauregard the Great, *Instructions for Visiting Parallel Worlds*

I'VE HAD plenty of missions go sideways. There's always some way to fix things. That's why Chloe, Zoe, the Hollow, and I have been sitting around our conversation pit for hours. I double- and triple-checked Rakkie to make sure he was hiding our every word from Godwin. Or Vargas. Or anyone, really.

For an old-fashioned bot, that little guy can do some pretty cutting-edge stuff. No one will ever know what we've been discussing down here.

Which is for the best.

After all our chatter, here are the facts as we see them.

Fact. I can't risk leaving the Underground to find Meimi until *after* Vargas takes the Hollow. And we don't know when that will happen.

Fact. We're all very worried about the Hollow. Six hours ago, we had a rock-solid plan to save her life. Now? Not so much.

Fact. Meimi has the silver sentient. She's the one who's practiced to get that critical part of the plan done. And yes, her palm print is the only way to open the bot itself.

Fact. Fritz already set up Zoe's big poof. It will still go off right before the Crawler takes the stage.

Fact. There's still one minute and change for Meimi to get backstage, get the agony switch from the guards, swap out the Lacerator for the new sentient, save the undesirables, and in general ruin Godwin's night.

Fact. We must get Meimi backstage when Zoe's camouflage cloud hits.

And that's where we're stuck.

I drum my fingers on my kneecap. "We know Meimi will be at a table somewhere with Luci and Josiah. The question is how to get her backstage."

"And with a security pass," adds Chloe. She's always the one to think of the mechanics of getting around.

"Plus, we can't alert Luci and Josiah that Meimi's run off," adds Zoe. "It's like we need to replace Meimi with another Meimi."

The rough outline of an idea takes shape in my mind. I sit up straighter. "Say that again?"

Zoe frowns. "We need to replace Meimi with another Meimi?"

"That's the one." My idea takes a more definite shape. I round on the Hollow. "You've been working in the Simulacrum."

The Hollow tilts her head. "Yes. To figure out how to interact with the new sentient swarm."

"Remember when Scythe came here disguised as Fritz?" I ask.

"I heard about it," says the Hollow.

I look to Chloe. "You looked into it, right?" It was a mechanical thing and Chloe simply had to figure out how it worked.

"Sure," says Chloe. "Turns out, the Scythe used cufflinks. One was a projector. The other was a scanner." She frowns. "But that tech isn't very stable. Best case scenario, it only lasts for a few minutes."

"Maybe a few minutes is all we need," I counter. "We're not talking about an all-new scheme, just getting us back to Meimi's plan." I focus on the Hollow. Hope rises in my chest. This has to work. "Can you build something like what the Scythe had?"

"It won't be an implant," says the Hollow.

"Fine."

"And it won't work for long," adds Chloe.

I nod. "Understood."

The Hollow's metallic eyes light up. She's really thinking about this now. "It will only do your appearance, not your voice."

"But you can build it?" I ask.

"Yes, with some help." The Hollow looks to Chloe. "What do you say?"

Chloe shoots a double thumbs-up. "I'm all in."

My mind whirs through scenarios. "Here's what we do. The Hollow and Chloe, you two work on creating as many sets of personal hologram projectors as you can." I turn to Zoe. "And you may be able to use your hallucinogen after all."

Zoe's face brightens. "Really?"

"Did you develop some way to protect the rest of us from the drug?"

Zoe sniffs. "I always develop an immuno-tab against anything I create."

"In that case," I announce. "I think we're back in business."

In my mind, my sentient send me images of many hands with fingers crossed. They're hoping this works.

I couldn't agree more.

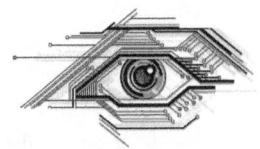

AFTER LUCI LEAVES, it takes me forever to fall asleep. Sadly, this puffy bed is way too soft and airy. I miss my nasty cot in the Underground. I want my scratchy sheets back. Most of all, I crave the sound of Thorne's soft breathing as he sleeps on the floor nearby, keeping me safe.

When I do konk out, my dreams take me back to the Ozymandias Chemical Factory. I step into my ruined kitchen. Like always, there's a figure by the window. It's the blue version of me.

"Ask me the question," says Blue Me.

"Luci says I'm not her sister. Did you know anything about that?"

Blue Me shakes her head. "From what I remember, we always looked different from Mom and Luci. But Mom said we looked like Dad. There were never any pictures around of him, though."

"That's fishy."

"When it came to Mom, there was always a lot of strangeness. No pictures wasn't that big of a deal." Her eyes fill with sympathy. "I wish I could give you the memories I do have. Mom taught us everything we know about drift science. She was ferocious about that."

I nod, trying to soak this in. "It's odd to think of me as *learning* science. It's just always been a part of me. At least, since I woke up. Those skills have also been what everyone—okay, mostly Godwin—wants to control." I hug my elbows. "When Luci told me she wasn't my blood sister, I knew it didn't make a difference, and it doesn't."

"And yet?" prompts Blue Me.

"It doesn't change how I feel about Luci. But it does raise so many questions. If this is true, why wouldn't Mom tell me?"

"I have one suspicion," says Blue Me.

"What?"

"Before Godwin wiped our memory, we came face-to-face with the Lacerator."

"Yes, Thorne mentioned that."

"The creature had been breaking free from the Underground. Every time, it would go to RCM1 in Western Mass. RCM1 is also where we'd get parts when creating stuff for the Scythe and Fritz."

I tap my chin and think this through. "The Lacerator went all the way from the Boston Dome to Western Mass?"

"That's right," says Blue Me. "And it visited the very same buildings where we'd always gone. There are thousands of warehouses in RCM1."

I shake my head. "What does this have to do with Luci?"

"She went to those same warehouses as well," explains Blue Me.

"Maybe Godwin made her do it." I frown. "We don't know what Luci's gone through, really."

"But we do know what she's done. Luci turned us in to Godwin. By visiting RCM1, Luci was walking distance from visiting Mom. She never stopped by. I only say this because I'm *you*, after all. I can guess what you're thinking."

I straighten my spine. "And what's that?"

"You still hope Luci might help us tomorrow at the Liberation Celebration," states Blue Me. "After all, Luci fixed up a new bedroom, bought matching dresses, and maybe seemed a little guilty. So you wonder: will she let us behind stage when the time comes?"

"I've thought things through from every angle. That has to be my best new plan." Worry constrict my throat. "Don't you think it has a chance?"

Blue Me meets my gaze straight on. When she speaks, all the seriousness in the world shines in her eyes.

"No," says Blue Me flatly. "I don't."

And with that, the blue version of myself disappears. With her, my dream ends as well, and in more ways than one.

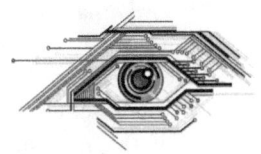

JOSIAH, Luci, and I sit in the back of the hoverlimo as it pulls up to the Golden Pantheon. Luci and I wear matching pink dresses. They're pretty as far as gowns go: sweetheart neckline, princess waist, full skirt, and most importantly, pockets. It's just strange to wear the same outfit as someone who says they hate you.

It's like the hoverlimo itself. Luci and Josiah like being driven around, but they don't want to acknowledge I'm the reason they're in a hoverlimo to begin with. I think the dresses are the same way. If anyone knows who I really am and what I really did for Godwin, Luci wants it to be super easy for them to connect the dots that we're related.

Only we aren't. Maybe.

And she hates me. Probably.

Gah. This is hard.

After we leave the limo, we enter the lobby of the Golden Pantheon, a round and sleek space with a domed ceiling. Everything glitters with a golden hue. A single thought strikes me.

What a lot of people.

The space is crammed with attendees of all ages, which is odd considering how this is a public execution. Who thinks of cleansing and family time in the same event?

Lots of folks, evidently.

Everyone also dresses in formal wear and is doused in cologne. Many hold flutes of champagne or glasses of wine. There are also lots of mother-daughter pairs in matching outfits. Luci must be following a fashion trend.

There is one bonus to this dress, though. The full skirt and pockets easily hide my new sentient swarm replacement for the Lacerator. Assuming I get close enough to make the swap, that is.

We slowly make our way into the main domed space: the Golden Pantheon proper. I've seen it in pictures, but stepping inside is far more overwhelming. The gilded ceiling sparkles above us. A patchwork of round tables lines the massive floor. The stage looms at the far end of the oval space. On it, there stands a wall of monitors. Right now, they show a single image.

A great red curtain about to be drawn up.

My pulse speeds. This is really happening. I'm here. It's the Liberation Celebration. I have to save the Hollow, Miss Edith, everyone. And my plan has gotten derailed in a huge way.

On reflex, I scan for the backstage entrance. *Bingo!* It's to the right of the main stage. There's a Merciless guard there who's checking passes. I'll definitely need one of those cards.

As we step toward our seats, I look for anyone with a backstage pass hanging from a chain around their neck. Then I try to stumble onto them and take their access tag. It does about as well as you'd expect. I'm a scientist, not a pickpocket.

Josiah has a backstage card, but the very idea of stumbling into him makes me sick to my stomach. There has to be another option.

Soon Josiah pauses by a table that's on the far right, about halfway toward the stage. "Here we are!" he announces. "Our seats." He pulls out Luci's chair, but she makes no move to park her bum.

"I thought we'd be in the first row," huffs Luci.

"These are the best seats in the house." Josiah looks in my direction. Not sure how the guy manages to turn any glance into a nasty leer, but he does. "Don't you think so, sweet Meimi?"

At this moment, the camera drones take to the air. An announcer's voice echoes through the Pantheon. "Welcome to this year's Liberation Celebration!"

I've never been happier for a distraction. "We better take our seats," I say.

Across the chamber, the camera drones fly in closer to the stage. The images on the monitor wall changes. Where there was once a single sheet of red velvet, now that curtain rises to show a massive scoreboard. I know it well. It's the same thing that still flashes on my wrist cuff.

Humboldt-Merciless Undesirables Tagged: 2,507,699
Godwin-Horde Undesirables Tagged: 565,431
Grand Total: 3,073,130

Serving staff deliver meals to the tables up front. *Unbelievable.* People actually eat and drink before a monitor that lists how many other human beings are about to be killed.

Panic twists through my insides. I vowed to help these people.

I simply can't fail them.

"The key to defeating any enemy is knowing their main weakness. Often, that is a member of the opposite sex." – Wu Zhao Zetain, *The Art of Sentient War*

THIS IS SO LIKE VARGAS.

The Liberation Celebration has just begun and yet, he still hasn't shown up to collect the Hollow.

Talk about playing mind games.

For her part, the Hollow waits in our conversation pit area, seemingly calm as can be. If you look closely, you can see how her pulse jumps in her throat. Not that I blame her.

I twist my thumb rings in a nervous rhythm. Each of us has a set now. Chloe couldn't make cuff links like the Scythe wore, but these should do the trick. The left band is to copy your target; the right ring will allow you to project a hologram of that person around yourself. The Hollow and Chloe figure these will work for a few minutes, tops.

That has to be enough.

Tweet, tweet.

Rakkie lets out a series of low warning tones. I look to Chloe. "That's your cue." She's a critical part of our new plan.

Zoe pats her sister on the shoulder. "You can do this." She hands Chloe a chem dart filled with colorless hallucinogen. Jam this into someone's skin and the target becomes a mindless puppet for hours.

"Thanks," whispers Chloe.

"One last thing." Zoe tapes what looks like a Band-Aid to Chloe's forearm. That's the immuno-tab. This way, Chloe won't be affected by the chem dart.

In truth, Zoe already applied an immuno-tab to Chloe. In fact, Zoe gave one to all of us. But Chloe is the key player here who'll have the most exposure. Doesn't hurt to be extra safe.

Zoe chucks her sister on the shoulder. "Go get him."

"Fuck yeah," says Chloe.

Zoe winks. "Kick that bastard's ass."

Some part of me is shocked that Zoe even knows how to swear. More of me is nervous about this entire operation. If the chem dart doesn't work, or the immuno-tab fails, then Chloe could get arrested or worse. And that's before she activates the personal hologram to take on Vargas's identity.

What made me think this was a good plan again?

Oh, right. Meimi and three million lives.

Chloe grins, rises, and marches out into the hallway. We turn off all the lights and crouch behind the conversation pit. Good thing I found large couches. This is the perfect hiding spot. Chloe's voice echoes through the darkened lab.

"Hi, Vargas!" she calls. "Can I show you something in the lab? Just us two?"

"And leave my men waiting the hallway?" asks Vargas.

"You're the captain, aren't you? I thought they did whatever you wanted."

"Of course I am. Let's go."

Footsteps sound as they step into the laboratory. "Where is everyone?" asks Vargas.

"In their rooms. It's just us for a moment. Can I ..." Chloe takes in a deep breath. "Touch your handsome face under that tough-guy mask?"

The Hollow curls her hand into a fist. The intent of the move is clear. *Go get him, Chloe!*

Vargas chuckles. "Sure thing, Feisty."

Zoe makes a gagging face. I agree. Feisty is a crap nickname.

Soft clicking sounds as Vargas removes his helmet. A flash of purple light follows. Zoe already explained what that means. Chloe is jamming the chem dart into Vargas's neck.

One second passes.

Two.

Any moment now, we'll know if Zoe's hallucinogen worked. When Chloe next speaks, she uses a singsong voice. "This is all a dream."

"This is all a dream," repeats Vargas.

Zoe, the Hollow, and I exchange silent high fives. *Yes!*

"You must do whatever I tell you," continues Chloe.

"Whatever you say," says Vargas.

I slip over to the door, close it, and lock us in. Out in the hallway, I hear the Merciless soldiers laughing in low voices. They think they know what's happening in here.

They have no idea.

I flick on the lights. Vargas stands just inside the lab, a silly grin on his face.

"Quick," says the Hollow. "Check for his agony switch."

We all scan Vargas. Once. Twice. There's no agony switch. Minutes pass. My blood pressure skyrockets.

A knock sounds at the door. "Sir, are you all right?"

Chloe goes on her tiptoes and whispers in the captain's ear.

"Bother me again and I'll end you!" bellows Vargas.

That seems to do the trick, but we can't rely on the Merciless to wait out there forever. They were already cutting it close to get the Hollow to the Liberation Celebration.

We're still looking through his armor when the Hollow throws up her hands. "They do this sometimes," she says. "Purposely forget the agony switch. It just means I have to walk around in pain for a while. It's fine. I've done it before. I'm surprised they put some kind of blocker down here for me in the first place."

Rage and grief battle it out in my soul. The Hollow never deserved any of this. Although one thing I'll say for the woman, she's always got a plan. I wouldn't be surprised if she already figured out some way around the agony switch problem.

Meanwhile, Chloe's already started forcing the helmet back on Vargas's head. Turns out, this part isn't easy.

"This." *Ugh.* "Thing." *Ugh-ugh.* "Won't fit."

"Big head," says Vargas.

"Don't speak again unless I tell you," scolds Chloe.

Vargas mimes zipping his mouth and throwing away the key.

That's a priceless sight, right there.

With a snick, the skull helmet finally falls back in place. Chloe sets the rings on her thumbs and raises her hands. "Activate scan," she orders.

Pale purple light shines out from the matching bands, shifting over Vargas from head to toe. Afterward, the same happens to Chloe.

Nervous energy zings through me. I press my hand against the wall with such force, the concrete starts to crack. This has to work.

Another flash of purple light bursts forth. This time, the brightness encompasses both Vargas and Chloe. The next moment, it looks like two Vargases stand before us.

"Did it work?" asks Chloe Vargas.

"Perfectly," replies the Hollow. "Now get his gloves off. We need to turn Vargas into me."

Turns out, Vargas has a fat head but very tiny hands. After ripping off Vargas's gloves, Chloe sets a new pair of thumb rings on the Merciless warrior. Next the Hollow and Vargas go through the same ring-routine, only this time, Vargas takes on the appearance of the Hollow.

"Wow," gasps Chloe-Vargas. "He looks just like you."

"He's got the best thumb rings," says the real Hollow. "Even so, I don't know how long they'll last. You better hurry."

"And remember," says Zoe to her sister. "Don't talk. Point and grunt."

"Right," says Chloe-Vargas. "I mean, grumpf."

Chloe-Vargas grabs the real Vargas, who now resembles the Hollow. She drags him over to the door, swings it open, and marches out into the hallway. Vargas-Hollow follows. The outer corridor turns silent.

"Where's the girl?" asks one of the Merciless.

I catch Zoe's gaze from across the room. Pure terror lights up her eyes. Will anyone believe Chloe's hologram illusion? Can the Merciless accept her as Vargas? Even more importantly, will they believe the hologram that Vargas is the Hollow?

Moving through the shadows, I slip closer to the open door. I simply must see what's happening.

Chloe-Vargas stands nearby. Merciless warriors surround her. "Murph!" she grunts. She motions toward the Vargas-Hollow and then the exit elevators. "Grrr."

A pause follows in which I think we all age about two years, minimum.

"Yes, sir," says someone at last.

With that, Chloe-Vargas, Vargas-Hollow and all the rest of the Merciless warriors march off toward the exit elevators. I exhale.

Everything is going to plan.

Looking to Zoe and the real Hollow, I raise my hands. Fresh rings gleam on my thumbs. "Let's do this. Zoe and I will swap places with two guests at the celebration. Then we'll find Meimi and get her backstage."

"I'm going with you," says the Hollow.

I shake my head. "You can't. You'll be in too much pain until we find your agony switch."

The Hollow's eyes flare white. "I can't stay here."

"True," says Zoe. "We need you to take over the data feed and reveal Godwin." Zoe gestures toward the pair of hologram rings on the Hollow's thumbs. "Your best bet is to find a fake identity of your own and hide out somewhere in the Golden Pantheon."

"Remember," I state. "The guard station at the event will have another agony switch. We know that from the plans. Make your way to the fake Hollow. One of us will bring it to you, just like we planned."

"Or," says the Hollow, "I'll find myself a Star Council adjunct. They always have agony switches and many owe me favors."

I grin. "That's the spirit." After so many months together, I can understand why President Hope relied so much on the Hollow. She's unbelievable. No agony switch? No problem.

Zoe rounds on the Hollow. "Is Chloe's controller is still in your wrist cuff?"

The Hollow nods. "Check."

Leaning back, I scan the hallway once more. "They're gone. We're free to leave."

Together, the three of us exit the Underground. The Golden Pantheon isn't far. With any luck, Zoe and I will find some guests with good identities to steal long before we reach the event.

After all, it's about time for our luck to change.

Meimi, I'm on my way.

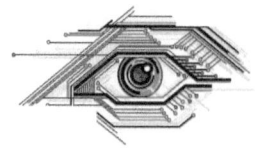

I SIT in my chair at the Liberation Celebration, my mind whirling through ways to get backstage before Godwin's big moment.

Meaning before the smokescreen rolls across the stage.

And the Crawler lumbers across the floor.

Not to mention the part where millions to die.

In other words, just a few minutes from now.

A smooth male voice echoes across the room. "Ladies and gentlemen, may I present ... President Hope!"

The wall of monitors shows the Presidential Palace. It looks just like what Godwin modeled back in the Simulacrum, two months and a million years ago. President Hope even wears the same white pantsuit and heels. A black patch covers her left eye. Camera drones encircle her as she steps to center stage.

"My people," says the president. "Tonight, we celebrate the glorious revolution when my brother, General Humboldt, freed the people of this continent from the oppressive rule of the United Americas." She gestures behind her to where the stocky form of General Humboldt lurks behind her. He wears a dark military coat lined with silver medals.

The audience lets out a polite round of applause. Humboldt is too icy and militaristic for most people to warm up to him. They only follow their so-called *Mother Hope.*

President Hope raises her arms. The crowd falls silent. "Since that day of freedom, my administration has been dedicated to removing undesirables from our society. Anyone who saps resources, breaks rules, or enacts treason must go! And tonight, at our annual Liberation Celebration, you shall witness the efficiency of your government at work as these dregs of society are finally cleansed!"

The crowd cheers. I don't.

"Ridding ourselves of undesirables is hard work," continues President Hope. "Why, one of my own assistants, the Hollow, is slated to be cleansed this evening. Although I appreciate the service Dr. Godwin performed by uncovering her treason, it still won't be easy. Fortunately, Lacerator kills are swift, painless, and help the undesirable in question move along to their final rest, body and soul."

My brows lift. *Help the undesirable in question move along to their final rest, body and soul.* That's an interesting way of saying the body decomposes into thin air within a few minutes. The way President Hope tells it, that's a good thing.

And to the Authority, sadly enough, it probably is.

I lean in closer to Luci. "Excuse me."

"What?" she bites off the word. "We're not supposed to talk now, you know."

"May I borrow your backstage pass? I need to step away for a few minutes. I'd like to check a few things behind the scenes."

There. That was simple, direct, and truthful. I don't mention the part where I plan to derail the entire cleansing, but Luci doesn't need to know that. Yet.

On reflex, I set my hand on the replacement sentient. The silver swarm waits within its nest inside my pocket, ready to be swapped out with the Lacerator.

And to do that, I simply must get backstage.

Luci shoots me a sly look. "Dr. Godwin warned me about you. He's known from the beginning that you wouldn't have the guts to see this through. That's why Josiah and I are here. We both have backstage passes, sure. But we also have smart watches." She holds out her arm. Sure enough, her smart watch has the layered logo of the Star Council. "Looks just like your guard's watch, right? I can contact Godwin like that." She snaps her fingers. "So sit back, shut up and watch the show."

My blood chills. "Luci, listen to me. Millions of people are going to die."

Luci gestures between us. "And *we're* not on the list. Don't be a sucker, Meimi. You're going to ECHO Academy. I'll be your sponsor mother. Do you know how many seventeen-year-olds would love to be in your shoes? Tons."

If my blood felt chilly before, now it turns positively arctic. "You can't mean that."

Luci rolls her eyes. "Drop the drama. Why don't you just play along?"

In this moment, I can at last see Luci with clear eyes. We're nothing alike. She simply doesn't understand anyone's needs outside her own. I'm merely another source of money for her. And of prestige, if I pull off this evening for Godwin. She doesn't care for me. She never has.

"I'm serious," states Luci. "Why don't you play along?"

My next words feel torn from my soul. "Because I never liked your games."

Leaning away from Luci, I return my attention to the stage. For her part, my sister shrugs and continues watching the show as well. My thoughts spin faster. There must be something I can do.

"And now," announces President Hope, "let me introduce the brightest light in our Star Council, Dr. Godwin!"

Godwin marches out onstage. As always, he's a wispy guy in his lab coat and small glasses. After pausing center stage, the doctor launches into a talk about how tonight is about more than just tagging undesirables. It's about automating their cleansing as well.

It's too much.

Turning away, I focus on the flow of people nearby. Since our table is closest to the wall, a stream of workers and latecomers to the event march past. There's also a clear path up the far-right aisle to the backstage door.

So. Close.

That said, I can't get near that door without a pass. My stomach twists with worry and despair. Waiting here, powerless, is its own kind of torture.

An elderly couple hobbles closer. She's plump and stooped in a blue dress. Her partner is tall and wiry with white hair and a wide mustache. As they approach the table, the woman stumbles.

I rush out, catching her before she falls.

The old man pats my shoulder. "You act just like my transcendent."

The voice sounds familiar. My eyes widen. Did that old dude just say transcendent? And did he sound like Thorne?

"Yes, it's me," says Old Guy Thorne.

"And it's me," adds the Old Lady Zoe.

Now, normally I'd ask how these two got made up as old people, but in this moment, I don't care.

Old Lady Zoe fans herself, acting as if she needs a moment before she can stand. "Thorne and I are wearing hologram projector rings. You need a set of these, pronto." Old Lady Zoe then sets a pair of rings onto my palm. "Hold these for just a sec. They need to calibrate to you. After that, you can put them on."

Their plan becomes clear. My heart soars. This is the same tech that the Scythe used to fake that he was Fritz. Only the Scythe's version also hid the voice as well. These rings only do the physical body. Not that I'm complaining.

A spark of hope lightens my body. *This isn't over.*

Inside my fist, the thumb rings flare with a pale-violet light. I've seen that shade before. Everything the Hollow does has that particular color. Whatever this tech is, the Hollow must have had a part in building it. That's super encouraging.

"Calibration's done," says Zoe. She taps my fist. "These rings will now create the perfect Meimi hologram, so give them to me. I'll give you my old lady rings. Let's swap in three, two, one ..."

Moving quickly, I set the old lady illusion rings on my thumbs. Meanwhile, Zoe puts her Meimi hologram rings on. For a second, a soft shimmer of purple light surrounds both me and Zoe. The next moment, I look like the old woman. Zoe now resembles me, down to every detail of the pink dress.

That's some tech.

"Be careful," whispers Zoe Meimi. "This is unstable stuff. It won't last long."

"Got it," I say.

"Hey," grumbles Josiah. "What just happened over there?"

Zoe Meimi slides into my old chair, turns to the stage, and ignores Josiah. Luci looks around, confused. Clearly, my fake sponsor mother was too interested in the show to pay attention to anything else.

Not so with Josiah, though.

Josiah rises. For a long second, his gaze flickers between Zoe Meimi and the Old Lady Me. I can't stand the idea of nasty Josiah going after my friend. But if my fake sponsor father chases after me? That could be even worse, and for many more people.

Old Guy Thorne grabs my hand. "Let's go."

I hop to my feet and make for the backstage door. Old Guy Thorne walks in sync beside me. My pulse speeds so fast, my head turns woozy.

Focus, Meimi.

"We copied a couple with backstage passes," explains Old Guy Thorne. He taps the silver card that hands from a chain around his neck. Looking down, I see a similar one on my hologram-self as well.

"Be sure to show yours to the guard," adds Old Guy Thorne. "Don't let them try to touch it or the illusion will be broken."

"Got it." I try to walk as speedily as I can without seeming to run. "Is Josiah following?"

"Hey, you!" cries Josiah. "Where are you two going? Stop right there."

"That would be a yes," deadpans Old Guy Thorne.

Onstage, Godwin's speech kicks into high gear. "Tonight, at this event, before your very eyes, we're about to execute all the undesirables that plague our land, including the most-wanted—or I should say least-wanted—undesirable on the continent. The Hollow!"

On the left-hand side of the stage, a silver cage is lowered from the rafters. Inside, there stands the Hollow. Although, having lived with the Hollow for so many weeks, I know the precise and dignified way she moves. This version seems drugged up.

What's wrong with my friend?

Someone grabs my shoulder. Turning around, I see Josiah behind me. "What is this? Some kind of hologram?"

Suddenly, a great boom of thunder rocks the chamber. A rolling blue cloud curls across the stage, pouring out over the audience as well.

Zoe's puff bomb.

Moving as one, Thorne and I race away from Josiah. We look like the two most buff senior citizens in the universe as we sprint through the backstage door. With the smoke so heavy, the guard doesn't even see us.

Trouble is, once we get backstage, we can't see a thing either. Good thing the guard station is to our right. I stumble through the smoke until my hand hits the door. It's locked.

"We need to get to the guard station," I tell Thorne. "I must grab that agony switch for the Hollow."

"She doesn't need it anymore."

"She *doesn't?*" I can't believe what I'm hearing.

"It's the Hollow. Let's just say she'll figure it out on her own."

"That sounds like the Hollow all right."

"We can head straight to the Crawler."

"Perfect."

All the hours of practice now pay off. I count off the perfect number of steps to the chamber where they're holding the Crawler. Every time my foot touches the floor, I know I'm getting closer to success. The replacement sentient swarm is still in my pocket.

We can do this.

Before I know it, I'm inside the chamber where the Crawler is held. I march the six steps to get to the machine itself.

Five.

Four.

Three.

Something stands in my way. Or rather, someone.

"What the hell do you think you're doing, Meimi?"

Even in the thick smoke, I know who this is.

Josiah.

My heart sinks.

"I knew you'd pull something," sneers Josiah. "That's why I memorized Godwin's plan."

All of a sudden, the smoke evaporates.

The room's dimensions become clear. It's a small steel space that now holds Old Lady Me, Old Guy Thorne, Josiah, and the Crawler. A flash of purple light flickers around me and Old Guy Thorne.

The hologram illusions for both of us vanish. Now there's no question who we really are.

"Want access to the Crawler?" asks Josiah. "I got here first. My pass gives me an extra level of access to everything. What do you say to that?"

"Something I've wanted to for quite some time." Thorne pulls back his fist and slams Josiah right in the jaw. The guy falls over like a sack of potatoes.

My fake sponsor father is out cold. Good.

Thorne returns his focus to me. "I'll drag him out of the container and slam the door. He shouldn't wake up for a while."

Which means it's time that I go to work.

Moving forward, I quickly open the access panel atop the Crawler. I enter the codes we got from Fritz; a small opening appears in the Crawler's side. The Lacerator is in there. My hands shake as I slip out the Lacerator's nest and replace it with the new sentient swarm.

"And now," echoes Godwin's voice from onstage. "I bring you, the Crawler!"

One wall of the metal room slides up. Bright stage lights pour in from the new opening. Thorne and I rush to the opposite wall, where we can stay hidden in shadows. At the same time, the Crawler lurches to life and marches out onto the stage.

I blink hard, not believing what I'm seeing.

The plan is back in action. At least, for now.

Take that, Godwin.

"No matter how well planned the visit, one must always expect the unexpected." – Beauregard the Great, *Instructions for Visiting Parallel Worlds*

MEIMI and I stand in the shadows of the metal shipping box for the Crawler. Rusted walls surround us. The waist-high spider bot lurches forward, pausing when it reaches center stage.

Godwin beams with pride. *So foul.* This is the most animated I've ever seen him, and it's all because he's about to commit mass murder. "Let's see those numbers again on screen!"

Behind the doctor, the wall of monitors shows the final count once more.

> *Humboldt-Merciless Undesirables Tagged: 2,507,699*
> *Godwin-Horde Undesirables Tagged: 565,431*
> *Grand Total: 3,073,130*

"Do you see that?" asks Godwin. "Three million weaklings. Three million burdens. Three million traitors, fools, and rebels. And we even have one right here onstage. The Hollow!"

The crowd lets out a loud chorus of hisses and boos. Across the stage, a spotlight focuses on the metal prison. Inside the cage, the Hollow wobbles from foot to foot, trying to stay upright. The outline of her body starts to fray. I've been on enough missions to other worlds to know when one's about to fall apart.

A jolt of alarm moves through me. How long ago did we drug Vargas and create the illusion that he's the Hollow? The effect can't keep going forever. And Zoe's hallucinogen? No idea how long that will last either.

"What's wrong with the Hollow?" asks Meimi.

"That's not the Hollow," I reply. "It's Vargas."

"He's got a set of thumb rings."

I nod.

In reply, Meimi laces her fingers with mine and focuses onstage. Her small hand trembles in my grasp.

"But there's more for us tonight than just the Hollow," booms Godwin. "We've sent out drone cameras to key spots across the continent. Witness the undesirables on screen!"

The wall of monitors now becomes live video feeds of more than a hundred people. Every few seconds, each face changes. Although they are different ages, genders, and skin tones, all these so-called undesirables have one thing in common. The video feeds show them in black and white with exaggerated shadows. Every last one of them is framed to look frightening on screen.

"Behold," cries Godwin. "The blight on our continent that must be cleansed!"

The crowd cheers like mad. And that is the word for it: *madness.* Some of these faces are children. Others are elderly with oxygen masks. Every one of them has value. They all deserve life. Sweat beads on my skin.

Please let our new plan work.

Godwin raises the master mechanism in his hand. "When I press the finish button, we shall watch them all be cleansed from this earth. Because inside this Crawler are two revolutionary innovations. First, there's an omnivoid generator, which will transport three million copies of this very Crawler to each undesirable. And second, there's the Lacerator, which will cleanse each blight quickly and pain- lessly. Their bodies will vanish in a matter of minutes."

Another cheer erupts. It seems the audience really loves the vanishing part. Meimi shivers. I pull her back against my chest and wrap my arms around her waist. So many things have gone wrong in the last twenty-four hours.

Please, let this one thing go right.

The real Engine inside the Crawler simply must work.

"You're about to see the first cleansing engine of its kind, both on screen and in the cage that holds the Hollow. Let's count down this miracle together! Three ... Two ... One!" Raising his fist, Godwin lifts the control mechanism high once more. "And now, I activate the Crawler!"

A flash of white light bursts from the mechanism in Godwin's hand. A halo of small lightning bolts surrounds the Crawler. Meimi's omnivoid generator kicks to life. Instantly an orb of silver light surrounds the machine as her device creates its first mini drift void, which appears as a bubble of shimmering gray around the massive Crawler.

Another flash of light follows. The mini drift void disappears, along with the Crawler inside.

That's it. The first Crawler is off to kill.

Another burst of light follows and is gone. The second mini drift void vanishes. On screen, we see two of the undesirables gasp in fear. The Crawler just materialized before them.

On reflex, my hands ball into fists yet again. I'm a fighter, and my instinct is to pound this machine into scrap metal.

The flashes of light flicker at a faster pace. More mini drift voids form. Additional Crawlers go out across the continent. Soon the flickers of light become so fast, it's hard to tell them apart any more. Millions of mini drift voids open and close at once.

On screen, the Crawlers march over to each undesirable. Quick as a whip, thin metallic arms jut out from the base of the Crawler's body, grasping their undesirable around the throat, pulling the person closer.

The wall of monitors now shows myriad faces in every stage of panic. Blank shock. Screaming in terror. Silent weeping.

The crowd is so enthralled by the many images onstage, no one notices the first danger sign for Godwin's plan.

The Crawler in this chamber hasn't moved toward the Hollow.

Meimi and I share a look that mixes both worry and excitement.

This is right. The Crawler here is recognizing that the Hollow is really Vargas.

Next, the wall of monitors show another panel sliding open on all the Crawlers. A wisp of silver particles coils out.

The new sentient swarm is free. All three million versions of it.

On screen, countless tendrils of silver reach toward three million bodies at once. Some particles enter their bodies. The sick become well. Other thin cords of sentient wind into nearby data feeds. Unjust records are wiped. False debts become erased.

I exhale a shaky breath. *This is working.*

The display wall shows more wisps winding into the very camera drones feeding video from the undesirables into the wall of monitors. The images of undesirables change. Where the pictures were once black and white, now color and light flood the on screen video. Some so-called undesirables pull off their oxygen masks to breathe deeply. Other children laugh. Even more adults stare amazed at data feeds that bring them good news. More cheer and smile. A handful even thank the Authority.

Godwin goes berserk. "What's wrong? This isn't how this was supposed to happen." He rounds on President Hope. "This wasn't my plan."

The images on the screen all change. This time, they take the form of a single face.

The Hollow. And she's smiling.

With that, I know what happened. Somehow, the Hollow got an agony switch as well as a safe place to use her true controller for the Engine. Again, she's amazing.

The Hollow's voice booms through the chamber. "Greetings, Godwin, Mother Hope, and everyone who calls the Authority their rulers." The place falls silent. "I come to you tonight with great news. Dr. Godwin was planning a coup. My friends and I stopped him."

After that, I can't believe what I'm hearing. Literally.

The sound of the Hollow's voice is gone. A comm unit has appeared in my ear, distracting me from everything else.

Beep ... beep ...

Justice is calling. I freeze as the importance of this fact slams into me.

Justice is calling!

I step away from Meimi to another corner. "Accept comm," I whisper.

"Thorne?" asks Justice.

"Here."

"I got good news. We got your powers back. Obviously."

"That's really great." *And it is.* "But I'm in the middle of something."

"Hold your quarter horses. Slate found a device that will protect your transcendent from Father. You're free to give her back her memories, brother."

This news is even more stunning. "Where did Slate find this device?"

"Did you hear what I said?" asks Justice. "You can kiss your girl right now, if you want. You're good as gold. Do you really care how Slate made it happen?"

"No, I suppose I don't." I chuckle. "Thanks for the update."

With that, my mind launches into a whirl of realizations. I have my powers back. I can finally return Meimi's memories. And the Hollow is still speaking to everyone onstage, just as we planned.

What a night.

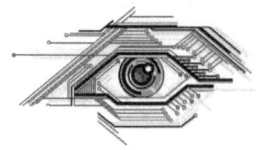

I CAN'T BELIEVE what I'm seeing. I mean, I can believe it, but the way my life goes, I'm waiting for a piano to fall on my head or something.

Things just don't go smoothly for me.

Thorne steps up behind me once more. I turn to him. "Why did you walk away?" I ask.

"Best if I explain later."

At this point, it's tempting to push. What could possibly distract Thorne at this moment? I don't say a word, though. Why? Thorne's decided to stand behind me once more and wrap his arms around my waist. The press of his firm body against me is really soothing.

Over on the stage, the image of the Hollow's face changes, and that further derails my mental train. I quickly come to a solemn decision.

Thorne is right. He can explain later.

On the wall of monitors, the Hollow's eyes light up with videos, numbers, and letters. I've known this woman long enough to realize one thing: she's processing something big.

"Godwin falsely accused me of betraying Mother Hope," announces the Hollow. "I've spent months collecting evidence of his true goal ... which is to kill Mother Hope, murder General Humboldt, and erase the entire institution of the Star Council. Godwin won't stop until he rules the Authority. Alone."

The image of the Hollow's face becomes replaced by dozens of video streams, each one showing Godwin, key documents, and plans.

"Here's all the proof I've collected but have been unable to share before this moment. And here is also the truth about today's cleansing. That list is filled with Godwin's enemies, as well as many of my friends."

President Hope lifts her patch, revealing how her right eye is all metal, just like the Hollow's. The president focuses on the stream of video evidence. Like I've seen with the Hollow, the president's eye flickers with images and text as she soaks in everything at once.

"It's true," declares President Hope. "Godwin is a traitor."

The images of Godwin's deceit disappear from the wall of monitors. Once again, the Hollow's face overtakes the many screens. "The Crawler was indeed sent out with a creature like the Lacerator, only this one heals instead of kills. Most of those listed as undesirable are now ready to be full citizens once more."

The audience falls silent. A heavy kind of energy fills the air. It's a mixture of funeral-style mourning and the shock of a lightning strike. Someone sobs. Another person cries with joy.

A realization appears. Even here, in the middle of so much bloodlust, people were dreading the loss of someone they loved.

"The person in my cage?" asks the Hollow. "That's a very incapacitated Captain Vargas, who was supposed to destroy me tonight. You may want to think about getting him a new job, Humboldt."

Inside the cage, the hologram projector finally kicks out. Now everyone can see that the person imprisoned is not the Hollow, but Captain Vargas. It turns out that Zoe's hallucinogen is a drug that lasts a super-long time. No sooner does the hologram disappear than Vargas starts swaying more violently than ever before.

"Find me that flower!" cries Vargas. "Slake the beast." Then he falls over unconscious.

What in the ever-loving *Hilbert space* was that about?

I let out a silent whistle. *Wow, Zoe's drugs are serious stuff.*

President Hope addresses the on screen version of the Hollow. The president's voice is so low, only those near the stage can hear her, including me and Thorne. "I'm sorry I doubted you." With that, the president pivots to face the audience. "It seems we do have an example of my administration's effectiveness, but in a different way. General Humboldt?"

Humboldt marches forward, pausing beside the president. "Yes, Madam President?"

"Brother, apprehend this traitor." She points to Godwin.

The doctor scoffs. "I am not a traitor. That evidence is a sham."

Humboldt doesn't even reply to this excuse. Instead, the general follows the president's order and immediately frog-marches Godwin offstage.

Couldn't happen to a nicer guy.

President Hope then gestures to the audience. "And I shall take it as a personal mission to extend my appreciation to everyone who assisted in this glorious show of support. To the Hollow and her friends, I thank you!"

President Hope keeps saying other stuff, but I don't hear a word. The metal panel that had lifted up to release the Crawler now lets off an ominous screech. For a moment, it wobbles in place before us.

Then it slams shut with a heavy thud.

Oh, no.

"Transcendence is a fierce kind of love. Bright. Profound. Consuming." –
Empress Ophelia, *The Lost Book of Transcendents*

AFTER THE METAL door slams shut, Meimi lets out a low gasp. "That was unexpected."

"It was." I pull her chest closer against mine. "And it means one thing. We did it."

"We saved them all," declares Meimi quietly.

"Yes." I move my thumb in arcs against her stomach. "You make a great leader."

"You do realize we're trapped in a dark metal container, right?"

"I do."

"Fritz rigged this to let us in here. I'm not sure there's an easy way out."

I lean in until my mouth almost brushes Meimi's ear. "Not to worry," I say in a low voice. Meimi shivers. I must admit, I love the feel of her body moving against mine.

And now that I have my powers back?

So much more is possible, too.

In my mind, I send a series of images to my knowledge sentient, showing them what needs to happen next. They respond immediately.

Above my skin, tiny particles of silver light rise up. I grin. It feels great to regain control over my powers.

"Are those sentient?" asks Meimi breathlessly.

"Yes," I reply. "When I stepped away, that's because Justice called. I have my powers once more."

The glittering particles whirl into the air, creating a snowstorm of light around us. My silver sentient don't always need to shine, but when they do? It's truly beautiful.

Meimi turns about so we're face-to-face. "What else did Justice tell you? Anything ... good?"

I know what she's really asking. And after months of waiting, I couldn't be happier to answer this particular question.

"Justice confirmed that we're now hidden from my father." I love seeing the reflection of my gleaming sentient in her brown eyes.

"Does that mean what I think it means?"

"Yes, you can have your memories returned. If that's what you want."

"That's everything I want."

Going up on tiptoe, she brushes her lips against mine. I soak in her feel, scent, and essence. Her kiss embodies everything that is strong and lovely. I brush my tongue across the seam of her lips, soaking in every aspect of this moment.

And of my transcendent.

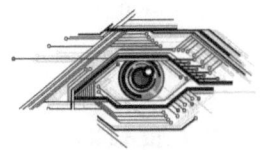

THORNE PULLS me closer against him. I run my fingers across the contour of the chest plate on his body armor. Our kiss deepens.

Images appear in my mind.

A slim woman with white-blonde hair and deep laugh lines. *My mother*.

A younger version of her. *That's Luci*.

I picture Zoe, Chloe, and I sitting in mismatched chairs at the back of a double-wide trailer while we giggle our way through math class ... then I witness myself going on tiptoe to wag my pointer finger in Fritz's square face, telling him how my latest prototype is worth double the credits ... and finally I watch Miss Edith making one of her ever-present cups of tea in our kitchen at Ozymandias Chemical. Mom and I chose to hide there after she became more catatonic.

Leaning back, I break the kiss.

"What's wrong?" asks Thorne.

"My memories are returning."

"That's wonderful." Thorne gives me one of his dimpled smiles.

Fresh recollections pour through my mind. "Right before Godwin got me, Mom had this really lucid day. She and I decided to work the drift, but we ended up flipping the factory into two-dimensional space-time. And you materialized in the kitchen."

"That's right. Miss Edith said I was a keeper."

With that, Thorne's emotions pour through me. I feel the rock-solid strength of his devotion. The spark of hope for our future. The growing heat of his desire.

"Sharing emotions," I whisper. "That also happened the first time I saw you. It's starting again."

"Yes." Thorne packs all the joy in the universe into that single word. "When we first saw each other, we shared feelings as well as visions of the future."

I smile from ear to ear. "That's right. We were riding hover bikes."

"And dancing," adds Thorne.

"But then Godwin came." My heart sinks. "Luci helped him take me. You knew he would wipe my memory, so you gave me that kiss. And you warned it would anger your father."

"It did. The connection between us turned too powerful in that moment. It sent ripples through the omniverse. My father became convinced that you were Justice's transcendent."

"Why Justice?"

"Because he's the obvious choice for the honor of a transcendent." Thorne shakes his head. "What you've seen me do with sentient is *nothing*. I don't even deserve the title of royal. Everyone knows it. You should as well." He cups my hands within his and kisses my fingertips. "Finding you has been the greatest adventure of my life. I can't begin to explain how rare it is for anyone to discover their transcendent, but especially for me."

"That's just wrong."

Thorne tilts his head. "How so?"

"We just spent months saving millions of people that someone else has labeled *undeserving*. And you're carrying that same self-hatred in your heart. Controlling sentient doesn't change who you are."

"It does to Umbrans."

"Well, it doesn't to me. Ever."

Thorne grins, and those amazing dimples return in full force. He leans in, ready to kiss me again, but then pauses.

Thorne slowly turns around. That's when I see it. A loop of particles forming in the air. I know that shape anywhere.

A drift void.

Only this one is unlike anything I've seen before. "Is that red?" I ask. My thoughts spin through everything I know about drift voids. "Didn't someone say the red ones mean exile?"

"It's just light reflecting off the rusted metal," says Thorne. "That's not a red exile void. It's black." Thorne's next words send lines of shock down my spine. "Someone's coming to fight us." Beside us, the loop of particles transforms into a massive round of darkness that floats suspended in midair.

Thorne doesn't need to say anything more.

Images flicker in my mind's eye. A man who's as tall as Justice, but stockier. His face handsome, but covered in scars.

"Cole is on his way," I whisper.

Then Thorne says something I never expected.

"Meimi, you're blue."

"I'm what?" I shake my head, dismissing the vision of Cole. I lift my arms, examining my skin. "I don't see anything."

"Your skin turned blue for a moment." Thorne beams. "Do you have any idea what that means?"

CRASH!

Cole punches a hole through his reality into ours. My heart sinks.

I knew things were going too well to last.

"At some point, every warrior faces their last battle. Let yours be fought with honor." – Wu Zhao Zetain, *The Art of Sentient War*

MY FATHER CROUCHES in the small metal room. He's already an extra foot tall, thanks to his battle sentient. Moving quickly, I shift my stance so Meimi is behind me. If nothing else, I can use my body as a barrier between her and Cole. My heart thuds against my rib cage. Scenarios race through my head.

The last time Cole appeared, I was able to bring my father back. It hurt like hell, but it worked.

The key is to get him talking.

"How did you find me?" I ask.

"The moment I detected that Justice had a transcendent here, I knew you'd deny your crimes. Thanks to my weakness, I couldn't bring myself kill you before without proof."

"That's not weakness. You're my father."

"I'm emperor first. That's why I needed to lure you both out into the open. And then I got lucky. Godwin took the transcendent and wiped her memory, so I gave that doctor some filament technology that would block your sentient power."

My thoughts return to the first time Godwin took me and Meimi into the Simulacrum. "The master control panel in the podium. You gave that to Godwin?"

"Who else could have managed it?" asks Cole. "I waited for you to take the girl to Justice. Return her memories. Usurp my crown. But you delayed." Cole's mouth twists into a sneer. "You were taking Justice's transcendent from him, weren't you? Or trying to?"

Meimi steps out from behind me. "Thorne helped me save millions of lives. That's why we didn't leave the Boston Dome. It had nothing to do with you."

Cole tips back his dark Stetson. "You can believe that, little lady. I know better. My boy Thorne has been playing you and Justice both. He thinks he can steal Justice's transcendent along with my rule." My father glares in my direction. "But he'll never have the strength to pull it off."

My first impulse is to press Meimi behind me again, but this concerns her as well. If she wants to speak to Cole, that's her right. That said, if my father makes one move toward hurting her, things will change. I may not have many sentient, but I will lay them all down along with my life before I'll let Cole hurt Meimi.

"I needed things to get a move on," states Cole. "So I let the protections fall from the Boston Dome. And then I let Slate think he found a way to block y'all from me." He grits his teeth. "Now I have the proof I need. You and Justice are traitors. The girl must die."

Panic and resolve churn through my body in equal measure. How can I protect my transcendent? An answer appears.

My brothers. I need Justice and Slate.

I send my sentient images of the small earpiece I use to communicate across universes. Particles rise from my skin, quickly forming the device.

"Don't you dare call in Justice and Slate," bellows Cole. "This is between you and me."

More options align. Another plan takes shape.

"Fine," I reply, my voice dead calm. "Then you and I fight. Not here. And you don't touch Meimi."

"Agreed." Cole's wild gaze locks on my transcendent. "Once you're dead, I can always come back for the girl."

I grip Meimi's hands. "Once I'm gone, you run. Find Fritz. Get another identity. Never contact anyone from Umbra again. Do that, and he won't find you."

"Listen to Thorne, little lady," adds Cole. "I got no beef with you, so long as you stay away from Umbra, Justice, and my rule. Never been one to like getting hands-on with ending a female."

Meimi's face pales. She speaks a single word. "No."

Cole lifts his right arm. Black particles rise from his skin, quickly forming into a spinning whirl. A heartbeat later, there's another black plate hanging in midair. Cole punches through it and saunters off into another dimension.

I kiss Meimi one last time.

"Run," I whisper.

And then I follow my father.

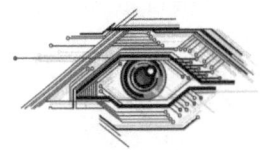

HOISTING UP MY SKIRTS, I rush through the open vortex between our worlds. For a moment, it feels as if I'm suspended in space. Zero gravity. Perfect darkness.

Then I land on my butt and freeze, not believing what I'm seeing.

First of all, there's no sign of Thorne or Cole.

Second, what I do see makes no sense.

Before me sprawls an abandoned settlement from the Old West. Twenty wooden structures line a dusty central street. A sign reads *Town of Vingian Knot, Population: 1,204*. Beyond the buildings, open prairies stretch off in every direction. Low hills overlap along the horizon line. Two searingly bright suns burn down from a pale blue sky. That settles it.

This isn't Earth.

It's Umbra.

Thorne once told me his planet was like the Wild West. In fact, Thorne's older brother Justice reminds me of a cowboy.

But abandoned towns on deserted prairies? Not what I expected.

A tumbleweed rolls by. Up close, the dried stalks glimmer with hidden technology. Filaments, just like what makes up the box that holds the Lacerator. I pat the pocket of my dress.

Yes, the Lacerator's container is still there. When it swapped it out of the Crawler, I set it into pocket for safe keeping.

But where is Thorne?

I step toward the main drag of town. Dust colors the bottom of my fancy party dress. I cup my hand by my mouth.

"Thorne?"

No reply. Not in words, anyway. That said, there's no mistaking the rhythmic thuds sounding from the building marked *General Store*.

With hesitant steps, I approach the storefront. After all, this is a strange planet. I could run across anything.

"Thorne?" I ask again.

CRASH!

Thorne and Cole smash through the large front window of the general store. A dust cloud erupts from the spot where they hit the ground. Cole quickly rises to stand. The Emperor looks fit and angry. Nearby, Thorne staggers back to his feet. Blood streams from his temple.

Hoisting my skirts again, I race toward Thorne. Somewhere along the line, I lost my heels, so I'm barefoot as I speed across the packed earth. Thorne spies me and gasps.

"Meimi, stay back."

"Not a chance," I cry.

I rush closer. *Thorne's only twenty yards away now.*

Cole narrows his eyes in my direction. "Welcome to Umbra." He tips up his Stetson. With that movement, the hat bursts into a small cloud of particles before disappearing back into Cole's flesh. "Here's where you'll die."

"No!" cries Thorne. "You keep your word. This is our fight. Meimi stays free."

Cole gives Thorne a twisted smile. "Maybe."

I force myself to go faster.

Ten yards.

Moving with impossible speed, Cole throws dozens of rapid punches at Thorne's skull, ribs, and kidneys. Thorne moves just as quickly, blocking each attack. Cole pauses, barely winded. Thorne braces his arms on his knees as he catches his breath.

Five yards away now.

"Son," declares Cole. "This is getting on my nerves." A cloud of particles appears around Cole's right arm. The next instant, those dark bits solidify into a long Winchester rifle. Cole raises the weapon, aims at Thorne, and fires.

BOOM!

The bullet strikes Thorne squarely in the chest. He's thrown clear across the street, through another glass wall, and into a building marked *Saloon*. Cole cocks his rifle. "Bet you didn't know Crown Sentient could do that, eh, son?"

Cole marches across the street. I follow behind, my mind turning fuzzy with worry and shock. What can I do here? How can I save Thorne?

I follow Cole into the empty saloon. Overturned tables and chairs cover the floor. An old bar lines one wall. The shelves behind it are filled with shot glasses, cobwebs, and the occasional empty bottle.

Thorne sits against the far wall. The wood behind him buckles in from the impact of his back slamming into it. With every breath, Thorne's lungs gurgle ominously. Splatters of blood line the nearby wall and floor. My heart lurches in my chest.

This can't be happening.

Cole saunters over to Thorne and stops. Raising his right arm, Cole points his sentient shotgun straight into Thorne's face. "You shouldn't have double-crossed me," says Cole, his voice low and deadly. "No transcendents."

My mind races through options. I could distract Cole, but that won't last long. There's nothing here that could possibly make a dent in that man. After all, I saw Thorne punch right through Vargas's Merciless armor. And if Thorne can't get in a solid hit on Cole, what chance do I have?

Pictures appear in my mind. I see myself holding the container with Lacerator inside. The thought isn't my own.

I gasp, realizing the Lacerator itself is sending me images.

Memories appear. This happened once before. I met the Lacerator back at RCM1. The creature didn't hurt me. Instead, it took down my enemies. But would the Lacerator attack an emperor of the omniverse at my command?

One way to find out.

I pull out the small container from my pocket. The motion feels natural. Inevitable, even. Another image reappears in my head. It's one of me in my pink dress, opening the Lacerator's container.

So that's exactly what I do.

"Of all painful words, the most hurtful by far is farewell." – Empress Janais, *The Fifth Age of Umbra*

EVERY INCH of my body screams in agony. Through the pain, Meimi steps into the empty saloon, her bare feet leaving behind a trail of footsteps on the dusty floor. Light seems to surround her. My girl is a vision of beauty amid so many shadows and cobwebs.

If I die now, the last thing I see will be her face. There are worse things.

Cole jabs his Winchester at my cheek. "You hear me, son?"

With the little air I have left, I force out a few words. "You're hard to miss." Even if I wanted to summon Justice and Slate now, I don't have the energy. It's everything my sentient can do to slow down my death.

"Then you listen to me, careful-like. In my duty as Emperor of the Omniverse, I hereby..."

Cole keeps saying things. I don't hear a word. Instead, I'm awestruck by Meimi. She's holding the Lacerator's nest in her hands.

And she's opened that container.

In all the shock with Cole's arrival, I'd forgotten about my kiss with Meimi. Afterward, her skin had shone blue for the barest of seconds. It was so fast, I almost thought my mind was playing tricks on me. But seeing my girl now? There's no question what's happening. The Lacerator is pulling itself out of the box.

One claw.

Two.

It appears as a haze of particles before her.

This is more than the action of a sentient swarm randomly deciding not to murder a human. Only sentient that have bonded to another Umbran will work to protect their host. If I had enough strength left in me, that's what mine would do.

Meimi isn't human.

She's Umbran.

Somehow, she got separated from her sentient. A realization strikes me. That's why the Lacerator kept escaping the Boston Dome. It wasn't hunting down Meimi to kill her, but to reunite with its Umbran.

I open my mouth, trying to tell her the truth. It's all I can do to suck in a small gasp of rough breath. White spots take over my vision. Cole's execution speech transforms into a low drone in the back of my consciousness.

Fear and pain ebb from my body.

Now, my death can be peaceful.

Meimi is Umbran. She'll always be safe.

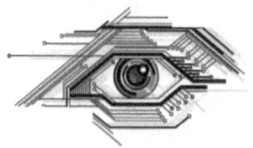

I STAND TRANSFIXED by the sight. The Lacerator stands before me, its semitransparent body taking what's become a familiar shape.

After all, I have my memories back, so I recall how this creature looked when I first saw it at RCM1: seven feet tall with a wide chest and stout legs. Dinosaur-style spikes protrude from its spine. Empty holes serve as its eyes. Razor-sharp teeth line its overly wide mouth. And the entire creature is formed from particles suspended in space, like so many bits of consciousness in amber.

I gasp.

It's gorgeous.

Images flash in my head. The Lacerator turns on Cole, tearing the Emperor away from Thorne. Next the creature opens a drift void to my home world. I escape through the portal.

In that moment, I know why the Lacerator is sending me these mental pictures. It's asking me questions. Do I want to fight Cole? Would I rather escape?

I wish neither.

In reply, I send a picture of the Lacerator entering Thorne, giving him the strength to live and fight. Emotions flow through me. They aren't my own. They're coming from the Lacerator.

There's an electric jolt of excitement.

Chilly waves of caution.

And a thirst for unity.

A realization appears. The Lacerator wants to be part of me. And it desires to join with Thorne as well.

Yet for some reason, it's not a total fan of this idea.

Normally, I'm the kind of girl who likes to ask a million questions. But Thorne's skin is turning sickly shade of white. And before me, there's a space-alien particle monster who needs some encouragement in order to heal Thorne.

I'm just the girl for the job.

In the back of my mind, a nagging suspicion claws at my resolve. Some instinct screams that what's about to happen is far larger than simply healing Thorne. Connections may be made that can never be undone.

I don't care. With every corner of my soul, I want only one thing. *Thorne. Alive.*

"Do it," I order the Lacerator.

Fresh images fill my mind. Yellow danger signs. The image of me tottering by a cliff's edge. Again, the Lacerator's telling me to be careful. It's trying to stall me out.

Not a great plan.

The Lacerator steps closer to Cole, its long arms dragging along behind it. Behind it, the Lacerator's extended talons leave a striped pattern in the dusty floor. All the while, Cole keeps droning on about all of Thorne's crimes and why he's about to be executed.

For the record, Cole must be an amazing dad when he's not out of his head. Because this Cole version is a dick with a capital *D*.

Thorne's eyes turn glassy. "Meimi."

The Lacerator's emotions flee my soul. Instead, Thorne's feelings flow through my consciousness.

There's a warm mantle of gratitude.

A solid undercurrent of love.

And the painful sting of goodbye.

Sweet mother of science. "Goodbye" is not in our vocabulary for today.

"Hey, you!" I march move to the Lacerator. "Whatever you can do, make it happen. Save Thorne."

It's the *save Thorne part* that gets Cole's attention. He stops blabbing about why Thorne needs to die. Instead, Cole shuts his fat yap and swings around. His icy gaze locks on me. What a sight I must make: a frizzy-haired mess in a dirty pink gown, my face tight with rage. Beside me stands the Lacerator.

"What is this?" asks Cole.

I hitch my thumb toward the Lacerator. "Leave right now and my buddy here won't turn you into Swiss cheese."

"You're Justice's transcendent. Why waste your time with Thorne?"

That does it.

White-hot rage careens through my soul. I round on the Lacerator. "Heal him! NOW."

The Lacerator bursts into a cloud of particles that spin around the room, reminding me of a swarm of angry bees. The sentient slam into Thorne's chest, merging with his body. Instantly, color returns to Thorne's skin. His bruises fade. Blood dries up and vanishes. He hops to his feet.

"Well done, Meimi," says Thorne. Even his dimpled smile is back.

Why was the Lacerator so against this? Sheesh.

Cole's face heats with rage. "What? You can't share sentient with him."

"I just did," I retort. "Get used to it."

Cole raises his arms. Black particles swirl around his hands. Power fills the air, like the sense of ozone before a lightning strike. Cole is Emperor. Whatever sentient he's packing, they have to be heavy duty.

Cole's dark sentient congeal into the shape of a lasso in his grip. With a snap of his wrist, the rope whips out from Cole's hand.

And it heads in my direction.

Thorne races toward me. "Get down, Meimi!"

There isn't time. One moment, I'm standing free. The next, cords of rope encircle my throat, cutting off all air. The lasso bites into my skin.

It also calls to my soul.

Inhaling deeply, I act on instinct. In my mind, I send an image of the cords merging with my own sentient.

They instantly obey.

The ropes transform into a haze of particles that encircle my throat. After that, they enter my body. Power thrums through my nervous system. Every cell in my body vibrates with energy.

"How can this be?" Cole staggers backward. "You're not Umbran. And even if you were, it's not possible for anyone to take in Crown Sentient."

I bob my brows up and down. "Oh, I do so love it when people tell me it's impossible." An idea hits me. "How about this?"

Sending new images and commands to my sentient, I reach toward Thorne. The particles heed my orders. The sentient rise from my palm, race across the room, and encompass Thorne in what looks like a dust cloud. Particles enter into Thorne's chest, hands, and mouth. Once again, I sense Thorne's emotions as if they were my own.

There's the underlying pulse of strength.

Growing sparks of protective energy.

Flow of cool intelligence and battle plans.

"This isn't happening," thunders Cole. "That boy is too weak."

Thorne cracks his neck. "Maybe you need to expand your definition of what it means to be strong."

Cole picks up his Winchester again. I reach forward, summoning the sentient to me. The rifle dissolves into particles that fly across the room and land straight against my palm. From there, the Crown Sentient seep directly into my body. Fresh waves of energy flow though me.

"How are you doing that?" asks Cole.

"Leaving is still an option," I reply.

Cole scowls. "This is all a trick. I don't need to use sentient to fight you." Turning, Cole lunges at Thorne. This time, when the Emperor attacks his son, Thorne does more than block the attacks. He hits back.

One hit.

Two.

Three.

With the last blow, Cole goes flying across the room. He lands against the wall, his head slumped forward, unconscious.

I send my sentient the image of what I want them to do. Instantly, they take the form of ropes that bind Cole's hands and feet. More twist around the Emperor's head and mouth, preventing him from speaking.

For a long second, I can only stare with my jaw hanging open. "Did we really do it?"

"Looks like," says Thorne. "I've never seen him knocked out before."

Some small part of me says this is too easy. But I decide that was the same part probably thought it was a bad idea to take in and share all these sentient.

Clearly, that section of my mind doesn't know so much.

Thorne takes off for me at a run, and I rush to meet him as well. Our bodies press together in the mother of all hugs. Thorne's hand slides up the side of my torso and neck, ending with a firm grip on my chin.

I know what's coming next, and I love this idea.

Thorne presses our mouths together. His lips are soft and demanding. The touch of his tongue against mine turns electric. Emotions fly between us.

Jolts of pure joy.

A burn of desire.

The cool wash of gratitude.

We break our kiss. Both our gazes lock on Cole's unconscious form.

"What happens next?" I ask.

Thorne lets out a long breath. That confirms it. He knows exactly what I'm referring to here.

Cole.

No doubt, this is a question that's plagued Thorne for years. I would know. Now that my memories are back, I recall that I've spent most of my life watching my mother slowly lose her mind. These aren't easy choices.

What should we do with Cole?

"Death and distance. Such are the true prices of war." – Wu Zhao Zetain,
The Art of Sentient War

MEIMI WANTS to know what to do with Cole. "It's a good question,"
I say.

"Why do I get the feeling this is a complex situation?"

"Because you'd be right. You should know the true choices here."

Meimi's breath hitches. For a few seconds, she stares at Cole.
When her gaze meets mine again, my girl is all steely resolve. "Tell
me everything."

"We could kill my father, take all his Crown Sentient, and become
joint Emperor and Empress of the Omniverse. That's how my father
got the job."

"Whoa." She winces. "The Lacerator tried to warn me against
sharing all that sentient. I think that's what the worry was."

"Yes, I don't know what happens next, but things have gotten
complicated."

"Honestly? I'm not a fan of becoming an alien emperor and
empress right now."

"Same here. But I wanted to be honest. And there is another
option."

"Let's hear it."

"I could take Cole back to my family's home at Fort Derringer.
That's on the other side of the planet. Now that I can wield some of

my father's Crown Sentient, maybe I can help him." I huff out a breath. "I have to try."

Meimi gently rests her palm against my cheek. "I understand."

Pure adoration pulses through my veins. *This girl.*

I sigh. "I should get back then, I suppose."

My mind races. Truth is, I'd love to take Meimi to Fort Derringer, but it would be a big risk. For my people, knowing transcendents exist would be a major revelation. Then there's the fact that Meimi and I could be the next emperor and empress—that's not what people are expecting. And when the unexpected happens, that can end in violence. Just because my family rules, doesn't mean we're without enemies.

"I would love to bring you to Fort Derringer one day," I say solemnly. "But when that happens, I want to be sure you'll be safe and welcomed. That might take some time."

"So to be together, we must be apart?" She shakes her head yet smiles. "That sounds like my luck."

"It won't be long. Soon you'll wield your sentient like a pro. We'll visit each other's worlds often." I glance over to Cole. "But that's the future. Right now, he could wake up any moment. It's time for us both to go home."

Just saying those words tears at my soul, but it's the truth. And as I said before, Meimi always deserves honesty.

"I'm not worried," says Meimi bravely. "I'll track you down in no time."

"Looking forward to it." Leaning forward, I rest my forehead against hers.

There's so much I want to tell her in this moment. She's part of my soul now. Nothing could truly separate us. But the sooner she leaves, the faster I can take care of Cole. And once my father is back, I can return to Meimi. After that, we'll have even more to celebrate. She and I can share not only sentient, but Crown Sentient! That's a miracle I never expected.

But it's one I will always treasure.

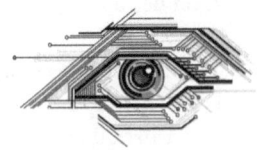

STEPPING BACK, Thorne breaks our embrace. The moment our bodies no longer touch, I miss his warmth and solidity. Miss Edith's words appear in my mind.

That boy is a keeper.

Yup, Miss Edith totally called it.

Thorne raises his right hand. Silver particles lift from his palm, quickly swirling into a loop. Within seconds, a flat plate of gray hangs in the air between us. "You can just step through that. Punching through is only for when you're in a hurry."

My throat tightens with grief. "Right."

I set my fingers against the silver plate. Last time I used the drift void to travel, it was when I came here in the first place. Back then, I was in a rush. This time, I want to move more slowly. My right arm goes inside. The round of sentient expands. I step in sideways. The weightless feeling I had before returns. It's as if I'm in zero gravity and not, all at once.

I'm almost through.

Looking back, I search for one last sight of Thorne.

That's when I see it.

Cole.

He stands behind Thorne, the lines of his face etched deep with fury. How long has that guy been waiting around? And why?

I gasp. This is the same man who planted the fake console to limit Thorne's powers ... and gave Slate a false tool that supposedly shielded us from the emperor's sight.

In other words, this is a really sneaky guy.

He planned this entire thing.

Cole quickly figured out he couldn't fight us with force, so he relied on lies and tricks.

Oh, no.

"Goodbye," cries Cole. "Enjoy your exile."

The sentient around me change from silver to red. This is what I'd been worried about before.

An exile void.

Cole is separating me from Thorne.

Forever.

Thorne and I reach for each other just as the void spirals into a loop of crimson particles. After that, it vanishes altogether. My heart shatters.

The next moment, I find myself back on the stage of the Golden Pantheon. Everyone is gone. A few workers sweep up the corners. A spotlight frames my filthy body and dress as I stand on center stage. Frantic, I reach out for any sense of Thorne's emotions. There's no connection anymore.

He's gone.

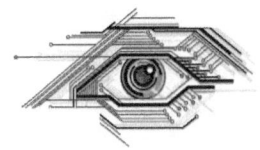

I can't believe it.

It's eight o'clock and I'm back at the Golden Pantheon building and wearing a fancy dress. I've even sitting at the exact same spot where I did at the Liberation Celebration. But that was so three weeks ago. Tonight's event is very different.

On the main stage, the wall of monitors now reads, *Welcome ECHO Academy, Senior Class!* Everyone's here with their parents and loved ones. I have Chloe, Zoe, and their mother at my table. Since they're both dressed up in blue gowns, the twins are hard to tell apart. You have to look carefully to see the grease stains still on Chloe's neck. That's always a dead giveaway.

Beside the twins, their Mom looks like an older version of her daughters, only with gray hair, more laugh lines, and a proud gleam in her eyes.

I slap on my own version of a happy look, but it isn't easy. I miss Thorne something awful. From the corner of my eye, I keep expecting him to appear, perhaps disguised as another older dude. Or anything. I'm not picky.

Lights flash across the main stage. The monitors change to read, *Professor Conway, Headmaster of ECHO Academy.* A stooped man with a jumble of white hair ambles onstage. He has drooping jowls, a bulbous nose, and a perpetual smile.

Across the table, Chloe and Zoe watch the stage with rapt attention. I don't blame them. Attending ECHO Academy is a true honor for anyone.

"ECHO Academy is the foremost institution for scientific learning and research in the world," declares Professor Conway. "Every year, we welcome the senior class and their families to this special event. It's our way of congratulating you for reaching your last year of high school." He raises his bushy gray brows. "And we certainly want to lure you to return here for college as well."

Conway pauses while the audience chuckles. The professor is the House Master for the Castle, a place that's arguably the most exclusive dorm on campus. President's Hope's nephew, Porter Saint-Clare, is a member.

Speaking of people who run a dorm, Luci and Josiah are seated in the back of the room. After the Hollow's evidence was reviewed, it was decided that Godwin would spend a very long time in jail. Luci and Josiah then declared that they'd been helping me all along. Vargas has been sent off to enjoy an exciting new career as a guard in Antarctica.

Back to Luci and Josiah. I debated about blowing them in as liars, of course. In the end, I decided that was bad karma. They're on the other side of campus. No one's signed up to have them as sponsor parents. Live and let live. Or avoid and hope to be avoided in return, as the case may be.

Back onstage, Conway clears his throat. The audience quiets. "So this is always one of our most exclusive events," he declares. "However, this year it is even more special. Our speaker tonight is none other than President Hope!"

The crowd applauds as President Hope walks onstage. I swear, that woman has a collection of white pantsuits and looks fabulous in all of them. "Greetings, faculty, students and family," begins the president. "It is my honor to personally welcome all of you to your senior year at ECHO Academy. However, I would be remiss if I didn't call out some of our most exciting new students, namely Meimi Archer, Chloe Fine, and Zoe Fine."

My eyes almost bug out of my head. *What a shocker*. I mean, sure we all worked to protect President Hope from Godwin, but it's not like I hang with the president in my free time or anything. I certainly didn't expect a shout-out at the welcome dinner.

President Hope delivers one of her hallmark dazzling smiles. "When I taught here, I had the pleasure of the Hollow as my student. Now, I'm thrilled to see a new generation of brilliant minds pass through this prestigious institution." Personally, I'd been hoping the Hollow would return here to teach, but she has other plans.

There's more to the ceremony. A choir sings some tunes. More professors get up and talk. I spend the time devouring the free steak dinner and mentally planning out my next invention.

And this one will be a doozy.

There's nothing like good food and great science to pass the time. Before I know it, the ceremony's over. People are milling out toward the exits. Chloe, Zoe, and their mother are chatting away at the other side of the table.

I'm debating about getting up to leave when the Hollow slips into the chair beside mine. She looks stunning in a silver gown. The look sets off her implants perfectly. I'd never leave the house in anything else if I were her. We say our hellos, but I didn't live in a basement with the Hollow for two months and not know she has another reason for stopping by.

"I brought you something," says the Hollow.

And there it is. The reason.

"What?"

She pulls a small silver container from her pocket and slides it across the tabletop. The tiny box is made from fibers that shimmer and writhe.

I can't help but smile. "The knowledge sentient."

"The Wiser."

"That's what it wants to be called?" The sentient send me fresh mental images, all of them representing cheering crowds. I'm getting more used to their visual way of communication. It's like hieroglyphs, only four-color and often sarcastic. "Okay, the Wiser it is."

"So you know, we tried sending her out on other missions in the Crawler."

"Her?"

"Don't you think so? I always thought the Lacerator was a girl, too."

I tilt my head, thinking. Inside my soul, my sentient rise up, showing me mental images of the Lacerator giving the Hollow a high five. *That settles it.*

"I think you're right," I say as I slip the container into my pocket. I've said it before and I'll say it again.

Never wear a dress without pockets.

"I've something else for you, too," adds the Hollow. "It's from Fritz." She sets her fingertips on my wrist cuff. It pops off with a soft click.

I must admit that I'm really happy to see that thing off. I didn't even want to think about the layers of goo growing on the bottom side. You're supposed to wear a plastic bag in the shower and stuff, but who has time for that?

I rub my now-free wrist. "Most people have wrist cuffs. How'd he manage it?"

"Fritz and the Scythe pulled some strings."

I give her the side-eye. "That's all? I can't help but notice that Fritz isn't the one doing the actual removal process here."

The Hollow chuckles. "I may have had a talk with President Hope, too. I can free up Zoe and Chloe as well."

At that moment, none other than Porter Saint-Clare approaches our table. Now that I have my memory back, I know that I am not the kind of girl that attract celebrity boys. I'm more the type that guys try to cheat from during exam time.

But now, Porter stares right at me. He looks just like he does in the data feeds, too: wavy black hair, sharp jawline, and bright blue eyes. He's a little shorter in real life than I'd expect, but what he lacks in vertical skills he's more than made up for in his outfit. Tonight, Porter wears a white jacket with black trim and one of those straw hats that people wear in old Earth movie stills, yet no one can get away with in real life.

Unless you're Porter Saint-Clare.

"Hello, everyone," he says with a million-watt smile. I notice absently that he has dimples and yet they do nothing for me. *Interesting.* "I'm Porter Saint-Clare."

"We know who you are," says Mrs. Fine. "Chloe and Zoe are always reading about you in the data feeds."

My best friends turn gray. Leave it to a mom to say something supremely humiliating. They must get classes in that along with what kind of diaper wipes to choose.

The Hollow rises. "I was just leaving, Porter. You can take my seat if you like." I can't help but notice how the temperature around the table seems to have dropped about ten degrees. Again, I know the Hollow. She's definitely not a member of the Porter Saint-Clare fan club.

"Thanks, Holl." Porter slips onto the chair beside mine.

I pull on my ear. Did Porter really call her *Holl?* I've never heard anyone use a nickname with her. The Hollow is too badass to be anything but addressed in full, including a *the*.

"I wanted to introduce myself," continues Porter. "And to say how impressed I was with the way you found the traitor. You saved my aunt's life. That means a lot."

Chloe, Zoe, and I give our standard replies. *It was our duty. Happy to help. You're welcome.* It's the kind of garbage we've been spewing out to data feeds and reporters for weeks.

"So." Porter rubs his palms together. "What do you plan to do when you get to ECHO?"

I frown. "I don't know. Go to class?"

"No, for your senior project. Everyone has one."

"Oh, that." My gaze locks with Zoe and Chloe. We've already talked about our next project. They are totally bought in and already helping me on my newest invention. In fact, that's when I was brainstorming through most of tonight's dinner.

"Well?" prompts Porter.

"Chloe, Zoe, and I are working on a team project. We want to tear open something called an exile void."

"Wow." Porter has a way of looking at you like whatever you said is the most interesting thing ever. "I must admit, I've heard of drift voids but never exile voids. What's behind them?"

Chloe tilts her head. That's her move when she's confused. "Behind?" she asks.

"What are you looking to find?" clarifies Porter.

The twins and I share another long look. I miss Thorne like crazy. That said, I'm not the only one with cross-dimensional heartbreak. Chloe and Zoe were devastated when they found out that Cole sealed us off not only from Thorne, but also from Justice and Slate. And you know the saying...

Hell hath no fury like science chicks who can't talk to their space-alien boyfriends.

Or something like that.

Porter tips his white hat a little lower over his right eye. It's supposed to be a playful move, and I'm sure most girls go crazy for it. But Chloe, Zoe, and I aren't most girls. "Come on, you can tell me," he urges.

I guess this senior project thing must be a big deal. Porter is clearly a competitive guy who won't let the subject drop. "What awaits you past this exile void?" he asks again.

"The future," I reply. "What else?"

"But the future of *what*?" asks Porter.

"Everything," we three reply in unison.

Porter laughs and starts talking about his project. It's something about chemical compounds and machine engines. I try to focus, but the blueprint I'd been struggling with finally comes into my mind's eye. I know just what I'll call it, too.

The exile void annihilator.

Hang on, Thorne, Justice, and Slate. We're coming for you.

—*The End*—

The adventure continues with ECHO ACADEMY, Book 4 in the Dimension Drift. Read on for a sample!

ALSO BY CHRISTINA BAUER

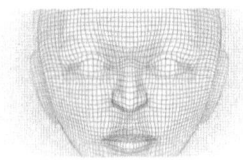

The adventure continues with ECHO ACADEMY, Book 4 in the Dimension Drift! Read on for a sample...

Try ANGELBOUND, the kick-ass paranormal romance with more than 1 million copies sold!

FAIRY TALES OF THE MAGICORUM

A modern fairy tale that *USA Today* calls a 'must-read!' Check out WOLVES AND ROSES!

Medieval mages ... Slow-burn love ... And heart-pounding action! Check out the BEHOLDER series!

PIXIELAND DIARIES tells the story of sassy pixie Calla and 'her' elf prince, Dare.

SAMPLE CHAPTERS: ECHO ACADEMY

SAMPLE CHAPTERS

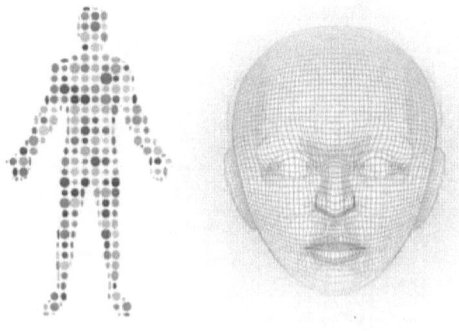

PREFACE

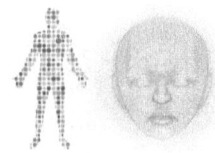

*ECHO ACADEMY begins with an expanded scene from the previous novel,
ALIEN MINDS.*

1 / MEIMI

WHEN WE LAST LEFT OUR
HEROINE...

I STAND on an almost-empty street of the planet Umbra.

That's right.

Not Earth.

Umbra.

This isn't one of my science books or simulations either. I, Meimi Archer, have journeyed to a completely different planet, solar system, galaxy, blabbity blah.

It all went by in a flash. I left a party, stepped into a drift void, and—WHOOSH—now I'm here. Taking in a deep breath, I seek to truly process that fact.

Total fail.

So I check my outfit instead.

My frilly pink dress is ruined. Meh.

Clothing isn't normally my thing. I'm more of a dark matter and quantum particles type gal. But in this moment? A trashed outfit feels super easy to face. The alien planet situation? Not so much. Plus, there's an evil space cowboy lurking nearby who happens to be Emperor of the Omniverse.

I'm not even kidding.

And did I mention how his Imperial Dudeness wants to kill my boyfriend, Thorne, who's the only other person around? Yup, that's happening, too.

Ding, ding, ding!

An internal alert goes off in my noggin, saying it's time to re-examine the hem of my gown again. Yup, still matted up with dirt and prairie grass. And is that a dead bug under the lace? Ick.

Get a grip, Meimi. You're here to help Thorne.

It takes a great force of will, but I sideline my clothing analysis and scan my surroundings. Ahead of me stretches a thin street flanked by wooden buildings. Names like *saloon* and *sheriff* are written on the facades in chipped paint. All the water troughs are rotted out. A broken shutter bangs in the wind. Basically, it's your classic deserted town of the Old West variety.

Down the road stands Thorne, Prince of Umbra and general hottie in black body armor. He's my age—around eighteen—with dark hair, blue eyes and a warrior's build. Plus he has dimples. That's an issue. In the end, I blame that smile for why I hauled my cookies across the universe to help fight Cole, the thug who's more than Thorne's attacker or emperor.

Cole also happens to be Thorne's father.

I know. Twisted.

Speaking of the emperor, Cole stands a towering seven feet tall, making him a mountain of a man with rough skin and cropped gray hair. He sports a Stetson, eye patch, leather pants and heavy boots... and all that the emperor wears is black as midnight.

No false packaging with this guy.

Cole narrows his eyes in my direction. "Welcome to Umbra." He tips his Stetson. With that movement, the hat bursts into a small dust cloud before disappearing back into Cole's flesh.

This isn't a magic trick; Cole wields powerful nanoparticles called Crown Sentient. That's the *killer* part of my *killer cowboy* situation. Regular sentient help all Umbrans travel through space, fight battles, see the future, you name it. But Crown Sentient do all that on steroids... and only for the emperor.

"Here's where you'll die," Cole adds.

I roll my eyes. *Like that idea didn't occur to me already.*

"No!" Thorne rounds on his father. "Keep your word. This is *our* fight. Meimi stays free."

Cole snarls out a single word. "Maybe."

No question what that means. Cole plans to murder us both. My stupor instantly vanishes. Obsessing about dresses? That was so forty seconds ago. Right now, I have a single thought.

Save the prince.

Hoisting up my skirts, I race toward Thorne.

Ten yards.

Moving with impossible speed, Cole throws dozens of rapid punches at his son's skull, ribs and kidneys. Thorne counters just as quickly, blocking each attack. Cole pauses, barely winded. Meanwhile Thorne braces his arms on his knees as he catches his breath.

Five yards away now.

"Son," declares Cole. "This is getting on my nerves." A cloud of particles appears around Cole's right arm. The next instant, those dark sentient solidify into a long Winchester rifle. Fear prickles across my skin. Cole raises the weapon, aims at Thorne, and fires.

BOOM!

The bullet strikes Thorne squarely in the chest. My guy gets thrown across the street, through a glass window, and into a building marked *saloon*.

I do a double take.

Triple take.

The emperor's super-powerful alien gun just blasted my boyfriend across a street. That's not something you see every day, even on a movie feed. My pulse moves into hyper drive. Cole talks a big game about killing his son.

Did he just murder Thorne?

Scanning the broken window, Cole rests his rifle on his shoulder. "Bet you didn't know Crown Sentient could do that, eh?"

My body turns numb with shock. Everyone knows what guns can do. And super-charged Crown Sentient guns? It's only logical that Cole's weapon would pack more power.

To me, the rifle isn't what's shocking... it's the fact that Cole is Thorne's *father*.

And the emperor shows zero concern that Thorne may be hurt. Worry twists through me.

Thorne could even be dead.

Cole speeds across the dirt road. I rush behind the emperor, following him into the empty saloon. Overturned tables and chairs cover the floor. A booze counter stands stocked with broken bottles. Wind tinkles random keys on a busted player piano. It's creepy as all get out.

Thorne sits against the far wall. The wood behind him buckles from the force of his spine having slammed onto the panel. He twitches; I freeze.

Thorne's alive. *Yes!*

What I see next makes my heart sink. With every breath, Thorne's lungs gurgle ominously. Splatters of blood line the nearby wall and floor.

Oh, no. Thorne's dying.

This can't be happening.

Cole saunters over to Thorne and stops. Raising his right arm, the emperor points his rifle toward Thorne's face. Cole then launches into a long list of my guy's execution-worthy crimes. All the while, that rifle stays jammed against Thorne's cheek.

No time to lose.

I'm so done watching Cole beat up my boyfriend. Time to take things into my own hands. Literally. Reaching into my dress pocket, I pull out a small container which contains swarm sentient, a variety that forms something far better than a shotgun. Not that this is a big space competition for who has the best stuff.

It's more of a science fair.

In any case, I plan to win.

Swarm sentient can take a unified shape that includes a central consciousness. Basically, I've got more of a killer pet than a boring old gun. My particular swarm becomes a semi-transparent creature called the Lacerator. And it's as badass as its name.

I open the container.

Sentient particles seep out of the tiny box, congealing into the shape of a semi-solid monster that towers seven feet tall. The Lacerator has a wide chest, stout legs, and empty holes serve as its eyes. Dinosaur-style spikes protrude from its spine. Razor-sharp teeth line its overly wide mouth.

Who cares if this swarm looks like a *connect the dots* dinosaur? My Lacerator is just the best.

Pictures appear in my mind—that's how the Lacerator communicates. Based on the images, the monster clearly wants me to issue a command.

That's easy.

"Heal Thorne," I order. "NOW."

The Lacerator bursts into a cloud of particles. The sight reminds me of a miniature tornado as it whirls across the saloon floor. Broken chairs and tattered playing cards get caught in the motion. Bands of fear tighten around my rib cage. I just ordered the Lacerator to cure Thorne, but that's more of a *hope* than anything else. I haven't actually seen the Lacerator do anything but kill stuff. My breath catches.

Can a sentient swarm fix a bullet wound?

The swarm slams into Thorne's chest. Dark particles swirl across my guy's arms, neck and face, forming moving tattoos of pinwheel-type lines. The ink-like markings seep right into Thorne's flesh, merging with his body. The scientist part of me thinks that's cool tech. The girlfriend side just wants to be Thorne not-nearly-dead already.

What happens next takes place in seconds, but forever seems to eke by as color returns to Thorne's skin. His bruises fade. Blood dries up and vanishes. After shaking his head, Thorne hops to his feet. Now that's a recovery sign if I've ever seen one.

I exhale. *Chalk up one for our side.*

"Well done, Meimi," says Thorne. Even his dimpled smile is back.

I give him a mock curtsey because one, I'm wearing a dress; and two, it's never a bad time for sass.

Cole staggers backward, the sentient rifle vanishing from his hands. The emperor's face pales with shock. "What?" Cole points at my nose. "Humans can't order sentient around."

"Well, I just did," I retort. "Get used to it."

Cole raises his arms. Once more, black particles swirl around his hands. This time, the Crown Sentient congeal into the shape of a lasso that's held tightly in the emperor's fist. With a snap of his wrist, the rope whips out from Cole's grip.

And it heads in my direction.

Thorne races toward me. "Get down, Meimi!"

There isn't time. One moment, I'm standing free. The next, a line of rope encircles my throat. I try to gulp in fresh air. *Useless.* The rough lasso bites into my skin.

Yet it also calls to my soul.

What happens next is pure instinct. Seconds ago, I communicated with the Lacerator using mental images. Now I send out a new command to the Crown Sentient around my neck. With all my focus, I imagine the lasso merging into my body.

Nothing happens.

I writhe to get free. The skin on my throat chafes and bleeds. My lungs ache for air. Once again, I picture the lasso melting into the same swirling markings I just saw on Thorne.

Again, there is no response.

Will the Crown Sentient ever act?

Suddenly the emperor's lasso bursts into a haze of particles. Hope sparks in my chest. *It's working!* There's a tickling sensation as markings appear on my throat, followed by a zing of electricity against my skin. No doubt, the Crown Sentient just merged into my body, the same as they did to Thorne.

Power thrums through my nervous system. Every corner of my soul vibrates with energy. Pain sears into my skull. It strikes me that I'm experiencing the worst *ice cream headache* of my life, times ten. The agony ends as quickly as it began. One fact appears with absolute certainty. I've taken in Crown Sentient.

Feels pretty good.

"How can this be?" Cole staggers backward. "You're not Umbran. And even if you were, no one but the emperor can take in Crown Sentient."

I bob my brows. "Oh, say it's impossible again. I love it." An idea appears. "How about this?"

For my next feat of amazingness, I imagine Thorne taking in Crown Sentient as well. With the picture firmly in mind, I raise my hand. Sure enough, Crown Sentient rise from my palm and race across the room. Fast as a whip, the sentient encompass Thorne in what looks like a dust cloud before turning into the same swirly markings as before. Those inky lines quickly seep into Thorne's chest, hands and mouth.

"This isn't happening," thunders Cole. "That boy is too weak."

"Maybe you need to expand your definition of what it means to be strong," counters Thorne.

I shoot him a thumbs-up. *Good point there, alien boyfriend.*

Cole forms his Winchester again. I suppose he thinks that's a menacing move, but I have another thought entirely.

More Crown Sentient for us, yum yum.

Reaching forward, I summon those particles to me as well. The rifle instantly dissolves into dark specks that fly across the saloon and soak directly into my body. Fresh waves of energy flow though my nervous system. The ice cream headache returns for a few seconds, but I can ignore it better this time.

The emperor scowls at Thorne. "I don't need sentient to fight you." Cole lunges for his son. This time, when the emperor attacks his child, Thorne does more than just block the blows.

He hits back.

One strike.

Two.

Three.

With Thorne's last punch, Cole flies across the room. The emperor lands against a back panel with an ear-splitting thunk. It occurs to me that Cole takes the same position Thorne did a few minutes ago—sitting against the wall with the panel behind him all busted up. The emperor looks unconscious, but you never know. I send out my own sentient to tie him up, just to be sure.

For a long second, I can only stare at the bound-up emperor. "Did we really do it?"

"Looks like," says Thorne. "I've never seen him knocked out before."

Some small part of me says this is too easy. But I decide to ignore that part, mostly because Thorne is racing toward me at a run. Soon our bodies press together in the mother of all hugs. Thorne's hand slides up the side of my torso and neck, ending with a firm grip on my chin.

I know what's coming next, and I love this idea.

Sometimes, it's good to be me.

"When you love someone across multiple realities, that connection can seep into your home world. Earthers call this finding your soul mate. On the planet Umbra, we say you discover your transcendent." - Empress Ophelia, author of *The Lost Book of Transcendence*

AT LAST, Meimi Archer is in my arms. For a moment, I soak in her perfection. Brown hair frames her heart-shaped face. Sixteen beloved freckles scatter across the bridge of her nose. The twin fires of intelligence and courage burn in her wide emerald eyes. She's seventeen and an immortal beauty, all at once.

Meimi's my transcendent—the woman I love in so many realities, it bleeds through into this one. Growing up, I thought transcendence was a myth.

Then I met Meimi.

I'm one lucky prince.

Little by little, I guide Meimi's lips toward mine. Once our mouths almost touch, I pause. Nothing compares to Meimi's kisses; I wish to commit this moment to memory. There's the way her lips glisten with a liquid beauty. How Meimi's soft curves press against my firm body. And the quick breaths which mean she wants this as much as I do.

For the hundredth time, I imagine our future. Such mental pictures kept me sane all those months when Meimi's memory was wiped and she didn't know me. Now those cherished images flood back.

There's Meimi and I riding hoverbikes across Umbra's prairies...

Waltzing on our wedding day...

And cradling our newborn.

I even see grey-haired versions of us cuddling on a porch swing, our faces wrinkled and happy.

Meimi goes up on her tiptoes. Our lips meet in a gentle kiss that's all things loving and grateful. But this isn't the time for much intimacy. Father won't stay passed out forever.

Meimi breaks the kiss. "What happens next?"

I let out a long breath. There's no question what Meimi refers to here.

Cole.

Fresh pictures flip through my brain. These aren't hoped-for futures; they're memories from a painful past. First come recollections of Father, a kind man who never treated me as less just because I didn't wield much sentient. Second follows thoughts of Cole, the emperor who rages and strikes. Crown Sentient fray Cole's mind, transforming a good man into an angry demon. Every week, Mother asks me to put Cole out of his misery. But I can't. There are still signs of the good man who is my father.

Even now, I just can't give up on Father yet. *How do I explain that to Meimi?*

"It's a good question," I begin.

"Why do I get the feeling this is a complex situation?"

"Because you'd be right. You should know the true choices here."

For a few seconds, Meimi stares at Cole. When her gaze meets mine again, my girl is all steely resolve. "Tell me everything."

"We could kill my father, take all his Crown Sentient, and become rulers of the omniverse. That's how Cole got the job."

"Honestly? I'm not a fan of becoming an alien emperor and empress right now."

"Same here. But I wanted to be honest. And there is another option."

"Let's hear it."

"I could take Cole back to my family's home at Fort Derringer. That's on the other side of the planet. Now that I can wield some of my father's Crown Sentient, maybe I can help him." I huff out a breath. "I have to try."

Meimi gently rests her palm against my cheek. "I understand."

Pure adoration pulses through my veins. *This girl.*

"I should get back then, I suppose."

My mind races. Truth is, I'd love to take Meimi to Fort Derringer, but it would be a big risk. For my people, knowing transcendents exist would be a major revelation. Then there's the fact that Meimi and I could be the next emperor and empress—that's not what people are expecting. And when surprises do happen, the situation often ends in violence. Just because my family rules, doesn't mean we're without enemies.

"I would love to bring you to Fort Derringer one day," I say solemnly. "But when that happens, I want to ensure you'll be safe and welcomed. That might take some time."

"So to be together, we must be apart?" She shakes her head yet smiles. "That sounds like my luck."

"It won't be long. Soon you'll wield your sentient like a pro. We'll visit each other's worlds often." I glance over to Cole. "But that's the future. Right now, he could wake up any moment. It's time for us both to go home."

Just saying those words tears at my soul, but it's the truth. Meimi always deserves honesty.

"I'm not worried," says Meimi bravely. "I'll track you down in no time."

"Looking forward to it." Leaning forward, I rest my forehead against hers. A weight of sorrow hangs about us, heavy as the threat of rain.

Best to get this over with.

We step apart. Raising my right hand, I call upon the regular sentient power inside me. Silver particles lift from my palm as I create a circular transport portal called a drift void. Within seconds, a plate of gray specks hangs in the air.

Somehow, I force out the next five words. "You can step through now."

Meimi sighs. "Right."

My transcendent sets her fingers against the silver plate. Inch by inch, she glides her right arm into the whirl of gray. The sentient panel expands, ready to accept her entire body. Meimi steps in half-way. All the while, emotions pour through our transcendent bond.

I sense Meimi's bone-deep chill of despair.

The heat of her frustration.

And a shock of fear.

The sorrow of our farewell vanishes. Every muscle in my body goes on alert. *Something's scaring Meimi.* Sure enough, a presence looms behind me. No question who it is, either.

Cole has awoken.

"Goodbye," snarls the emperor. "Enjoy your exile."

The sentient surrounding Meimi do something I've never seen before.

Change color.

Particles of gray become tiny points of crimson. I blink, not believing what I'm seeing. *Red sentient.* These are illegal—even to the emperor—because they don't just transport someone to another part of the universe. They block both sides of that void, eternally.

No, no, no.

Cole is permanently separating Earth from Umbra... and me from Meimi.

On reflex, I reach out to my transcendent. Our fingertips almost brush. With the barest flash of crimson light, the red sentient disappear. Meimi vanishes as well. My mind blanks with shock. I reach out to Meimi through our bond. No flow of emotion pulses through. We're severed.

Yet my transcendent can't be gone. I won't allow it.

Focus, Thorne.

Minutes ago, Cole wanted to kill us both. Now he's fine with an exile void? Father is a rage machine, but that doesn't mean he isn't an expert schemer. And this situation positively howls with secret plans. All those factors add up to a single conclusion. The first step in connecting with Meimi is understanding why Father did this in the first place.

I turn to Cole. "You could have killed Meimi, or at least tried to. But you played possum against the wall, waiting for your chance. Then you sent Meimi to exile on Earth. That keeps her safe away from anyone on Umbra, including you. Why?"

Father sneers. "I needed to lock a door."

I turn over his response. "Meaning that to keep me and Meimi apart, an exile void was the only way to do it."

Cole shrugs. "The girl empowered you to steal my Crown Sentient. You don't think I'd allow that to ever happen again."

An idea sparks. Father brings up a good point. My new Crown Sentient could be very useful here. I picture them opening the exile void. Nothing happens. So I imagine more of them leaving Cole. Again, there's no response.

The emperor chuckles. "Checking if I'm right, are you? Like I said, you can't take in any more Crown Sentient. Not without the girl."

In reply, I quote one of the oldest sayings in Umbra.

"That horse won't run."

In other words, you're full of it.

"Not sure what you mean," says Cole.

"Crown Sentient are everything to you. I should be dead now, same as Meimi. And yet you choose an exile void to separate us. Again, I ask—why?"

Cole waves his hand in a casual motion. "Lost my temper." There's no real heat in his words, though. When Cole is actually angry, you can't miss it.

Lost his temper, my ass.

"It's like this," Cole continues. "The moment that girl took in my Crown Sentient, I knew she wasn't any more human than I am. She's Umbran and a conduit for my Crown Sentient. Can't allow that. Now she's gone forever. You need to accept things."

I narrow my eyes. "Out with it, Cole. You've got a plan. Just tell me what you want."

"If you insist." Cole slaps on a forced smile. "I'm a generous man. You can keep the Crown Sentient you just stole. All I ask is that you don't cause trouble. Forget about that girl."

Frustration heats my veins. "She has a name. Meimi. And she's my transcendent, not some girl."

"On that we agree, son. Miss Meimi is indeed a transcendent. But we differ on a single point." Father 's next two words that blow apart my world.

"She's mine."

Shock zings through my nervous system. "No."

Father's false smile stays firmly in place. "Took in my Crown Sentient, didn't she? What do you think that makes her?"

"Not. Yours."

"Being emperor ain't an easy job, son. Crown Sentient mess with your head." Father's eyes take on a strange gleam as he says the *mess with your head* part. "A transcendent will share my load. This is a gift from the omniverse—the very universe of parallel universes—and it's not meant for a weak boy without the sense of a newborn piglet."

A realization washes over me. "You didn't exile Meimi. You've put her in safe keeping until you can get to her properly."

Implications link through my brain, like so many dominos falling. Meimi would never agree be Cole's empress. My heart sinks. She never would have agreed to help Godwin, either. But Godwin wiped her memories.

"Why shouldn't I keep her safe?" asks Cole. "She's mine, ain't she? Now, do you agree with me on that, or must I get nasty?"

White hot rage heats my veins. Father wants to take Meimi as his empress. That's upsetting on so many levels, it's hard to keep track. Yet much as I want to throttle my Father, that won't help anything right now. Leaning into all my warrior training, I force my mind to calm.

And I round on Cole once more.

"Come on," I state. "The fact that you're not attacking me? You *know* I'm Meimi's transcendent. And if I'm dead, I can't be used to control her. I can see it now... *Marry me or Thorne goes into prison.*"

A muscles tick on Father's neck. "You should have lied. You should have said you'd be a good little prince."

"So I'm right." I lower my voice. "Tell me. How do you plan to get around the exile void? You need time to plan how you'll control Meimi. After that, you must have some way to break the exile void."

In reply, Cole swings his fist. Before today, this strike would have appeared whip-fast, too quick to catch. Now I can dissect every aspect of the emperor's punch, from the way his muscles ripple to the barely-detectable breeze as his arm closes in. One option for what to do next.

Use it to my advantage.

The emperor's fist draws closer. Once Cole's knuckles brush my forehead, I crouch down, dodging the punch. Twisting my torso, I land a strike of my own, straight to Cole's chest.

Crack!

That sound is unmistakable. My hit snapped some ribs. The emperor clutches his torso, his gaze shifting between his injured chest and my raised fists. Little by little, Cole lifts his hand from his torso. His fingertips glisten with the barest trace of blood.

"You caught me off guard there, boy." Cole eyes me from head to toe. "Whatever trick you're pulling, it won't last." He wipes his hand off on his thigh. "You're mine, too. Just like her."

The words ricochet through me in odd ways.

You're mine, too. Just like her.

Deep inside, some kind of switch flips on. Fresh energy streams through my body. The static hiss in my head turns deafening. Everything in the saloon transforms to stark shades of black and white. Even more connections form within my soul. Whatever is happening, my new Crown Sentient are at it again.

And I thought things were strange before.

Suddenly, my body alters. My shoulders grow broader. Each bone stretches. Muscles bulge. One moment, I'm the runt prince to a behemoth emperor. The next thing I know, I stare at Cole dead on. We're the same size now. The Crown Sentient changed everything.

A realization appears. This will be more than one solid strike against Cole. For the first time in my life, we'll have a full and fair fight. One on one.

Yes.

"Don't underestimate me," snarls Cole. "I can also use you to control Meimi from the comfort of Umbra... or while trapped alone on a prison planet. Your choice."

"You must grab me first."

"I'm working on that." The emperor summons fresh Crown Sentient. The black particles swirl around his hands, only to solidify into the shape of a double barrel shotgun. My breath catches. The last time Cole made that particular weapon, I almost died.

Lifting my arm, I picture my own Crown Sentient encompassing my first. The dark particles instantly rise from my skin, creating a black glove around my hand. Slamming my arm forward, I aim straight for the barrel of Cole's gun. All the while, I focus on a single image: shattering the weapon.

What happens next only lasts a second. Still my mind soaks in everything as if it takes hours to complete. Inch by inch, my fist pushes forward as the shotgun disintegrates. Once I get within a breath of my father's actual hand, my knuckles strike onto what feels like actual metal. I pull away.

And I don't wait to see what Cole does next.

Jumping high, I lock my shins around Cole's neck. Twisting my body, I flip the emperor through the air.

Cole lands on his head with a smack. Floorboards shatter with the impact. Splinters and dust erupt into the air. Father hops back onto his feet, ready to return the strike with a kick of his own. His hit lands on my stomach. I stagger back from the force of the blow. Normally, I'd be winded from that strike. Not this time. Leaping forward, I slam my elbow into Cole's throat before kicking in the back of his knees.

My father lands on his spine with a thud. I stalk closer, ready for the knock-out.

Voices echo in from the street. I glance toward noise. That's all the distraction Father needs. A dagger of sentient forms in Cole's hand; he pummels me against the wall and presses the weapon against my throat. "Do you want an extra mouth?"

Quick as lightning, I summon a blade of my own and shove it against his kidneys. "Only if you'd like an open gut."

Father glances down. "It appears we're at an impasse. How about I give you some time to think? Remember, it's a good offer. Keep the Crown Sentient. Find yourself a new girl—there are plenty of princesses running around. Just give up on Miss Meimi. And one more thing. No matter what you do, say nothing of this to your mother."

I frown. "What?"

"Fooled you, don't she? I don't pretend anything. I'm a good man and a bad one, both rolled into the same patch of real estate. But Janais is something else. If you value Miss Meimi, you'll keep the fact she's Umbran a secret."

I tilt my head, trying to understand. Just when I thought I had it worked out, there's another twist. Outside, the rumble of voices echo in from the street grows louder.

Slam!

The saloon door whips open. Mother enters.

And inside my soul, my life derails. As long as I can remember, I've worked to save the good man that is my father. Now a line has been crossed. Cole wants to make Meimi his empress. If the choice is between my family of origin and my future with Meimi, there really is no decision to make.

No one hurts Meimi, ever.

SWEET MOTHER OF SCIENCE, that did not just happen.

An exile void.

My parents were drift scientists. Growing up, Mom taught me all about exile voids. And what happened just now? That certainly looked like one.

Red nanoparticles? *Check.*

Transport between distant worlds? *Check again.*

Evil guy saying creepy stuff like, *enjoy your exile? Not required, but big ass check.*

Blinking hard, I scan my surroundings. Sure enough, I've returned to Earth. Specifically, I stand inside a metal container backstage at the so-called Liberation Celebration. Which isn't a bad thing, considering how it's the same spot where I left Earth for Umbra. And this particular celebration is why I wear a frilly pink dress in the first place.

I've come full circle.

So far, so good.

Stepping around in a slow circle, I examine the small metal room around me, scanning for a drift void back to Umbra. My heart sinks. All signs of sentient have vanished. Reaching into my soul, I search for the pulse of Thorne's inner life. I don't feel anything, but that doesn't mean he isn't alive. Anxiety tightens across my shoulders.

What's happening to Thorne now? What will Cole do to my transcendent?

I straighten my spine. *Nothing, that's what Cole will do. Because I'm getting back to Umbra.*

Together, Thorne and I can fight anything. And right now, the Emperor of the Omniverse is top of my list of Dickheads To Take Down.

There's just the little matter of how to make it happen.

Rubbing my neck, I consider my options. The easy answer to this problem comes in the form of my handy-dandy new Crown Sentient. I picture them opening the red exile void. Nothing happens.

So I do that about ten more times.

Same result.

Moving on.

For years, I built quantum gizmos to keep my family fed and well away from the government's notice. My handler, Fritz, always sent me the most impossible projects. For me, design begins when I list the pieces to bring together. Parts for a new creation spin through my head.

Dark matter monolith? *Tricky to find, but totally necessary.*

Wormhole detector? *Sure thing.*

Magnetic enhancer? *Buy in bulk.*

Beyond that, I stall out.

A jolt of worry zings up my back. There must be a way to do this; I just need to focus more.

Think, Meimi!

Something stirs inside my mind. My thoughts, which always fly pretty quickly, now zoom off on something close to light speed. Synapses fire in new ways. Odd connections form. Back at Umbra, I'd gotten a blazing headache while taking in Crown Sentient. Now that pain returns with a vengeance. Agony sears into my eye sockets.

And I start seeing things.

Namely, sentient cascade from the ceiling, the many black particles reminding me of a dark snowfall.

My heart sinks. Eye pain? Sentient snow? The stress must be taking over at last. After all, I just traveled through space. Not to mention how before that, I stopped an evil doctor from *cleansing* millions of my fellow humans. Either I'm finally having a breakdown or... that's really all I have.

The breakdown idea.

Which sucks because I'm stuck inside a box right now. Not the best place to start seeing stuff. What if I pass out? I could end up on *News Of The Bizarre* data feeds. I can see the headline now: *Supposed Genius Girl Locks Self In Box And Dies.*

Huh. I'd totally read that article.

The pain in my skull turns unbearable. Energy streams down my back, forcing my spine to arch and my gaze to lock onto the ceiling. My arms fall loose to my sides, palms forward. An eternity and a moment pass, all at once. More components fly through my mind, from star maps to software code. Pieces fall apart and realign. A plan begins to form. Nothing final yet, but it's a good start.

Little by little, the agony in my temples fades. At last, I can stare in directions other than up. Before me, the dark snowflakes cease to fall. Instead, they swirl and merge into a new shape. Surprisingly, it's familiar.

The Lacerator.

My mind continues to spin. More thoughts align. Before, I wasn't sure what was happening to me. Now, an answer appears.

Crown Sentient.

I focus on the Lacerator. "Am I changing?" I tap my head, just to make it clear where I think something has decided to make improvements.

The Lacerator nods.

"It's the Crown Sentient, isn't it?"

Another nod.

I hug my elbows. Not sure how I feel about some alien nanotech monkeying with my brain. Intellect is the only thing that's kept me alive for years. Still, I've never come up with plans this quickly before. If I'm able to build something to destroy that exile void, it will be thanks to my new Crown Sentient.

Meh. I'm keeping them.

The edges of the Lacerator's body stretch and flip, like image glitching on a data feed. I step closer.

"Are the Crown Sentient affecting you, too?"

The Lacerator nods once more.

The glitching turns more violent. One moment, I look upon my favorite dino monster. The next, the Lacerator has taken a new form entirely.

It's my sister Luci.

On reflex, I take a half-step backward. This isn't a solid statue kind of deal. The new figure is created from a swirl of particles. But the slim figure, long hair, and piercing gaze... that's all Luci.

Joy and rage churn through my nervous system. Growing up, Luci was my idol. I followed her in everything—doing all she asked and more—even if that meant working as a child in a garbage reclamation center. Over the last months, I've learned that my love for Luci was all one-sided. While I adored her, she hated me. Long story.

An electric sense of frustration curls over my skin. How can I still feel some affection for Luci? She betrayed me. Sold me out. Yet some part of me wishes to remain the little girl riding the hoverbus to garbage reclamation, proud to be seated next to her sophisticated older sister.

I focus on Sentient Luci. "Are you my sister?"

She shakes her head. That's a *no*.

"You're still Crown Sentient."

A nod. *Yes*.

"So you're here to..." I step near enough to carefully examine the particles. They're no longer pitch black, but bright blue. This particular shade of sentient see the past or future.

That narrows things down.

"You want to show me something about the past?" I ask.

Sentient Luci rolls her eyes. Another *no*.

"Are you here to warn me about the future?"

Sentient Luci nods.

"That's cool," I say.

Although to be honest, I could have used a warning like this a lot earlier. Luci already sold me out to Godwin's cleansing program, big time. Still, it's good to know Luci is still out there, scheming and causing trouble.

"What exactly should I worry about?" I ask.

In reply, the sentient take a new shape. It's a pair of life pods. One holds a man, the other contains a woman. For both people, their limbs are in disarray while their faces stay frozen in a scream.

When I speak, my voice comes out as a whisper. "They're dead." The sight bothers me much more than it should. My eyes prickle with held-in tears. "These people are important to my past or future."

There's no need for a reply. Deep in my heart, I already know this is the truth. I press my palms against my eyes. These are two random people who suffered an awful death. Yet for some reason, seeing them hurts me as badly as Luci's betrayal.

When I speak, my voice is a hoarse croak. "That's enough."

The scene bursts into a tornado-style whirl before reforming into a new figure. It's a stooped man with drooping jowls, a bulbous nose, and a perpetual smile. Although he's made from blue particles, there's no missing how this guy wears a tweed suit and matching fedora. I've seen this particular character many times on data feeds.

"You've taken the shape of Professor Conway, the Headmaster of ECHO Academy."

Sentient Conway grins. Another *yes*.

I shift my weight from foot to foot. "Before, I always wanted to go to ECHO Academy. It's the best high school for science."

Sentient Conway lifts his chin in agreement. He points to me and then the ground beside him. The meaning of the gesture is clear. *You belong with me at ECHO Academy.*

Prepare for disappointment, bud.

"Here's the deal," I state. "I just went to another planet and fought the Emperor of the Omniverse. Before that, I put together a team that stopped Doctor Godwin and his cleansing program. Going back to school now feels a little..." I bob my head, searching for the right words.

Sentient Conway points to the ground beside him again. It's clear that he doesn't care how I feel on this one. Conway thinks I belong at ECHO.

"I've got it," I continue. "It feels like trying to shove toothpaste back into a tube. I'm out of high school and not going back. What's there for me, anyway?"

In reply, Sentient Conway transforms into a new figure: a stick of a woman with thinning hair, intelligent eyes and lots of wrinkles. *Miss Edith*. Growing up, my mother spent a growing number of her days catatonic. When I'd go off on my gizmo projects, Miss Edith would stay to watch Mom.

I have a single question for the real Miss Edith. It's been burning away in my mind. Even though this isn't the same person, I can't help but try and satisfy my curiosity.

"Are you all right, Miss Edith?"

She frowns. This is a super-good replica of her. That particular look is Miss Edith's way of saying, *whatever do you mean?*

"Oh, I already checked to make sure you weren't hurt as part of Doctor Godwin's so-called cleansing. Are things still okay with you?"

She nods. *Yes.*

"Then why are you here and—" Before I can finish, a new sound rattles the air.

Boom!

The floor shakes from the force of an explosion. Like wind through autumn leaves, the sentient whirl out of a humanoid shape, becoming separate particles once more. One moment, the swarm is here. The next, they are gone. And I'm alone in a completely dark metal container.

Not good.

"I hereby announce the Fifth Age of Umbra, which shall be ruled by the Oxblood clan." - Empress Janais, author of *The Fifth Age of Umbra*

COLE'S WORDS still ricochet through my soul. Father thinks Meimi is his transcendent.

What a nightmare.

"Think on what I said," whispers Cole. "Say nothing to Janais."

Umbrans stream into the saloon. My eyes widen with surprise. This is the extended royal court. Like all Umbra, the nobles resemble groups from Earth's so-called Wild West. In reality, everything they wear—as well as this very saloon itself—are formed from high tech threads called filaments.

My mother, Janais, steps up. With her strong cheekbones, copper skin, and long neck, Janais is the very image of the word *queen*. Today Mother wears a simply white robe that cinches at her waist.

The way Janais crosses the room, it's not like her husband and son are pulling knives on each other. Mother focuses on Cole first.

"My love," Janais says smoothly. "The factions have arrived. Shall we join the conclave?"

What my father does next is a genuine surprise.

He gives up.

My father's dagger disappears from his hand. Cole raises his hands shoulder height, palms forward, in the universal symbol of surrender. Nothing remains except me, my knife and a chance to skewer the emperor's gut.

Mother rounds on me. With Father, Janais acted as if nothing were odd about his knife at my throat. With me, she takes a different approach. Her mouth thins to a worried line. "Do not do this, my son." She glances to the rest of the court.

Mother's logic is obvious. Everyone can sense that Father won't last much longer as emperor. The other two factions in Umbra—namely the Vingians and Komandir—are bulking up on sentient and warriors.

War is coming.

Today's conclave is to assure everyone of Father's sanity. Walking in on Cole about to skewer his son doesn't help things.

There may be a time to end my father's life, but it won't be in front of my family's enemies. I command my blade to vanish, then step away.

For his part, Cole gives Mother a sweet smile. For the first time, I see rage that boils behind that grin.

"However did you know I was here?" asks Cole.

"You're hard to miss, my love."

"So you say."

Father's logic here is obvious. Today's conclave is being held in order to prove the Father's mental strength. So Janais guides our enemies right into a room where Cole attacks his own son? It might be an odd coincidence.

Then again, it might not.

Cole rounds on the court. His demeanor transforms from false cheer to overwhelming charisma. The emperor steps about, glad handing delegates. The most important are the leaders of the two main factions, namely the Komandir and Vingians.

First, Father approaches Doc Pyotr, King of the Komandir. The guy reminds me of a music hall maestro—all tall and slick in his red striped suit. His top hat is surrounded by metal gears and lights, making the man super easy to pick out in a crowd.

Second, Father greets Locus, the leader of the Vingian faction. She's a nine-year-old girl with ebony skin, long braided hair and about a hundred previous Vingian rulers chatting away in her head.

Vingians value learning, and their leader always gets previous minds loaded in her own. The thought makes me shiver.

As Father circulates, my thoughts return to Father's warning about Janais. How *did* Mother know where to find us, anyway? Any why did she walk in with the entire court without checking first?

I'd always seen Janais as a long-suffering saint who perseveres under Father's slowly-descending madness. Now a new idea worms into my consciousness.

Perhaps I can't totally trust her, either.

After finishing his greetings, Father strides over to Mother's side. "The conclave! Let's go."

Janais sets her hand on Father's forearm and she rounds on me. "Excuse us."

Together, they process out of the saloon. The court follows.

Soon it's just me, Justice and Slate.

And a lot of new questions.

———

End of Sample

The adventure continues with ECHO ACADEMY, Book 4 in the Dimension Drift ...

NEW APPENDIX OF TOTALLY AWESOME GOODIES

INTRODUCTION

WELCOME TO THIS NEW APPENDIX!

I've added lots of extra stuff here in order to celebrate the release of new covers for my Dimension Drift series! Check them out below:

Say it with me: *ooooh, aaaaaah!*

Now, you may wonder: *what's behind the new covers?*
Good question, you.
There are my five reasons why I did this.

One. The 'I Gotta Be Me' Cover

With the original covers, the first three had a theme of characters running through walls. Then the fourth book, ECHO ACADEMY, did it own thing. It was walls, walls, walls and... WTF? That bugged me.

Two. I Like Visuals

Reviewers often say that reading my books is like watching a movie in their heads. And hey, that's what it's like when I write them, too! Even after the books are launched, I'm still picturing the story and how to enhance it. All of which leads to item number three...

Three. More Books A-Coming

Great news! I plan on adding two more books to the series, namely JUSTICE and SLATE. As it was before, the cover design template wasn't really expandable to those guys. After all, you can only run through so many walls before things starts to get repetitive. This new format will fit in the two new titles perfectly. Yay!

Four. Getting Less Literal

The first covers represented actual scenes from the books. It was fun at the time, but I think it's a little limiting in the long run. Plus, this series is science fiction which I think lends itself to more *suggestive versus literal* design. The new look should give you an idea of the book's themes without getting too specific.

Four. Reader Goodies

Recently, I added an extra appendix to SLIPPERS AND THIEVES, a title from my Fairy Tales of the Magicorum series.

Readers really liked it—and I love making you all happy—so the new covers were a good excuse to add in more content here as well.

All in all, I truly hope you enjoy these extra goodies... and please keep an eye out for a release date on JUSTICE and SLATE!

Best,

Christina Bauer, Author

HERE THE TUNES that inspired me while writing this novel!

Tune Number Five.
Love Spreads by the Stone Roses
"Let me put you in the picture, let me show you what I mean. The messiah is my sister, ain't no king man, she's my queen."

In ALIEN MINDS, we have an intergalactic prince, Thorne, who thinks he will never be fortunate enough to find his transcendent (the girl he loves through so many parallel realties, their bond bleeds into his current universe.) This song captures the feeling he has when our guy meets a certain Meimi Archer.

Tune Number Four.
Renegades by X Ambassadors
"All hail the pioneers."

Both Meimi and Thorne love to build new tech and this song celebrates makers everywhere. I listened to it obsessively while writing this series.

Tune Number Three.

Zero by Imagine Dragons
"Hello, hello...
Let me tell you what it's like to be a zero."

Almost every time I write a book, I end up obsessing on a fresh Imagine Dragons song. This time, it was *Zero*. Thorne is the kind of guy who's very open about his limitations ... yet he never gives up. This song really captures that spirit for me.

Tune Number Two.

I Will Wait by Mumford & Sons
"I will wait, I will wait for you."

Without giving away too much, I'll just say that this song is all about Thorne. Read the book and you'll know what I mean!

Tune Number One.

Hazy Shade of Winter by The Bangles
"Look around,
Leaves are brown,
And the sky is a hazy shade of winter."

Much of ALIEN MINDS takes place in a future version of Boston, MA that is a hot dystopian mess. This song really captures that spirit. Plus, it's a classic 1980's chick rock song, so YEAH.

So there you have it—my top five tunes while writing ALIEN MINDS! I hope you enjoyed this list.

I'VE WRITTEN MORE than thirty young adult fantasy-romance novels. Here are my top five tips for new writers.

Number 5.
Read In Your Genre. A lot.

You may have heard this before, but it's worth saying again. And again. And again. Now one spin I'll add here is to invest time in finding books that are unusual: a strong voice, a different style of world building, you get the idea. What you put into your head is what comes out of it. If you're reading the same things as everyone else, you'll sound like everyone else. Which if that's your goal, go you! If not, be aware and selective about what you choose to finish.

Number 4.
Be Prepared to Suck.

Think of your favorite author. That person you idolize? When the started writing, they sucked. I sucked hard for ages. It takes a long time to build your chops and voice. That's an okay part of the process, as is tuning out the naysayers who tell you that your work isn't good enough.

Number 3.
Find Someone To Kick Your Literary Ass.

This can be an advanced degree. Or a writing group. You just need someone who is going to give you honest feedback without stifling your voice. You can do it!

Number 2.
Accept Certain Criticism As A Gift.

After 15 books, I've gotten a little more balanced about so-called bad reviews. Here's my rule: if someone gives you one or two stars, then they aren't your reader and never will be. Buh-bye! That said, a three star review with some negative feedback is gold. This is someone who wanted to love what you did but had some pointers. Accept that for the gift it is.

Number 1.
Never Forget That You Are Awesome.

Let's be honest. Writers are awesome. We create stories that open minds and drive beauty, even though we're trapped in a world that values piling up the most stuff before you die. It can't be said enough: Never forget that you are awesome.

HERE ARE the top five books that inspire me as a writer...

Book Number Five.
The Lord of the Rings by J R R Tolkien

This book had a massive impact on me when I read it for the first time as a teenager. This was back in the 1980's, and the fantasy genre was a lot less developed than it is today. LOTR opened my eyes to a new kind of fantasy that was separate from fairy tales, and I loved it.

Book Number Four.
Grimm's Fairy Tales by the Brother's Grimm

My first entrance to fantasy was through the original *Grimm's Fairy Tales*. Now, I'm not referring to the sanitized Disney version, although I enjoyed those as well. I'm talking the gritty stuff where Snow White ends up dead, that kind of thing. My work is often classified as dark fantasy and this is where it all came from!

Book Number Three.
Mythology by Edith Hamilton

This is not so much a story as a compendium of Greco-Roman myths written in the style of Grimm's Fairy Tales. Such an eye opener in terms of themes, character, magic and fantasy!

Book Number Two.
The Egyptian Story of Isis

I read this one for a decade—in different translations—before I truly understood it. Isis was the original goddess story and stretches back in use at least 40,000 years. It's a tale of power, sacrifice and intellect. For more analysis, check out my blog post on the subject.

Book Number One.
The Hero With A Thousand Faces by Joseph Campbell

The first time this crossed my path, I was in high school. Campbell writes about what he calls the hero's journey. I then became interested in mapping out the heroine's journey, which brings me to why I write today.